Watch for More Novels by Sarah Jilek
from Indigo Sea Press

www.indigoseapress.com

Jiada

By

Sarah Jilek

Abyss Books
Published by Indigo Sea Press.
Winston-Salem

Abyss Books
Indigo Sea Press
302 Ricks Drive
Winston-Salem, NC 27103

First Abyss Books edition published
February, 2016
Abyss Books, Moon Sailor and all production design are trademarks of Indigo Sea Press, used under license.

For information regarding bulk purchases of this book, digital purchase and special discounts, please contact the publisher at www.indigoseapress.com

Cover design by Stacy Castanedo
Cover photo by Sarah Trostle
Map design by Chloe Helser

Manufactured in the United States of America
ISBN 978-1-63066-220-2

To everyone and everything that has made the journey so far worthwhile.

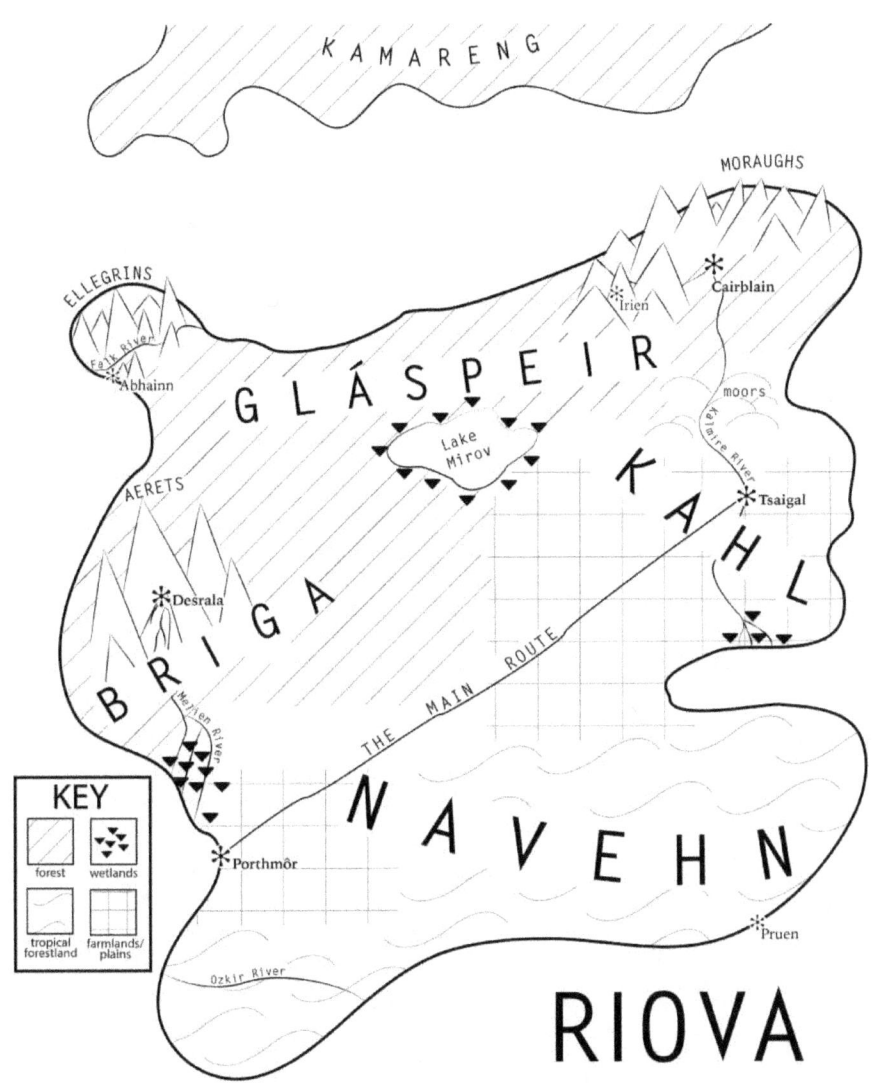

Prologue
An excerpt from *Existence*

...All came from the Thinker. He was the Ethereal, or Rhumein. Whatever he thought, was. He thought of the earth itself, dreaming it into being. But he could not think of a way to fill it, or to create light. Instead, he created Nharyav, who was a god like him, but dark in matters of spirit. Nharyav did not have the power to create. And so the Thinker destroyed him in frustration. For five thousand years he buried himself in the earth to think as Nharyav's mangled spirit roamed the empty earth. As the Thinker slept, he dreamed of beauty and so created it: it became a root that grew from his head up to the surface of the earth. A flower sprouted and grew into Aluveina, the Everlasting Melody. She was afraid of the thick darkness, so she screamed. With her scream, she created lightning. The light fascinated her and she realized that her voice had created it. She began to sing very softly and created a tiny pinprick of light that fell into her hand. She sang louder to it until it became the sun, and she also made the moon and stars in a similar way. Then the evil spirit of Nharyav came upon Aluveina and forced itself upon her, using her screams to create fire, chaos, and pain. The earth became a fiery wasteland until finally, the Thinker awoke. With Aluveina's help, he banished Nharyav deep within the earth, and he remains there. The Thinker and the Everlasting Melody also took their leave of the earth and together dreamed humans from afar. Nharyav still found ways to influence these new beings, and he chose some for his own, scarring their faces and chests. He ordered them to do his work, in order that someday he might be free of his earthy prison. He called them the Draougari, or Death-bringers, and hid them from sight...

Chapter 1
I

She was having sex with her professor when there was a knock at her front door. "Don't you dare," he whispered into her ear. His breath was warm. The tiny hairs on her ear tingled. She smiled and gently bit his lower lip. They waited, his hands pressing into her back as she sat, bare thighs resting on top of his. Beads of sweat slowly trickled down their temples. Audric glanced around her dimly lit bedroom and then at her, his eyes glinting. Jiada waited until she could only hear her ears ringing. Then she pushed Audric back onto the soft, thick mattress, her slender fingers pressing into his chest.

A while later, he was sleeping. Jade stepped onto her terrace with a cup of tea, her bare feet on the cool stone. She wore her floral pink silk robe and nothing else. She watched the tendrils of steam from her ceramic cup snake away towards the falls. She could see the falls from her balcony. The water crashed loudly, spilling over slippery, jagged boulders. Desrala, the Bright City, illuminated by its wisdom, was built around the falls. The city began with a group of intellectuals who set up a camp high in the Aeret Mountains where the falls spilled over into the dense forest far below. It was the perfect place for them to study water levels and the effect they had on wildlife. Word traveled about their studies and bright young minds left their dull farm lives and made their way to the Aerets, and the first stones of Desrala were lain. Today, every avenue was paved with bright, gleaming white stone. The houses, thin two-story white stone buildings, were arranged in military fashion, cozily beside each other. The city was built into the mountainside, the streets sloping up, and when twilight caressed the watchtower on the highest point of the city, it could be seen for miles.

"Beautiful, isn't it?" Audric called from the doorway. Jiada turned. He was naked. His black curls were stuck to his forehead with sweat. He leaned against the doorway, the muscles in his arms tensed, beads of sweat glistening on his sculpted stomach. He wouldn't come further than the doorway. Jade knew that.

"Yes. I've lived here all my life. It's funny how I'm still captivated," Jade replied. Her long auburn curls blew gently over her shoulder. She

2

shivered in her thin robe.

"I've given my life to this city as well. Just being a part of something that's lived for so long, and is making such great strides..." he trailed off. She was facing the city, staring out at the deepening darkness. All the roofs like perfect black triangles, each shingle standing at attention.

"Due to my work, of course," she said. Audric laughed.

"Of course."

It hadn't been a joke. Jade's research in astronomy had propelled Desrala to the discoveries of new stars and the development of better technology and the evolution of new theories on the celestial world. Her work was what the astronomy professors taught. And it was only her second year attending the university. But Audric had sat her down before and explained to her that even though her work was revolutionary, the fact was that she was a woman. Because of that, her theories would need patronage, support, from a man; specifically, him. Thinking about that made her shake her head sometimes, made her clench her teeth at the injustice. She and her female classmates had been given a disadvantage, before they were even born. But yet, her work held promise. Her pulse raced as she thought of all the possibilities. The astronomy tower named after her. A new apartment on the north side of the city, overlooking the gardens. Extravagant parties in her honor—fountains of champagne; glittering dresses; every eye on her.

"Come here," Audric called impatiently. Jiada continued to look at the city. "Please?" She turned, a small smile on her lips. She lifted one bare foot, toes flexing, as if to take a step. One graceful eyebrow rose above a blue eye. Audric's eyes lingered now on the flexed muscle in her calf, now the breeze that played with her robe, now the soft curve of her hip. She felt that lingering look, as strongly as she felt the evening breeze. She felt it and loved it and she knew it made him sick. Jade set her foot down.

"Don't tease me," Audric said. There was no smile on his face.

"Why not?"

"Just...just come inside, okay?" His eyes darted around. She was in love with the fact that he would risk his job for her body. He made her feel like a goddess. Not directly, of course; they both tried to refrain from giving each other any power. But the way he looked at her when he was teaching, the way he melted beneath her hands, the furrowing in his brow when they had sex; that gave her all the power she needed.

"How long do you think this will last?" Jade asked, wrapping a long strand of hair around her finger.

"What?"

"This." She gestured quickly, a flash of her white hand, at him and then at herself. "You sneaking in and out of here."

"Haven't really thought about it," Audric said, staring at her.

"Liar," she said, smiling. A cold breeze ruffled her robe again.

"Okay, I've thought about it. Okay, it scares me. You already knew that. Would you please come inside?"

"Do you love me?"

Audric tilted his head and gazed at her body, his eyes moving slowly up and down. She let him fumble for the right words for a moment longer.

"Never mind," she said with a mocking smile. She walked past him into the bedroom. Audric quietly closed the door behind them.

II

As usual, Audric left early the next morning. This was the part he hated. The way her door swung shut behind him with a sound that was really only a soft thud but for him was a clang so loud it echoed deep in his skull, rattling, making the hairs on the back of his neck prickle. He always cast frantic glances around the empty streets in case anyone might have heard. Then it was the hurried walk home, fifteen blocks uphill to his apartment down the paved, trudge-smoothed avenue, walking so fast his legs strained, but knowing that he could not run. His leather shoes always hurt his toes. His gray trousers, waistcoat, and jacket seemed to strangle him.

Each avenue in Desrala was lined with maples, fragrant and budding. The houses on either side of the street seemed to lean in above him, close and frowning, the sun warming their white stone. As soon as he crossed the midway and passed the apothecary with its unpredictable smells— cloves; dried eel; pumpkin—and the bakery where the baker yawned over the floured pastry dough, and the dark, silent toy shop where dolls and sculpted animals sat waiting for the bright eyes and sweet, sweaty hands of children—when Audric passed the familiar midway and the sun began to rise over the gardens ahead of him, he slowed his pace. His legs began to relax, now tingling with too much blood. He breathed deeply.

4

Jiada

Rosemary and lavender perfumed the streets in the northern part of Desrala; the closer to the university, the better it smelled. After a long winter—or rather, one that had seemed long because of its uncommonly brutal chill—, spring was palpable. It grew every day inside the waxy green leaves of the redbud trees. It hummed deep in the throats of slippery frogs, who splashed from rock to slimy rock near the precarious falls. The professor, all hurry forgotten, decided to walk through the gardens even though it would take him a good twenty minutes longer to get home. There was something too irresistible in the perfectly pruned hedges. Glancing over his shoulder, he turned onto the garden path and slipped between the two lines of hedges. Not a single twig protruded from them, he noted with satisfaction as he strolled along the neat cobblestone path. He passed beautiful, perfectly shaped flowerbeds—octagonal patterns, delicately planned and kept. Rows of pale pink tulips, reluctantly opening. He was comforted by the focus of the tulips. He admired it and tried to concentrate in the same way as he strolled within the pleasant confines of the tall hedges. He tried to focus on his lessons, his research. His real research was what kept him up at night; what made him pore over ancient texts in the dim light of the library until his eyes crossed. An age-old question. But the university couldn't know; not yet. So he played his part and dissected plants and animals too. He was currently working on a project that, if successful, would allow scientists to replicate the attributes of certain plants—namely, plants with healing qualities. When those qualities could be duplicated, medicines would make a huge leap forward. Apothecaries could be always fully stocked with every kind of medicine. They could be easily transported to the outlying towns. In the event of an epidemic—horrible as it might be—Desrala would be prepared. Audric had only to do more research, to find out how to extract the qualities and duplicate them quickly. As he sat on a bench sifting through thoughts, he picked a leaf from a small bush. He rubbed the jagged edges of the small mairen leaf between his thumb and forefinger. If he could somehow make a pill that contained whatever it was in this tiny miracle of a leaf that cured nausea…

Mairen cured nausea. Jiada had been chewing the leaves during morning classes yesterday. She was nauseated in the morning. Audric's stomach lurched. Pregnant women got sick…four to six weeks in. Four weeks ago…he couldn't remember. He had to see her. No, no he didn't. It was too late in the day already. Too dangerous. His head pounded as he

5

stared at the delicate leaf. He swallowed the smells of the garden. Today they made him sick. He shredded the leaf with his fingernails, stripping the green to reveal a pale yellow skeleton, as he left the garden the way he'd come and hurried home.

III

Jiada Ansel sat in the bustling café in her blue riding breeches and white lace blouse. Every now and then, an older woman would look twice at her clothing, she herself wearing a long pastel muslin gown, her hair perfectly curled and pinned. Jade was used to the glances at her clothing: she and some of the other girls that went to the university wore pants and shorter dresses instead of the outdated long-skirt fashion.

In her favorite booth, the one with the squeaky leather in the far corner, by the window that overlooked the waterfall, she read an astronomy textbook and scribbled notes on its thin pages. The café smelled of expensive coffee imported from Pruen. Morning light poured onto the smooth table and Jade's book as she scanned the text.

"Good morning, Jade," a voice squeaked. Jiada recognized the excited chirp and reluctantly lifted her gaze. Lottë Friere gazed expectantly back. Her blonde curls hung limply around her moist, plump cheeks. She was wearing an olive-green dress that reached to her knees and hung unflatteringly on her bulging waistline.

"Hello, Lottë." Jade returned to her studying.

"Hello. I was wondering if I might study with you?"

Jiada gestured weakly at the booth opposite her. Lottë grinned and flopped all one hundred and eighty pounds of herself onto the seat. Jade sighed.

Lottë was also an astronomer, although Jade knew she'd never do any worthwhile research. She was too eager to please and too rigid in her morals. She was in most of Jiada's classes and since they started two months ago, Lottë had been slowly attaching herself more and more to her.

Glancing up at Jade, Lottë pulled an identical textbook out of her bag. She sighed melodramatically as she thunked it onto the table. Jade's eyes flicked up, but her head stayed in place. Lottë smiled apologetically at Jade's glare.

"Sorry." Lottë opened her book and flipped loudly through the pages.

6

Jiada

"Do you even understand what we've been learning? I'm so lost." She giggled.

"I understand perfectly."

"Right. Of course." Lottë bit her lip. "Could you...um...maybe explain it to me?"

Jade sighed. "I don't have time right now. I should get to class. Maybe you should ask the professor. I know I'm more qualified than him to answer your questions, but I just don't have time," she muttered as she stood up and gathered her books.

"Sure, right," Lottë called softly after her, cheeks burning.

IV

Audric was staring out the open window of his empty classroom when he caught a glimpse of auburn hair. Jiada was slowly climbing the wide sunlit steps outside his building. When he saw her, she was staring right at him. She slightly inclined her head to the left, and then veered off the same way, towards the courtyard between the chemistry and biology buildings where students often studied. His heart beginning to pound, Audric looked around his classroom. Desks perfectly aligned like a battalion. A chalkboard on the wall next to his desk, scrubbed clean and black. Long sticks of white chalk. In the back of the classroom, a black microscope sat like a large bug on each wooden laboratory table. Behind the tables, the far wall was lined with sinks and with cases of chemicals: glass cabinets filled with acid and salts and copper and silver filings, each labeled neatly and organized in alphabetical order. A door at the back of the classroom led to his tiny office, which was packed with boxes of beakers and flasks and crystallized iodine, not to mention his own experiments: a frog hung suspended in formaldehyde; filled notebooks were crammed into each bookcase.

The classroom, which had been Audric's home for the past five years, smelled of pencil shavings, sulfur, and mercury. The air burned his nostrils like an old friend. Audric walked as calmly as he could out of his classroom, down the hallway, out the heavy doors and into the blinding noon heat. The courtyard was surrounded by tall stone buildings and covered in lush grass and thick-trunked linden and maple trees that had been there first. The lindens were still mostly skeletal. A few students were clustered on the far side of the shaded, perfectly trimmed lawn.

7

Jade sat cross-legged under a maple. Her white blouse caught a gust of wind and blew tightly against her skin and Audric could see the outline of her breasts. He sat down next to her. She was squinting her eyes against the sun.

"So," Audric said when Jiada had been gazing at the sky for a few moments. She took out her chemistry textbook and began leafing through the pages. Their public meetings were always under the premise of tutoring. "Why are you here, Jiada?"

"Our lesson," she said, confused. Audric had forgotten about the lesson they'd planned. His cheeks burned. He'd hoped she'd had an important reason to come to him. The reason she had these private chemistry lessons was to get the subject out of the way as fast as possible so she could focus on her astronomy. Suddenly, Audric felt the question rising in his throat, like an insect crawling up from his lungs to be coughed out and grimaced upon as it lay between them, slimy and writhing. Jade was looking at him, her head tilted and her eyes narrowed to slits. She looked like the insect, he noted. Audric cleared his throat and focused on the blade of grass he was tearing apart. "What?" Jade asked, her voice biting.

"Are you pregnant?" Audric asked, and there was a horrible few seconds of silence as the question hung between them. He couldn't look at her.

"Yes, I am." He still couldn't look. He scratched his head violently and rubbed his face as his stomach dropped.

"Well." Audric sighed. His heart was pounding. It was like he looked at the world around him—the courtyard, the buildings, Jade's textbook—through a straw. All his research, his years at the university, his prestige—it all depended on Jade. "What will you do?" he whispered. He finally looked up at her. She was smiling, a cold grin the lioness gives the antelope.

"Don't worry. I'll take care of it."

Audric felt the weak relief of a sick patient who has finally begun to feel normal again. Now that it had been established, all feelings of tension and even intimacy—although it was the wrong kind—faded. All he wanted to do was leave. His mouth was chalky.

"It'll be a relief," he said.

"Definitely. For both of us."

Audric nodded. If news had gotten out, they would both have lost

8

their dreams. Now that his was secure, the professor felt he was wandering in a dreamy haze. "Well, back to our lesson?" he asked reluctantly, for he only valued the time they spent alone together, time when he could see more than just the curves under her blouse, when she was his to touch, malleable and glistening with sweat.

"Back to our lesson," she affirmed, sounding just as reluctant as he had.

V

The chemistry classroom was mostly empty, except for a few early students. Lottë Friere scanned her notes furiously, trying to somehow prepare herself for the test she had to take in ten minutes, but her notes were only incoherent scribbles and the boy behind her was humming off-key and the girl in front of her was clicking her nails on the table. Lottë finally shut her notebook and sat in a cold sweat until the classroom was full, her stomach pulsing like a scared animal in her abdomen. Jade wandered in, looking disinterested, and took a seat across the room. Lottë could see her in her peripheral vision. Her mahogany hair shone and she wore a navy blue sweater. As Lottë watched, Jade pulled a mairen leaf from her pocket and placed it on her tongue. Lottë blinked. Morning sickness? She sat back in her chair, eyes wide. The classroom door opened and Audric strolled in, wearing his usual waistcoat and trousers. He seemed to have a matching pair for every day of the week. Today it was slate-gray, and his shirtsleeves were rolled up to his elbows like usual. He scanned the full room and Lottë watched him make eye contact with Jiada and look her up and down quickly. She did the same to him, sat up straighter and slowly brushed her hair off her shoulder, all the time staring at him with her sapphire eyes. No one who wasn't looking for it would have noticed. Lottë sat back in her chair with a satisfied smile.

As Audric was about to pass out the tests, the door opened again. Twenty heads lifted in unison. A tall woman strolled in and right over to Audric, who had frozen and was staring at her, along with everyone else. She wore unusual hide boots and skin-tight leather pants, with a starched white shirt belted into them. The fashion was unusual, but the clothes hung elegantly on her thin figure. Her hair was the color of a lemon's insides.

"Is this the chemistry class?" she asked, and the whole class shifted in their seats at her unmistakable northern accent. So she was from Gláspeir. It explained how she had almost floated into the room, carrying inside her strange clothes the scent of snow and chrysalithe. She stood two inches shorter than Audric. He did another quick look-over. Lottë glanced at Jade, who was glaring at this northern beauty.

"Yes. Why don't you sit right up front here?" Audric suggested, gesturing at an empty seat in front of Jade, who was staring into Audric's eyes. He never returned her gaze. "We're taking a test right now, so you can just—"

"May I take it?" she interrupted.

Audric narrowed his eyes. "This is very advanced material," he warned. She laughed, remarkably like the sound of a bell. Audric smiled at her smile.

"I'm sure I can manage," she said.

"Well, here you are..." He held her test as if waiting for something.

"Daina," she supplied.

"Daina," he repeated, placing the paper on her desk. "Welcome to Desrala."

Jade rolled her eyes.

VI

After class, the students had all handed in their papers and filed out of the room except for Daina, who still sat with her legs crossed and her lemon head bent over the paper.

Audric slowly walked to her desk. "I'm afraid that's all the time I can give you," he said.

Daina looked up at him with a shy smile. "Well, I did the best I could," she said, shrugging.

"I'm sure." Audric slid the paper off her desk and placed it on the stack. When he turned back around to face her, she was stretching in her seat, her back arched and her head thrown back. With a soft moan, her chest lifted until Audric's hands began to tremble.

Daina lifted herself back up with a sigh. "Professor—"

"Audric. Call me Audric."

"Audric. I was wondering if you had time to give me a private lesson. So I can catch up with the rest of the class," she said.

"Of course."

"Good." Daina grinned. "Tomorrow afternoon in the courtyard?"
"I'll be there." Audric smiled.

As Daina left the room and walked into the hallway, she caught a glimpse of auburn hair and a navy-blue sweater disappearing down a different hall.

VII

Jiada Ansel counted the days until her doctor's appointment. Five, counting that day. She could count on one hand, and she held that hand with the counted days against her chest. She sat on the edge of her bed, dressed in only her robe. No class today, so she'd slept in until noon. She considered studying, but lately she hadn't been able to focus, so instead she closed the curtains, turning her bedroom into a soundless, murky cave, climbed back into bed and pulled all the blankets up around her, making a cocoon. She pressed on her stomach until she got nauseated and finally fell asleep.

When she woke, she knew she was late. She changed quickly and left for the courtyard. As she approached the chemistry building, she heard laughter above her. Looking up, she saw Audric's light on. As she watched, Daina passed by in the window, giggling.

Jiada shook her head. She'd have to learn chemistry by the book, she thought as she turned around to walk home, her fists clenched.

VIII

Lottë wasn't accustomed to walking the streets of Desrala at night. Normally, she'd be in her house on the west side of the river with cup of lemon blossom tea and the doors and windows locked and curtained. To Lottë, everyone became a murderer during the night. She clomped along as quickly as possible down the maple-lined, stone-paved avenue, crossing the bridge, skin prickling at the roaring of the falls. The night breeze blew her hair in her face. She shivered. When a door opened, she whimpered. But still she walked, her hands wringing above her distended stomach. At last she reached the house she was looking for. Swallowing her fears and wiping any evidence of them from her face, she knocked on the door. Just when Lottë was starting to panic, Jiada opened the door.

Lottë smelled vanilla wafting out of the warm house. Maybe it was from Jade herself.

"May I come in? I have something important to tell you," Lottë said. Jade looked her over, grimaced slightly, and moved aside to let her in. Lottë gathered all her confidence as she looked around the small living room. A creamy silk blanket lay wrinkled on the richly upholstered sofa. Articles of clothing cluttered the cozy room and crumpled sheets of paper lay in and around the wastebasket. Lottë couldn't help but look around at the house and see Jade everywhere; in the black dress that had hugged her body at last week's garden ball, in each note scribbled on each paper in the café and brought back here to be scrutinized.

She remembered herself. Remembered Jade and Audric. She saw the house now through a microscope, saw Jade as simply a pair of legs and lips and breasts in a silk robe. No longer on some pedestal the likes of which Lottë herself could never attain. Had she and Audric sweated with desire on that sofa? Were there still traces left? Did the room smell like him—acid and parchment?

"What do you want?" Jade asked after closing the door. She stood right next to it, waiting to open it again and shoo Lottë out.

"I know about you," Lottë began, and as soon as she did and saw Jade's eyes narrow, all of her fear melted. She had her. "You and Audric."

Jade swallowed, her trachea bulging against the taut skin of her throat. "What about us?" Her voice lacked its usual richness. Flat, it stuck in the air like ice.

"That you're pregnant. It's his, isn't it?" Lottë almost beamed when she looked at Jade, skinny and vulnerable and furious. She never was one for keeping emotions under the surface. It was too easy for them to poke through and play across the delicate cheekbones and smooth milky skin. Jiada crossed her arms and glared out the window. "I wonder how much you've gotten ahead by sleeping with him."

Her glare shifted to Lottë. She began to pace. "That's not why I do it. I'm the best damn astronomer in the world because I was born with the mind for it." Jade flexed her toes as she spat the words at the ground. "I don't need his help."

"Then you're in love with him," Lottë declared, nodding her head. She watched Jiada laugh a deep, throaty chuckle, her head tilted back and her curls falling like auburn silk.

12

"Wrong again."

"Then why risk everything?" Lottë whispered, a sense of uneasiness creeping up from her toes, like she was intruding on a private show, Jiada here in her robe, musing over Audric with a sensual laugh.

"I don't. He does," Jade said flatly, finally meeting Lottë's eyes. Her smile still played at the corner of her mouth. She leaned her head against the wall, her arms still crossed under her breasts. "He has his career at stake. I could always turn him in it if got ugly. I'd do it, too. But I don't want to. Maybe after he's taught me everything he knows. The only reason we do it is we're both here and willing. It's fun." She picked at her nails, chewing on them in the silence. "So what do you want? What's your price for keeping this quiet?"

"Your notebook," Lottë replied. She was sweating.

"My notebook? Why?"

"When I introduce your latest research as my own, you won't argue. If you do, I'll make sure everyone in town knows all about what happens in here when the curtains are closed, and about what's growing in there," she said, pointing at Jade's abdomen. She was surprised at her command of the situation. Her voice didn't even sound like her own. The sharp sounds issuing from her throat ensnared the beautiful Jiada as clearly as a pair of shackles. Lottë saw it in her eyes. The two of them stared at each other, Lottë panting and Jade glaring.

"Fine," Jade said. Lottë felt her eyes widen in their sockets. Jiada picked up her notebook from the small table next to the sofa. She leafed through the pages one last time, slender fingers caressing the familiar binding, before handing it to Lottë. As Lottë was about to close her fleshy, moist fingers around it, Jade pulled it back. She gave Lottë a sharp azure stare. "If word gets out about this, I will slit your throat."

Lottë swallowed, feeling saliva trickle down that very throat and trying not to think of it gutted and crimson. She nodded at Jiada, who stood nearly five inches taller than her, and pulled the notebook out of her hands.

"Get out of my house," Jade snapped and turned away. Lottë rushed past her to the door. It was hard to believe that the dark streets frightened her less than a warm home had. Clutching her prize, she hurried home, unable to shake the vision of her own throat gashed and Jiada's cold eyes.

IX

Five days later, Audric lay in Daina's bed. She was still asleep. Dawn was burning on the horizon, and dank gray light seeped around the curtain. Audric rolled over onto his stomach and gazed down at Daina. Her lemon hair was tousled on the pillow and her chest rose and fell slowly. Audric pulled down the sheet and kissed her breasts, stroking them gently and then, unable to stop himself, more firmly.

She gasped as her eyes opened. When she saw him, she laughed sensuously and pressed her cheek into the pillow, eyelids fluttering.

"Good morning," Audric whispered, kissing her lips.

"Mmm," she replied, stroking the back of his neck.

With Jiada there was never this intimacy. She never wanted to be close to him after sex, and he never wanted to admit that he still longed to touch her. He wouldn't give her that power. But Daina, with her fluttery eyes and soft moans, would probably let him do whatever he wanted. To test the theory, he pulled the sheet off the bed and spread her legs. She moaned loudly as he put himself inside her and wrapped her legs around his back. Audric thrust until they both were exhausted. Then he slumped on top of her, sweating into her skin, smelling her body.

"Can I ask you a favor?" she asked when they could breathe normally again. He rolled off of her and lay beside her, stroking her stomach.

"I'll give you anything," he said, and he almost meant it.

"That girl Jiada," Daina began.

"She's nothing," Audric interrupted. Daina raised one eyebrow.

"I know you have history. I see the way she looks at you. She wants you."

Audric's fingers trailed down to caress Daina. "She wants attention. She's mad I found someone better," he said as he slipped a finger inside her. Daina closed her eyes and moved her hips for a few seconds before placing a firm hand on Audric's arm. He went back to tracing circles on her stomach.

"Get rid of her," Daina said. Audric's finger stopped.

"Jade won't be a problem."

"If she wants you, she's already a problem. What if she attacks me? Will you let that happen?"

Audric sighed and rolled away. He didn't care if Jade attacked Daina.

14

Hell, why not just let the two of them fight it out? He chucked to himself as he pictured it. No, he couldn't have that.

"Maybe you're right."

Daina smiled, nestling her head on Audric's shoulder and stroking his chest.

But how best to get rid of her? Give her an assignment that took her away, sure, but for what purpose? And it came to him there in Daina's bed as an elusive final note plays into a composer's mind, clear and beautiful.

"How will you do it?" Daina asked.

"Oh, I'll think of something," Audric said, grinning.

X

Jiada sat in the operating room, dressed in a crinkly white paper gown. It smelled like bleach and human flesh. Underneath her bare bottom was the cold metal operating table. It felt like sitting on her own coffin. It was a new procedure. There had been so much talk about how it would cause a revolution. Jade didn't trust new things, didn't like the sound of the procedure at all, but there was no alternative, and it meant that she'd be free. She didn't know anyone who'd had it done, but the doctor had assured her it was perfectly safe. Anatomical sketches adorned the walls, done by anatomy students at the university. Jade read the spidery handwriting with her head tilted sideways. Uterus. Birth canal. Her skin prickled as she glimpsed the steel surgical tools lying on the counter with open, gaping mouths. Some sharp, some with clamps like animal traps. Glinting. The doctor entered with a flourish, the way doctors usually do.

"Good morning," he said flatly, without looking at her. He walked right to the tools and picked each of them up, inspecting. Jiada's heart began to pound. Tears held pressure behind her eyes, a wet tourniquet. She breathed deeply. It was perfectly safe. "Lie back," the doctor ordered. He was a gruff man with chubby fingers and a double chin. His eyes were always narrowed, creating deep furrows in his forehead. A few inches above that, his few remaining hairs were combed over in greasy waves. Jiada lay back on the table, cold seeping into her skin. She shivered. The doctor lifted her feet into stirrups so her legs were spread. She felt nauseatingly exposed. "Drink this," he ordered, handing her a

15

cup of some foul-smelling liquid. She raised her eyebrows in question. "It'll numb your body," he answered. She gulped it down, trying not to cough. Her heart hammered as he picked up a clamp. She twitched as it touched her. It was inside her and he began to open her up. Every once in a while as he worked, his fingers would slip and touch her. She shuddered. When she was open as far as possible, the doctor picked up a steel rod and Jiada squeezed her eyelids shut. She could feel it and wasn't she supposed to be numb? The liquid still left a bitter taste in her mouth.

"I can feel that," she told the doctor.

"Mmph," he grunted. "Too late now." She whimpered. "I'll be done soon."

Jiada tried to breathe and all she could feel was cold, piercing cold and an ache deep inside. It was like being skewered. She pictured herself as a pig, slowly turning on a spit. "I'm going to be sick," she whispered. The doctor ignored her.

"I can't get to it. There's something in the way," he muttered. Without warning, he pulled out the rod and Jade's stomach lurched as she realized how deep it had been in. All she wanted was to get out. The doctor picked up a hideous sharp tool. Jiada began to cry as he settled himself again and pushed it slowly into her. She didn't feel it at first, but then it touched flesh, deep secret warm flesh, and she shrieked as it pierced her. Slowly, warm blood trickled down.

"There," the doctor said. He pulled out the tool and Jiada felt dizzy when she saw the blood, almost up to the handle. "Sit there until you stop bleeding," he ordered, gesturing at a tub in the corner of the room. Jade stood up and hobbled over to it. The doctor left the room and Jade sank down into the tub, crying as she watched the blood leak from her body, holding her stomach and trying to rub warmth into it. Her body shook with sobs. The paper gown was bathed in her blood. She felt something move out of her, something bigger than just blood. A tiny mess of skin lay in the tub. She fainted.

XI

Later that day, Jade went back home. Fatigued, she climbed into bed and made her cocoon. She was asleep within seconds. When she awoke, her legs were encrusted with a sticky liquid. She frantically threw off the sheets and sobbed. Her bed was covered in blood. Jade dried herself off the best she could, her fingers shaking, and stuck a towel in her underwear. She went back to the doctor as quickly as she could run. He grumbled when she came in and told her to wait. She sat rigidly, feeling warmth spreading between her legs. The waiting room was empty and cold. Nothing on the walls. A blank white tile floor. When the doctor finally came to see her, she was in a panic.

"It's a perforated uterus," he told her after looking at it. "I'm afraid yours is the worst I've seen."

"What...what does that mean?" she stammered.

His eyes were dull. "It means you'll never have children," he stated flatly.

Jade swallowed. "Oh," she said, her voice breaking.

"These will stop the bleeding," he said, handing her a cup of lithel berries. "Come back if you still have problems." And then he was gone again.

Jade didn't know how long she sat on the operating table, slowly crushing the bitter green berries between her teeth.

XII

Audric opened the door and entered the full classroom. Students immediately quieted. He breathed in the satisfaction of that power. The first thing he noticed was that Jade was back. She'd been gone for a week. Her desk had sat empty, gathering dust. No other student would sit in it. But there she was today, wearing loose clothing and a bleak, far-off look. She glanced at him and then away. Audric knew she'd taken care of the pregnancy. He didn't care to wonder what it had cost her. He glanced at Daina next. She had seen Jade too and was giving him a pointed look. He knew what came next.

"Jiada Ansel has decided to join us," he declared, gesturing at Jade. She didn't look up. Some students glanced at her. "Jade, you missed Lottë's presentation yesterday." Jade lethargically lifted her eyes to Lottë, who smiled smugly.

"I'm sure it was unbelievable," Jade grumbled.

"Indeed. And I was waiting for you to come back so I could tell you about your special project. I'm assigning each student one for the end of the year," he explained. She raised one eyebrow. Daina was smiling down into her desk.

17

Audric cleared his throat. "You'll be traveling," he began.

"Traveling where?" Jade asked, her voice rising. Audric knew she'd never left Briga; she had barely ever left Desrala.

"You'll be looking for the Draougari," he said, and the room fell silent.

Jade's mouth opened, trying to form words. "I thought the Draougari were only a legend," she snapped.

"Part of your project is to find out if that's true or not," Audric said. He walked to his desk, pulled out a drawer and lifted a thick book out of it. "This book will tell you everything you need to know." He placed it on Jade's desk. She stared at it like it was a dead animal.

"So what exactly do I do?" she muttered, opening the book and leafing through it.

"You leave after class," he replied flatly. Jade's eyes snapped up at him. He turned his back as he prepared for the day's lesson.

"I'll leave now," Jade snapped, pushing herself out of her seat. Audric turned but said nothing. She paused at the door. "Don't think I don't know why you did this," she spat, glaring at Audric, and then at Daina, before throwing the door open and storming out.

XIII

Jiada Ansel's feet clomped down the hallway, echoing. As she turned the corner, she bumped into a late student. He apologized profusely, but she didn't really hear him. She walked faster. She climbed the stairs to the astronomy tower two by two and yanked the smallest telescope from its stand, shocking a student. She gave him a glare and ran back down the stairs. Jade passed the midway like a horse wearing blinders. She smelled yeast and chocolate glaze from the bakery. Her heart thudded and her eyes threatened angry tears. She passed two girls playing with rocks near the orphanage she grew up in. Her feet slowed and she watched them shout and scamper around with glee. They weren't like the other city children. They wore rags instead of jumpers and shiny buttons and dresses like frilly pink cakes. Jade stopped and gazed up at the building. She passed this way when she was in a hurry to get to class, but she usually tried not to look at the brown bricks, the grimy windows, and the unevenly trimmed lawn. She wondered if Mother Lissette was still slaving over the hot stove, boiling carrots for soup or baking warm crusty bread, or maybe picking up dolls and toy boats from the hallways, or scolding children. At night, she'd always tuck the small children in and then sit at the end of the hallway mending clothes or knitting socks. Jade remembered she smelled like lavender. The two girls had stopped playing and were staring at her. One of them sucked her thumb, and the other fidgeted with her dress. Jade turned away and kept walking, still fighting tears. She reached her house and went inside, closing the door behind her. The air was stiff and warm. She sank down to her knees and leaned against the door, closing her eyes. Slowly, her breathing became more labored until she shot up from where she was kneeling, grabbed the nearest flower vase from the table and threw it across the room. It shattered, deafening. Shards of glass littered the floor. The doomed roses lay like wounded soldiers on the sofa.

"Fuck!" Jade cursed, and startled herself with her own voice. She screamed and pulled her own hair. She kicked over a chair. When she'd tired herself out, she lay panting on the kitchen floor. Every now and then she kicked her legs like a toddler. She was so close. She'd dreamed of publishing famous research here in Desrala, and now maybe that would never happen. Lottë had her notes, even though she was probably too stupid to do much with them. If her presentation hadn't been earth-shattering, then she hadn't been able to figure out Jiada's advanced work. "I'll be back," Jade whispered. "I'll be back." She picked up a bag and began frantically tossing in supplies—food, clothes, mairen, bandages, a map. And the book. She stood with her hand on the doorknob for five minutes, intermittently closing her eyes and opening them to look around the living room. She wanted to be back in her blanket cocoon.

Finally, Jade opened the door and breathed in Desrala's air. It was chilly, the nip of winter still hiding under spring's crispness. She locked her door and threw her bag over her shoulder. Jiada walked on stiff legs down the street, her heels clicking on stone. That sound had raised her.

Chapter 2

I

The stars were veiled in a thin fog. The king's breath clouded in the night air. His large, rough hands gripped the cold stone wall before him as he gazed out at the plains and forests of Gláspeir. From his home in the fortress of Cairblain, the kingdom spread out before him into the horizon. The ground through which the frost seemed to seep up—as though it was created inside it, manufactured by the firm Gláspeir earth—was and always would be home. The forests of evergreens that he'd run through as a young prince, the mist-covered Moraugh mountains always at his back, the very stone of Cairblain, weather-worn but strong, tough, like the hands of the men who'd built it long ago. The stone fortress was rooted in the earth like it had been formed at the beginning of time with the Moraugh foothills. Sven leaned his head on his hands like a sleepy child. The four stars of Hiri's sword glinted on the blanket of black velvet sky. He wondered if the other kings were using those stars as a guide. Tomorrow morning they'd meet in the great hall of the fortress for their yearly meeting. Alain of Briga, encrusted with jewels and with an undoubtedly larger belly than last year. Nikola of Kahl, the youngest of the four, with his unruly dark hair and timid, beady eyes. And of course, Edmund of Navehn, who'd step out of his carriage still reeking of the fishy Porthmôr harbor, with greasy black hair and wild eyes set in his thin face, grumbling about the long journey.

Sven lit his pipe and breathed in the minty chale leaf smoke. He scratched his blonde head, leaning on the battlement. They'd talk about the usual subjects tomorrow—taxes, armies, renewing the old alliances— but there was something new on Sven's mind this year and he wasn't sure if he should share it with the other kings of Riova. His colony to the north—the treacherous, icy land of Kamareng—was proving somewhat of a burden. The kings still resented him for snatching up the largest colony for his empire, so how could he ask for their help in keeping rebels in line? His army was fearless, it was true, but he wasn't sure how much longer they could keep them at bay without reinforcements. But if he were to bring it up as they all sat in the hall, oh, he could just imagine the smirks. No, he couldn't bring it up. And the last report he'd received from General Karl had been alright. He took one last look out at the countryside from his stone perch and sought the warmth of his bedroom. He strolled through the hall, where all the preparations had been made, and through the kitchens, where the orders had been given to prepare a feast of roast seal, roast caribou, boiled potatoes, lamb stew, leek soup, goat cheese fritters, lingonberry bread and cinnamon pudding. Above all, tankard upon tankard of Abhainn's finest ale. Sven passed through the busy kitchen and opened the bedroom door. The air was warm and heavy, insulated by the tapestries adorning the walls and the furs covering the floor and the bed. He went to his dressing room, closing the hide curtain. He'd never cared much for that expensive silk. Nice enough, but it seemed to reek of tropical sweat. Maybe that was just his imagination because he knew it was from Pruen, that haven of disease and grimy, dark-skinned natives, but he still preferred leather and coarse bear fur to silk. He liked the scratchy feeling; it was from the land.

Sven struggled out of his ceremonial hide armor. He could have had a footman to dress and undress him. He told himself he didn't have one because he didn't want to keep a soldier away from where he was needed in Kamareng, and that was part of it, but the truth was that there was no one in Riova that Sven trusted enough to make his footman. That and the whole business seemed a little silly to him anyway. If he couldn't dress himself, what kind of a king was he?

"Not a very good one, apparently," Sven grumbled as he threw off the chestplate, panting. He put on his night shirt and climbed into bed, but he wasn't tired. He left the lamp burning and watched the light flicker on the wall, illuminating the adventures of his father, Falk, depicted on the tapestries. There was a particular one that had always been Sven's favorite. It was a picture of King Falk riding his favorite horse, Evening Storm, a cloudy gray stallion with a black mane and tail. In the picture, Falk was loosing an arrow at a black caribou. Sven remembered sitting in his bed when he was a child, furs piled around him. A blizzard was drilling snow into the walls of Cairblain. His mother Gemma was away for some forgotten reason, so it was up to his father to tell him a bedtime story. The frigid wind howled on stone and Sven's skin prickled.

"I'll tell you the story of the black caribou."

Sven's eyes brightened. His father had promised to tell this story when Sven was wise enough to understand it and use the knowledge to help the kingdom. He nodded eagerly.

"Are you wise? Do you feel wise?" the king asked, his thick blonde eyebrows knotted together above his nose.

Sven took a moment to think. He was ten years old. Was he wiser than he had been when he was nine? Yes, he was sure he was. "I feel wise, Father," he answered confidently.

"Well, then I guess you're ready." Falk cleared his throat. Sven felt as if he were being admitted to a grand treasure room inside his father's head. "Now this is a somber thing," Falk warned. Sven had an inkling of what 'somber' meant. He'd heard it once at his uncle's funeral, and that was enough. "You know about black caribou, don't you?"

"Know what?"

"That they're magic, of course."

Sven's eyes lit up, and then narrowed.

"You're just storytelling," he said.

"I swear to you on the frost-bitten soil of Gláspeir, this is not make-believe." His eyes were stern. That was enough credibility. Sven believed every word after that. "When I was a young king, I learned that if you wound a black caribou and then get to it before it dies, it will prophesy for you. So, I went out hunting and I scoured the forests for a week. Just when I was ready to give up, I saw one through the trees. I was on Evening Storm and I grabbed my bow and—faster than I'd ever done—stuck an arrow in him two inches left of his heart. See, I didn't want him to die straightaway, but I didn't want to make him suffer much either."

Sven was enraptured. His hands tightly clutched the fur covering him.

"I got over to him and knelt down by him. By the gods, what a sight. Fur blacker than General Karl's beard. And so soft…like the coat of a new lamb. My arrow'd been a perfect shot. He had maybe a minute left of life. So I knelt down real close, like this." Falk leaned in until his face was inches from his son's. Sven didn't dare recoil. He stared at the wide bridge of his father's nose, his lion's mane of blonde hair. "And I said, 'I've caught you, so you must give me a prophecy.'"

Sven felt compelled by his father's sharp gray eyes. He felt trapped, like the caribou.

"And he said—"

"He talked?"

Falk tilted his head. "Well, how else does one say something? Now listen. I'll never forget it, and neither should you. He said, 'Your line will soon end if your eyes are focused elsewhere'. And then he died. Just like that."

Sven turned over the phrase in his mind, settling it in. He knew it was important because of his father's tone.

"Your mother and I tried for a very long time before we had you, and we won't be able to have any more children. So you see, Sven Falbjorn, you are the hope of Gláspeir."

II

Edmund's carriage arrived first the next morning. He was early and Sven had just finished dressing when he saw the gilded blue-and-gold carriage through the window. He rushed to the kitchen and gave orders for the servants to prepare something, anything, for Edmund. Sven ran down the stairs and out into the courtyard. Winter still clung to the land, and a chilly wind whipped through his blonde Falbjorn mane as his thick leather boots sloshed through dirty snow. The gate was open and a flock of servants surrounded the carriage. One opened the door and out stepped a black boot, followed by purple silk pants, a jeweled chestplate, and greasy black hair.

"His Highness Edmund of the House of Vahir, King of Navehn," a footman announced. Edmund squinted against the white slate of the Gláspeir sky, making his beaklike nose even more prominent, and pulled his furs closer around his shoulders.

"Sven." Edmund nodded at him.

"Edmund," Sven returned.

"You remember my valet, Ahmar." Edmund waved his hand at a tanned man next to him who was trying not to shiver. Sven had thought it was warm today. He nodded, although he didn't really remember.

"Breakfast is ready. Follow me," he said and turned to lead the way.

Edmund was wide-eyed, dodging every snowflake. "Wretched stuff," he grumbled.

"So you have no fond memories of the snow, I see," Sven observed.

"How could I?" Edmund said.

"How long since it's snowed in Porthmôr?"

"I'd say ten years," Edmund mused.

"I'd miss it."

Edmund let out a hoarse chuckle. The two kings stepped inside the doors of Cairblain and into the long hallway decorated with tapestries, paintings, and animal heads. A large fire burned at the end of the hall.

23

"Your room is at the end, on the left. I'll meet you in the great hall, up those stairs."

Edmund nodded.

Breakfast was seagull eggs, fresh whitefish, and toast with wild blackberry jam. Edmund seemed unsure of the fish at first, probably mistrusting the pallid color, but upon tasting a bite, he seemed satisfied and asked for two more fish, all the while letting his eggs get cold.

"I've been landlocked for five weeks. Fish is wonderful," he said. It was rare for Edmund to express any approval. "Of course, we salted some and brought it with us, but there's nothing like fresh fish."

After breakfast, Sven showed Edmund the grounds. They walked on his favorite trail through the forest, to the ford where they watched small ice floes float down the Kalmire. They'd melt as they reached warmer water further south, and finally the ocean.

"I'll never understand it," Edmund muttered, shivering.

"Understand what?"

"Your fascination with this icy wasteland."

"Ah, but I see no wasteland," Sven said, as if comforting the nearby pine trees. "Ice maybe. But no wasteland." He picked up a handful of flat black rocks from the riverbank and began to skim them across the river's surface. They hit and bounced like dragonflies.

"So still no Queen Falbjorn?" Edmund asked.

Sven threw the last rock. It sunk instead of skimming. "Not yet."

Edmund dug his boots into the dirt. "You know, a man changes when he's married. When he's a father. There's some'll tell you a man never changes, but it's not true. Well, it depends on the man how big the change is, but there always is one. See, men are…well, they're like beaches. The same beach is there for decades, but it's not really the same, see? The grains of sand are all different. And sometimes you'll get a huge wave to knock out a big chunk of sand and wash it out to sea."

Sven was watching Edmund. He'd never heard him talk so much at once before.

"Is that what happened to you? Was Sema a huge wave?"

"She was," he said, smiling at a distant memory. "I used to be even more taciturn before I met her."

"I remember."

"And Sarila and Emre. My children made me more patient. But they also made me more paranoid."

Sven chuckled, and then remembered what his father used to tell him when he'd caught him running through the forest alone or playing with fire. He'd say, 'You take a year of my life every time you do something reckless, son.' It was a burden Sven had to bear, being the 'hope of Gláspeir'.

"Some men aren't suited for marriage, though," Edmund continued.

"I believe I am. But I'm not sure I could ever find a woman I trust enough to marry," Sven explained.

"Ah, but trust and love are so wound up together that you don't even notice your guard's down until she could steal everything from you."

"Yes, that's what I'm afraid of, I imagine," Sven muttered. Just then his servant Fyn came panting into the clearing.

"My lord, two carriages have been spotted," he rasped.

"Thank you," Sven said. He and Edmund began to walk back to the fortress with Fyn trailing behind, out of earshot.

"You trust him, don't you? That's a step," Edmund said, jerking a thumb in Fyn's direction.

Sven raised his eyebrows. "I would have made him my footman if I didn't know he swigged whiskey in a corner of the kitchen when no one's looking."

In the courtyard, Nikola was surveying the high stone walls with his hands on his hips. He wore a dark blue cotton shirt and pants tucked into his boots. His lips were tinged with blue and his wild black curls were piled on top of his head and held in place by a leather strap. Alain was struggling his way out of his carriage as Sven and Edmund reached him.

"Ah! My old friends. Help me out. I seem to have—humph—gained a few inches around the middle since our last meeting."

Sven and Edmund each took an arm and helped pull him out. His chubby feet touched snow and he righted himself, red-faced, and straightened his elaborate gold crown.

"There we are," he breathed. He was a tall man, but not as tall as Sven. "Met up with this fellow a few leagues back south on the Kalmire." Alain waved his hand at Nikola, who nodded austerely.

"Welcome," Sven said, and led the three kings inside.

III

25

Jade sat on the carpet of dead leaves and grass. She felt as near to the ground as a dormouse. The oaks and maples towered above her head and made a wall surrounding her on all sides, blending together in the twilight into a single, leafy brush stroke. She warmed her hands over the soft green spring branches, which smoked and crackled. Jade's stomach grumbled and she fished a handful of lithel berries out of her bag. They barely soothed the hunger pangs, but it was too late to hunt—not that she knew what that would entail either. The darkness was gathering like a storm cloud into the forest. Twilight had disappeared, faded into black before Jade knew it. The stars shone like bright pinpricks in the sky. Jade let herself relax. There was nothing more she could do tonight. She'd climbed down the Aerets and now she was exhausted. She bunched her bag into a pillow and rested her head on it, each exhale spreading through her body, loosening the muscles she'd spent all day straining. The tiny flames licked before her eyes, swimming orange and gold sparks.

Jade awoke to the stench of smoke choking down her throat. Coughing, she sat up and waved the fumes away from her watery eyes. The trees were outlined with a dull gray and the air was freezing. A twig snapped and Jade whirled around, sticking her hands into the damp leaves. Audric stood behind her, leaning on a tree ten feet away. He was naked from the waist up. Jiada's eyes lingered on his stomach as she remembered the way the muscles clenched.

"Audric," she breathed. He began to walk slowly toward her, his face blank.

"Come to Draoul, Jiada," he said, but it wasn't Audric's voice; it was a guttural moan. Jade's head swam. As she watched, two identical cuts opened on Audric's cheekbones. They began to drip blood. A gash began to open up all the way down his sternum. He closed his eyes and grinned, opening his palms and raising his arms as the blood turned black and congealed into batlike forms that crawled out of his chest and flew in circles around his body, cawing fiercely.

Jade gasped and awoke, her chest drumming. The sun was peeking through the treetops above her. The forest floor was speckled with new light. Jade sighed and wiped cold sweat from her forehead. The damp ground had crept into her skin and she shivered. The charred wood was barely smoking. Just to be sure, she threw a glance over her shoulder.

The trees swayed and sighed in the breeze. She breathed deeply, calming her heart's race. There was something wet on her face. Jade's hand flew to it and wiped mud off her cheek. She glanced around wildly for her leather bag and spotted it ten feet away. Crawling over to it, she found it torn open. All her food, gone. She cursed softly and sat back on her heels. The book was still there, but it wasn't much use if she couldn't find any food. She'd never had any hunting or trapping experience, so the best idea would probably be to find berries. She could hear the river rushing in the distance, so she threw the remains of the leather bag over her shoulder and began to walk toward it. The morning air was wet and cool. The Melien river, the same one that fed the falls back home, was a welcome sight. Jade scooped handfuls of cold water into her mouth until her stomach ached.

IV

Nikola awoke with a start. A cold film of sweat covered his tanned skin. He shivered and pulled the bear fur over his legs. He'd kicked it off in the abyss of some nightmare. Strange, how his nightmares were always instantly forgotten. It seemed like he'd been having nightmares for weeks. Ever since the winter storms began. In Kahl, the storms were nothing compared to what Gláspeir's or even Briga's must have been, but no other province relied more heavily on agriculture. If storms damaged the early planting, there would be less food. People would starve. That made him bite the inside of his cheek, staring at nothing. He rubbed his eyes and swung his legs over the side of the bed. He was accustomed to sleeping naked, since often the nights in Tsaigal made him sweat through the cotton sheets of his bed. But here in Cairblain, he felt exposed; the cold seemed to be tearing the fibers of his muscles with each shiver. Nikola lit a candle and began to rummage through the wardrobe in his room. He found a fur coat and slipped into it, his breath sticking icily in his throat. The fire was dying in the hearth, and Nikola tried to revive a flame from the glowing embers, but the firewood was mostly ash. He knelt on icy stone and placed his palms near the orange and black remains. When his skin had seemed to meld into the fur and gain its warmth, Nikola began to pace the small room. Sleep was now a shiny trinket dangled above his head. How could he sleep here, with all this new air around him, making his head spin with the feeling of being severed from the thread of his homeland and floating dangerously high above the earth? He longed to be sweating through his sheets back home. His stomach churned the sickening remains of the roast seal he'd eaten for dinner. Now he understood why everyone from Gláspeir could withstand the cold. The seal fat they ate insulated them. Nikola sat on the edge of the bed. The sun would rise in a few hours and with it would come the hunt. It was a tradition whenever they met in Gláspeir or Briga. As a young boy, he'd hunted on the plains of Kahl with his father and uncle. He shuddered when he thought back to those trips. The shivering rabbits that would bleed out the last few seconds of their lives, warm against his shirt, as he hurried them back to his father. The plains of Kahl were barely conducive to careful hunting, so most of the time the king and his hunting party led ostentatious charges against herds of groaning buffalo or knock-kneed elk. Nikola remembered the trophies they brought home—antlers attached to heads with gaping, blood-crusted mouths, sawed-off hooves to be hollowed out and made into cups. Nikola's worst fear growing up was that his father would show him the hunting room. He'd have to stand there among all those skulls and remember how the bodies of the animals had gone limp and landed, sprawled on the grass with a sickening crunch. His father would be staring at him, boring holes into him with his steel-gray eyes, so he'd have to gaze in wonder at every single head, pair of bony antlers, and dislocated jawbone. Worst of all, he'd have to turn to his father and smile.

Nikola, lying back on the scratchy dead animal skins, fell asleep to dreams of skinned elk roaming about the plains, naked and cold, their secret pink skin twitching.

V

The sky was preparing for the sun's arrival, spreading out layers of blushing pink clouds, as Edmund joined the others in the courtyard after breakfast. Their exhalations fogged around their heads like smoke around a volcano, slowly drifting upward. The others were all on horses already, Alain and Sven looking regal and Nikola mostly just out of place and tired. Edmund clambered onto his chestnut mare and the four of them clomped out of the courtyard and into the forest.

The sun never seemed to touch the ground there in the forest, even though the kings hunted until well in the afternoon. The sky was slowly getting darker, and clouds were beginning to bunch together, clumps of dark gray. Edmund had been hanging back the whole day, letting Sven and Alain track and shoot and exult in their victories. Nikola was even further behind, grimacing whenever a bowstring snapped. Edmund rejoiced with Sven whenever he was shown an elk or rabbit or fox, but that was the extent of his participation. He would rather have been at home on a silk cushion watching the latest opera. He longed to smell fish in the air and feel the sun's heat on his skin. Here the sun was perpetually swathed in freezing clouds.

"Shouldn't we head back? There's a storm coming," Edmund called ahead to Sven, who looked up at the sky through the treetops.

"Is it evening already?" he muttered. "Time rushes by while hunting, does it not?"

Alain grunted his agreement. Nikola looked hopefully at the sky.

"Well, it must be close to dinnertime anyway. Let's head back." The four kings turned their horses back the way they'd come and began to trot back. Sven and Alain chatted side-by-side. Edmund and Nikola followed silently behind. From time to time, Edmund heard the bellow of Alain's laugh.

"Why don't you like hunting?" Edmund asked Nikola, who had ridden up next to him. Edmund looked sideways at him. He looked like he'd been caught stealing cookies.

"Why don't you?"

Edmund laughed. "I think it's a waste of time." Nikola didn't answer. "Your turn."

He sighed. "I never liked it. Bad experiences."

Edmund's eyes narrowed.

"Fair enough."The forest was eerily silent except for the thump of hooves on frozen ground. No bellowing laughter. "Do you see them?" He asked Nikola, pointing ahead into an ink well of darkness. He wasn't sure if his aging eyes were failing him.

"No. I—I haven't been watching," he admitted, looking around. Edmund saw the whites of his eyes.

"Let's hurry," he said, and the two of them spurred on their horses. A few feet ahead, Edmund heard a thump and a groan. "Are you alright?" he called.

"I hit my head on a branch. We have to slow down. I can't see anything."

29

They slowed to a walk, and as if on cue, the skies split open. Lightning washed the trees in a blinding flash. Edmund closed his eyes and still saw bright light on the inside of his eyelids. Thunder pounded in his ears, and his heart began to knock against his ribs. The trees were closing in around him. Torrents of rain began to fall. He shouted for Nikola. No answer. Lightning flashed again and his mare reared up on her hind legs, pawing the air with a fearful whinny. Edmund was thrown from the saddle. His skull crunched against a tree trunk.

When he slowly opened his eyes, the rain was a cold drizzle stinging his raw cheeks. The forest was still dark, but he could see further than before. The moon had appeared from behind the clouds. He pressed on the back of his head and felt sticky, warm blood. Willing himself not to faint, he sat up.

"Your majesty," a voice said. Startled, Edmund turned around. A blonde woman stood behind him. She was dressed in a black robe and had two puckered scars across her cheekbones.

"Who are you?" He had a strange feeling in the pit of his stomach, like something with claws was trying to escape.

"A messenger. Your homeland is in danger. You must return at once."

"Why should I trust you? Who are you?" Edmund repeated, this time louder.

"Your family needs you." The woman's eyes jerked up to the trees behind Edmund. He followed her gaze. When he turned back around, she was gone.

"Wait—" Edmund sat on the ground, dumbfounded. His head still ached. The other kings tramped into the clearing on foot a few seconds later. "Did you see her?" Edmund demanded.

"See who?" Sven helped him stand.

"Never mind," Edmund muttered and let himself be led back to the fortress, all the while glancing back over his shoulder.

VI

The great hall blazed with light and warmth from the fire. Servants glided around from the table to the kitchens, lifting and balancing plates effortlessly. Sven noticed that Edmund hadn't touched his fish.

"You're not still shaken up, are you?" he asked. Edmund glared and sliced the fish open.

"Well now, are we ready to talk business?" Nikola asked. He, too, seemed to have no appetite.

However, Alain had already finished three plates. He wiped his beard. "What's the hurry, lad?" He laughed.

"With respect, Alain, at your pace we'd be here for a month," Nikola said. Edmund scoffed bitterly.

Alain nodded. "You may be right. Well, Sven, what should we discuss first?" Sven cleared his throat. All he could think about was Kamareng. He pushed his oysters around on his plate. "What about the alliance? Shall we renew that first?" Alain suggested.

"To renew alliances before settlements seems most unwise," Nikola interjected.

Alain raised his eyebrows. "Only if you're planning on not honoring the alliance," he replied. Nikola shifted in his seat.

"I don't think that's what Nikola had in mind," Edmund said wearily, rubbing his cheeks so that the bones pushed up closer to the skin.

"You speak for him?" Alain shot back. His cheeks were reddening. "He's barely warmed the throne and you trust him?"

"He's been king for five years," Edmund interjected.

"Let me know when it's been forty," Alain boomed.

"Alright, that's enough," Sven rose his voice over the argument.

Alain sat back in his chair, fuming. Nikola was glaring at the wall above Alain's head, refusing to look him in the eye. Edmund and Sven's eyes flashed from one to the other, and finally back to their plates in silence.

"If it were up to him, we'd all just let our people fight to the death whenever they felt like it," Alain muttered.

"Alain—" Edmund began.

"Of course you would say that. You've never seen a fight in your life. Of course it's the customs you don't understand that you attack," Nikola spat.

"I understand perfectly. That you're all barbarians," Alain snapped.

"Clever insult. I've never heard that one before," Nikola said drily. "If you're not going to be civilized—"

"What? Leave? You'd throw me out? With what authority? I'd crush you. You and your entire country of sweaty, olive-skinned mongrels!"

"Enough!" Sven shouted, slamming his fist on the table. The silverware rattled. "Now. Can we be civilized or not? I will not put up with this in my home." Alain grumbled something incoherent and returned to his potatoes.

"Perhaps, Nikola, you could enlighten us on the topic of fighting?" Edmund began. Alain scoffed. "It's a topic we've skirted in the past, and I'm curious."

Nikola was leaning back in his chair, his arms crossed. "It's very important to the province of Kahl. It's a coming-of-age ritual, a way to settle disputes, and a true art form. Arrows and swords against woodland creatures? That's heroic." Nikola rolled his eyes. "But man against man, wits and strength evenly matched, there is real heroism." He leaned forward and pounded the table with his fist. "And, contrary to popular belief, these fights almost never end in death. Of course, accidents happen. But we are not so barbaric as you foreigners believe us to be."

"Maybe not, but you must admit it is a jarring concept," Edmund stated.

"For you and Alain, maybe, who sit on silk cushions all day."

"Now wait—" Edmund began.

"How fitting, how perfect, that you cry over the newest opera and eat imported chocolate while your disease-ridden citizens die in the stinking streets," Nikola snapped at Edmund.

"Porthmôr is the most prosperous city in the—"

"Actually, Desrala is the richest—"

"And in both, the poor kiss the feet of the wealthy and there is nothing for them to do but die."

"Better to die in Desrala than in the sun-scorched, barren plains of Tsaigal!" Alain grumbled. Nikola shot up from his chair, knocking over his glass of wine. The red liquid oozed like blood over the planks of the wooden table. Sven, seeing his glare, stood up just as quickly.

"I think it would be best if one of you two left the room for a while," he said.

"I'll go. I'm already standing up. We wouldn't want the king of Briga to lift a finger," Nikola said. He stormed out of the hall.

Alain tossed back the rest of his wine. "Young idiot. I remember when I was an idealist."

"He just wants what's best for his people," Sven said wearily.

"And the sooner he realizes that he can never please all of them, the better off he'll be."

"So, what shall we discuss?" Edmund asked.

"Am I correct in saying that your armies are all deployed, Sven?" Alain asked. Sven's cheeks burned.

"Yes, almost all of them," he mumbled.

"And where are they?"

"Kamareng." Sven saw Edmund hide a smile.

"Is there a problem?"

"Actually, there is." Sven stood up. "Nikola should hear this, too." He opened the door for Nikola, who strode in without glancing at Alain. "We were discussing a problem I'm having with a colony," Sven told him as they both settled back into their seats.

"Kamareng?" Nikola asked with a smirk. "So it's not such a valuable asset after all."

"Slaves have begun to rebel. It won't be long before they organize themselves and try to take back their government." Sven paused as all the kings shifted uneasily in their seats, fearful of what was next. "Gentlemen—" Sven sighed, "I'm asking for a new alliance tonight. This alliance will bind our armies in the event of war with Kamareng."

It was as if the air had been sucked out of the room. Alain stared at Sven. Nikola refilled his glass and drank a large gulp of wine. Edmund shook his head at his lap.

"How did we not see this coming?" Edmund muttered.

"I did," Alain said. "Sven, I'm afraid my allegiance is impossible to pledge. Briga cannot afford to be swept up in a war."

Sven's stomach dropped.

"I'm glad you said it first. Sven, my response is the same," Edmund said. Sven sighed. He was hoping for help from Porthmôr's navy. Now it would have to be a land battle.

"I will back you," Nikola said, the first one to meet Sven's eyes. Sven smiled in relief. Nikola's soldiers were well-trained; combat knowledge was important in Tsaigal.

"We'll discuss terms tomorrow. I will rest more easily now," Sven said, and lifted his mug of ale in Nikola's direction.

VII

Jade had spent the entire day hunting and had only managed to find a bird's nest. The eggs, fried unevenly over a fire, had only made her hungrier. She had promised herself she'd read more from the book about the Draougari before she went any further, but when she stared at the pages, the letters swam. She had found her way back to the Melien River and was curled up on the muddy riverbank, listening to the rushing of the water as her hunger pangs came in waves. She knew there were fish in the river that she could catch if she made a spear, but she only wanted to sleep and dream of roast duck, dripping with grease. The sun was setting, dipping below the horizon like a broken egg sliding into a bowl. Jade felt surrounded once again by wave after wave of blackness. She curled herself more tightly. Her stomach churned, and she felt a different kind of pain along with the hunger. It was as if her entire abdomen was hollow. Gutted. She felt the cold pierce of steel inside her. She remembered the tiny thing that had once lived there. Jade rolled over and retched. Nothing came out. She heaved over and over again until she couldn't breathe, then collapsed onto her stomach, her face in cool mud.

VIII

From the balcony Nikola watched his servants readying the carriage. His fingers were numb with morning cold. He was going home to beautiful, open plains and cornfields. All the trees here made him feel smothered. He longed to feel warm wind whipping through his hair again.

"Heading home, eh?" Alain muttered from behind him.

"Yes."

"Listen, I know we don't get along very well. But…if I said anything…you know, the wine…" Alain rambled.

Nikola sighed. "Alright." He walked down the stairs into the courtyard, not giving Alain another glance. At the banquet the night before, with all of Sven's court in attendance, as the guests danced, Alain had suggested they play a game: whoever held a position of any power at all—counts, earls, dukes—was to dance. Then whoever held their position the least amount of time was to leave the floor first. Alain had smirked as Nikola stalked off to the table and sulkily chewed a leg of elk. The banquet was a tradition for the last night of the meeting. Nikola wasn't sure why; it always left everyone with an awful hangover for their journey home. Not the best parting gift.

"I hope you enjoyed yourself," Sven said, grasping Nikola's wrist in the ancient farewell ritual.

"Indeed," Nikola replied.

"Thank you again." Sven's smile disappeared as he bored into Nikola with his eyes. "I hope we never have to join our armies."

Nikola nodded. "As do I." He stepped into his carriage and let a servant close the door. The wheels creaked and groaned to life, grumbling along with the trotting of the horses. The Gláspeir countryside flowed by like the Kalmire they followed all the way home.

IX

Jade sat in front of her tiny fire, celebrating her first kill. She'd rejoiced over the squirrel when she'd first hit it with her makeshift slingshot, but now that she had skinned it and was roasting it, she was rather disappointed. There was hardly any meat on it. But still, it was a step. She could barely wait until it was cooked before she ripped into it with her teeth. She felt whole again, or as near to whole as she could possibly feel. Jiada lay back, one side of her face warmed by the fire. She had no idea where she was, since hunting had taken her far off course. It was noon, so she had a decent amount of sunlight left to hopefully find her way back to the river. She decided she'd look for animal tracks and hopefully follow them all the way back.

Four hours later, she'd followed the tracks of a rabbit, a moose, a deer, three different kinds of birds, and a raccoon. The sun was beginning its descent and she felt like giving up for the night. Jade sat down, and then spotted a beaver track. She eagerly followed the tracks as best she could in the dimming light, squinting. After losing the trail several times and spending an hour following it altogether, she heard the rushing of the river. Relief swept over her, and with relief, energy. She vowed to walk until she couldn't anymore, and hopefully reach Porthmôr within a week. She planned on following the Melien until it reached the sea, and then veering southeast to the harbor city. She hadn't been able to discern any definitive direction she should be heading from the Draougari book, and Porthmôr was the nearest city, so logically, it was her best option. Jade set off down the riverbank, walking with the help of the moonlight.

X

Four days later, Jade, exhausted and hungry, noticed that the ground under her feet was becoming mushy and unstable. The forest was also beginning to thin out. Every step she took, she sank a little more into muck. It felt like walking over a bruise. By the time she reached the edge of the forest, her boots were nearly ruined. There was an undeniable marshy stench in the air. Jade pulled out her map and saw that three tributaries of the Melien fed these mires on their way to the sea. She set down her bag on the driest spot of ground she could find. She ate the remains of the deer she'd killed earlier and settled in for the night. In the morning, she'd start for Porthmôr. Jiada closed her eyes and huddled next to her fire for some kind of warmth. Her teeth chattered and her eyes kept opening even though she was fatigued. The wet ground was seeping into her skin. She sat up and rubbed her hands together. The wind died for a moment and she heard a faint humming. Jade tried to hold her breath, listening for it again. It sounded like the echo of a plucked guitar string. Jiada looked around, searching for the source. Across the river, there was a tiny white glow. She picked herself up and waded across the cold river, her feet slipping on mossy rocks. When she reached the other bank, she saw that the glow and the hum were emanating from a flower. Jade dropped to her knees to examine it. The glow inside its delicate white petals reminded her of the paper lanterns that decorated the cafés at Eventide, everyone's favorite holiday. Good food and public intoxication: what more could you ask for?

"Lumale," Jade whispered, remembering the flower's name from botany class. It was supposed to cause a deep sleep, which was exactly what she needed. Jiada plucked the tiny flower up, roots and all. The humming died instantly, and the glow began to slowly fade. Jade knew she had to eat it now, or it wouldn't work, but she also knew that it acted fast. She had to get back to the other side of the river first. She sloshed through the water as quickly as possible. She felt a shooting pain in her leg, like a bite. She cursed and clambered onto the riverbank and stuck the flower in her mouth, lying down again. The silky petals tasted bitter as she crushed them between her teeth. Her limbs became warm and heavy. She closed her eyes, and this time they didn't open.

She was sweating when she awoke. The sun beat down on her skin. It was noon, and her face burned. She'd been out in the open all morning. Jade wiped drool from her cheek. She gasped and sat up when she saw black saliva on her hand. The sharp intake of air made her cough. Her chest burned. Her calf ached. Remembering the pain from the night before, she rolled up her pant leg to inspect it. "Oh," she whispered. There was a red mark where she'd first felt the pain, and three red rings encircled it. Jiada sighed. She tried walking, and it seemed bearable enough. It just felt like her leg was numb. She picked up her bag and threw it over her shoulder. She could see the coastline in the distance, and she decided to follow it all the way to Porthmôr.

XI

The next day, she threw up a total of eleven times. Each time, only a thin string of slimy black saliva came out. Her empty stomach grumbled, but she had no appetite. The rings on her leg were beginning to darken. The spot itself was black. Jade tried to clean it, but it only hurt more, so she left it alone, thinking it would scab over, only to find pus leaking out of it the next time she looked. It was getting more difficult to walk. Each step with her left leg sent pain shooting up to her hip. She had to rest every half hour or so.

That night, Jiada didn't sleep one minute. Her leg was pulsing. Each breath was labored. "I'm dying," she murmured around the phlegm in her throat. She coughed and spat and sweated through the night, shivering. When the sun rose, Jade stood up and immediately lost her balance and fell to her knees. Her head was spinning like a carousel out of control. She accidentally ripped her pant leg trying to roll it up. She sobbed when she looked. Each ring was black and had opened up, oozing foul-smelling pus down her leg. A black line on her arm caught her eye. Her blood vessels were black. Jade sobbed and lay down on her side, pulling her legs in close, her one good leg and her numb, injured one. She lay there, crying and thinking of her blanket cocoon back home. She'd never get back. She knew now that Audric had wanted her dead, and he'd get his wish soon enough. It was like her own body had turned against her. All she wanted to do was sleep. She was so tired…

"No," she shouted, making herself sit up. "I won't let you die out here." She stood up on shaky legs and fought nausea. Some voice in her head reminded her to grab her bag, and she was on her way again. Every step was a struggle, and eventually she was dragging her right leg behind her left one. She promised herself she wouldn't stop until she reached Porthmôr. She wouldn't let herself stop. Not when she was so close. When her mind wasn't consumed with pain, she looked at the countryside. It had slowly been flattening out over the week she'd been gone. She now saw plains in front of her, and forested mountains behind her. The light hurt her eyes, so she closed them as she walked, only opening them every now and then to make sure she was still going southeast. She walked night and day. She knew stopping meant sleeping, and sleeping meant dying. Her right leg became completely useless. She fell often. Her skin became red and itchy from the sun. The heat often made her dizzy and nauseated. At times, she found herself crawling without remembering falling. She escaped with her mind, remembering Desrala. She remembered the smells of the garden in the spring. Trees afire with fall foliage. The bakery, the art museum. The squeaky leather on the seat of her favorite booth in her favorite café. The seat by the window that overlooked the falls. The water misting in the air above the falls, falling far to be collected in the forest's basin below. Cool, clear water. It came from some secret place high in the mountains. She would love to swim in it right now. Be clean. Climb into bed and feel warm blankets smothering her body.

Maybe days later, she saw the first glimpse of Porthmôr. She had no way of knowing how far away it really was, or if it was there at all. Maybe it was just a mirage. Either way, she shed a tear of happiness. "Thank you," she whispered to no one in particular. She found that every now and then when she looked up, the city looked bigger. Jade began to walk faster, dragging her dead leg like a creature from a nightmare. Every one of her blood vessels, even the tiny capillaries in her fingertips, was black, she noticed. Panicking, she whimpered and thought of morgues and anatomy dissections back home. That afternoon, the spires of Porthmôr seemed so close she could reach out and touch them: shining silver between her fingers. She smelled fish in the air. Jade could see people walking in and out of the city gates, maybe carrying crops from the fields or goods to sell in town. They got bigger and bigger. Jade tried to run and tripped. She tasted warm earth, and even that made her heart leap. She was close. Her aching muscles pulled her up and she walked on. By the time she got to the gates, people were shrieking in terror and running from her. "No...wait," she cried, not realizing she was slurring her words. Her left eye must have closed up sometime, but she didn't remember when. It didn't matter. She was here. She looked up at the stone walls and walked through the open gate. There was a sickly smell of fish and a bustling marketplace. Jiada collapsed and closed her eyes. Someone screamed. There was a hand on her back. She felt like a string had been snipped, and her brain had shut off.

Chapter 3
I

The foamy sea swelled underneath the ship. Sven stood at the helm, his hair whipping behind him, the salt spray stinging his face. He breathed the clean, cold air. He loved the cold, but admittedly, the vast expanse of water frightened him. He'd rather be surrounded by trees. Still, every now and then, the ocean was invigorating. The water rolled past the ship with every drumbeat and stroke of the rowers, who sweated and grunted as their muscles worked the oars back and forth.

"Nearly there, your highness," Captain Olander said. Sven hadn't noticed him standing behind him.

"Very good," he replied. The trip to Kamareng had only taken a day. The coastline began to emerge out of the fog. Sven sighed. He only had to see General Karl. Then he could leave. He told himself that there was nothing wrong, that the general had just been unable to write recently. There was nothing wrong. Unless, of course, something had happened. Sven stepped onto the creaking dock and walked along the frozen planks to the snow-covered ground. Snow-laden evergreens surrounded the small harbor that his men had built and rebuilt after every native attack. Down the forest trail a half mile was the general's camp. Sven trudged through the snow, surrounded by five soldiers. He constantly scanned the trees and underbrush, his hand resting on the axe hanging from his belt. The warriors of Kamareng were notorious for ambushes. Sven had tried to disguise himself to look the same as the other soldiers for safety, but even though he didn't look like a target, he was still in danger. Snow crunched underfoot. No one spoke. When they reached the camp, which was set in a clearing, Sven breathed a sigh of relief. It was bustling with soldiers. Not a panic, but a healthy scramble, soldiers preparing to make their daily rounds. Sven jogged to General Karl's tent and opened the canvas flap. The general sat at his desk, poring over documents. Sven was struck by how old he looked. Karl had been a general since Sven was a boy. He'd always been part of the backbone of the crown. And now that backbone looked like it was about to break. His beard seemed grayer that the last time Sven had seen him, and his blue eyes dull and gray as well when he met Sven's gaze. It made Sven's chest ache.

"Your majesty," he greeted him, standing.

"As you were," Sven said, and Karl sat back down.

"I apologize for not having written recently. We're in the middle of a transfer of soldiers. New batch," he said, returning to his papers.

"Of course. I just had to make sure nothing was wrong. You look tired."

Karl feigned a smile. "Just busy."

"You're sure? Because if there was something wrong, you would tell me immediately. Or lose your position."

Karl met Sven's eyes. His were exhausted.

"Your highness," Karl began, even though Sven had told him countless times to call him by his first name. "Please sit."

Sven's stomach churned.

"I'll stand. What is it?"

"The situation has become precarious," Karl stated. Sven swallowed. "We're using all of our manpower just to keep the villagers in line. They won't stay unorganized for long, especially with some of the things our men have been doing." Karl shook his head. "And we're outnumbered. We need more men."

"How long can we hold out?" Sven demanded.

"A few months, maybe. No more. But even so, it's a waiting game. Sooner or later, Kamareng will reject us."

Sven stared at the wood grain of Karl's desk. He couldn't give up Kamareng. It was his greatest asset. But he couldn't ask Nikola for help so soon, either. He sighed. "How do you feel about weddings, Karl?"

II

Jade had been vaguely aware of a room for a long time. Sometimes she'd wake up and find the small, white-walled room cold. Sometimes the air felt boiling. She always fell back asleep. The scents of fish, sweat, and vomit pervaded her dreams. Jiada lay in a sweaty half-consciousness for an eternity. She felt time moving on, but not the way it usually did; it skipped and slid, jerking ahead or crawling forward. Her body ached. She felt anchored to the bed. Her heart thrashed like an air-poisoned fish in her few moments of awareness, but most of the time it rolled lethargically in the blood soup of her chest. One moment, she opened her eyes and was able to keep them open. The room hurt them. The wall lamps illuminated the white paint. There was a door directly across the room from where Jade lay. There were no windows, not even on the door. The bed she lay in had only thin, scratchy blankets. Jade lifted herself onto her elbows and sat up, straining her neck muscles. Black spots appeared all over the room. Jade's eyes stung. She lay back down quickly, panting and blinking until her vision cleared. She took a deep breath and tried again, more slowly this time. She felt a pressure behind her eyes that became almost unbearable, but she squeezed them shut and panted through it until the pain ebbed away. Jade opened her eyes and sighed at her clear vision. Bracing herself, she looked underneath her blanket. An involuntary groan escaped from her throat. On her right calf was a huge puckered sore, black and oozing. It looked like maybe it had gotten a little better, but it was hard to remember how it had looked the last time she'd seen it. A tingling sensation radiated from the sore. Jade carefully swung her bare legs over the side of the bed. She was wearing a knee-length, stiff cotton gown. Her feet touched something wet on the cold floor and her stomach churned when she realized she'd just stepped in her own vomit. She wiped her feet off as best she could, and then saw that her sheets and gown were both stained yellow. Jade backed away from the bed, from the stains and foul-smelling fluids. On her way to the door, she caught her reflection in a small mirror on the wall. Slowly stepping closer, Jade touched her face and watched her reflection do the same. So it was herself she was looking at. That pallid, gray skin stretched thinly over protruding cheekbones was hers. Those eyes, oh, she remembered their piercing ocean stare. Now they looked dull, nearly black. The gleam was gone. Her auburn hair, thin and fraying. All she could think about was how close to death she had come. How long had she been unconscious? There was no way to know. Jiada hobbled to the door, her right leg a dead weight. It was stiff, like the flesh of a corpse, she realized. For an awful moment she thought she was dead. She took a deep breath. "Can't think like that," she muttered. Jade reached for the doorknob. It felt cool against her clammy palm and her fingers closed around it like it was a lifeline. She turned it. The door didn't move. She tried pulling the knob toward her. Her yellowed nails scraped against metal as she held on. Nothing budged. She pushed instead. Throwing her shoulder against the door, she leaned into it with all of her weight, which couldn't have been more than one hundred pounds. Her bare feet slid across the cold floor. She lost her balance and fell to her knees, bruising her shins and landing hard on her right leg. She bit her lip and managed

41

to keep in her scream. A whimper came out instead, a sound so pathetic that Jade exhaled through her nostrils and stood up to try the door again. She slammed her weight against it again and again, and when her shoulder began to ache, she pounded on the door with her fists. "Let me out," she shouted over and over. Even her voice sounded different. It was a dry, scratchy growl. Jade thought of what she must look like. An animal in a cage.

III

Desrala was alive with spring. Buds bloomed on every tree, flowers burst open, the sun burned the leaves. Students sprawled lazily on the grass in the courtyards. Children squealed in the streets. The gardens were perfumed with heavy floral infusions. Bees buzzed clumsily from tulip to purple coneflower, drunk on sweet pollen. The sky was a painful blue, too bright and clear to look at. Audric couldn't help but feel inspired by the season. He saw beauty everywhere. In the wind-dancing trees, in the tiny birds' eggs, in the rosy cheeks and blowing hair of the college girls. They had begun to wear shorter cotton skirts. Audric loved their bare legs.

After class one day, Daina came to his house. He opened the door, but didn't let her in.

"Daina, I've told you not to come here. I'm in enough trouble. The dean suspects something. I feel him watching me."

"I just thought you'd been looking a little tense lately. That you could use some…relaxation," Daina whispered. She was holding her necklace, and then she slowly let her fingers trace a line down the middle of her chest. Audric's eyes followed them.

"We can't." She looked hurt. Audric remembered the last time they'd been together. "Not here. Go home. I'll come later." Audric closed his door and wiped his face, sighing. He couldn't go yet. He still had work to do. He sat down to grade papers, but he couldn't concentrate. He was able to wait five minutes before grabbing his jacket and rushing out the door.

IV

Daina stood in her front yard, holding a letter that had been waiting in her mailbox. The crest on the seal told her it was from the hospital. Her heart quickened and thudded in her ear like hearts do when they want to be noticed. She hurried inside, glancing over her shoulder. She felt the whites of her eyes glaring out at whoever might be watching. Daina locked her door and threw off her jacket. She placed the unopened letter on her table and backed away, like it might explode at any minute. She forced herself to pick it up and open it. Her fingers shook as she read it. When she heard a knock at her door, she jumped. Audric. She couldn't breathe. She saw her whole future: sent away like Jade, forced to die alone in some strange wilderness…Audric couldn't find out. But he would sooner or later.

"I have to kill it," she whispered. But even if she did, even if she took care of the problem growing inside her, what would stop Audric from leaving her when he simply got tired of her? He knocked again, more urgently, as if to remind her that he might only be there for a short time. Daina nodded to herself. "I have to keep it." A smile grew on her face. Audric would have to take care of his child. In secret. Or tell everyone the whole story. He knocked a third time. Daina hid the letter under a couch cushion. She tousled her hair, took a deep breath, and opened the door.

V

Jade sat on the cold floor, leaning her back against the door. She'd given up pounding on it and was now reading the book. She carefully flipped from page to page, so as not to tear the old, musk-scented paper. It was yellow and it crinkled a little when she turned the page. She squinted in the soft beams of light that the lamps gave off. The writing in the book was thin and cramped. She'd already read the disclaimer at the beginning and it had made her laugh bitterly in the middle of the forest. It read:

The exact location of the Draougari, if there is one, is unknown.

She remembered she'd tossed the book away in frustration, and that

43

was when she'd decided to get to Porthmôr as soon as she could. She hadn't opened the book since. Now she began to read it, all the way from the first page. The lamps lit page after page as she discerned the text. Jade was reading the chapter on their appearance when her stomach dropped.

The Draougari all have three scars, which are presumed to be part of their initiation ritual. These scars are located across both cheekbones and down the sternum.

Jade thought back to the nightmare she'd had during her first night in the forest. The one with Audric. The scars on his body had been the same scars described in the book. Jade flipped furiously through the book until she found the section on the behavior of the Draougari. She read that they were known for invading nightmares. Jade heard wind whistling outside and glanced around the room. She shivered. She felt violated. If the Draougari could enter her dreams, could they read her mind, too? What was the extent of their powers? The book didn't go into great detail. What had the fake Audric said to her?

"Come to Draoul, Jiada," she heard the raspy voice moan. She hadn't thought twice about it back then, but now she felt compelled to. Like it was the most important thing in the world. But what exactly was "Draoul" and, more importantly, where was it? It wasn't on any map. Jade's head began to ache. Her stomach gurgled loudly. How long had it been since she'd eaten? She couldn't remember the last time she'd been hungry. A wave of panic washed over her as she remembered that she was trapped. She was about to pound on the door again when it opened into a hallway. Jade stumbled away. In the doorway stood a young woman who looked as shocked as Jade felt. They stared at each other like two young girls meeting for the first time for a play date, trying to hide behind their mothers while they sized each other up. The girl had black hair tucked into a white bonnet. It looked greasy, Jade thought, and then remembered the state of her own hair. The girl wore a long, thin dress. It was gray and plain, slightly wrinkled. She stared at Jade comically, her mouth gaping open.

"What?" Jade snapped. The girl seemed to recover and blinked. She gestured past Jade and cautiously walked into the room, placing a stack of clean sheets on the bed.

"I—I was told you'd be dead," she stammered.

"Well, I'm not. Why did you lock me in?

The girl began to strip the dirty sheets from the bed. "You were sick with something we'd never seen before. No one wanted to catch it."

"Some hospital," Jade scoffed. "But that means you'll probably catch it."

"We'll see," she said. "But I don't think so. The sore on your leg, I believe that's the only way to become infected. I've studied airborne diseases for some time, and they normally don't produce such substantial external symptoms."

"Huh. I'm impressed."

"By my medical knowledge? We have schools in Navehn, too, Brigan," she said drily. She began to put the clean sheets on the bed.

"I'll do that," Jade said, taking them from her. "Just find me some clothes and something to eat."

VI

Audric sat in the café, in the seat that overlooked the falls. Seated across the table from him was a first-year student in his chemistry class. Her name was Colette.

"I'm so glad we could meet in person," she said, beaming as she brushed her red hair out of her striking green eyes. "Well, I mean, we meet in person every day in class, but—" She sighed, smiling. "I wanted to talk to you alone."

"Why is that?" Audric asking, smirking at her eagerness. She had a nice face, he thought. Good bone structure.

"Well, you're a genius," she said, leaning toward him, as if she was telling him a secret. As if he didn't know that he was a genius. Audric glanced at the bit of skin that peeked out at him from under her blouse as she leaned over the table.

"You flatter me," he said, sipping his coffee.

"What are you working on right now?" Colette asked, folding her fingers together and resting her chin on her hands.

Audric searched for the right words. "It's not exactly public information…"

Her eyes widened. "And it will stay that way. I promise."

Audric fought an urge to laugh at her serious face. "It's a mystery

45

that has existed since the beginning of time," he said, dropping his voice to barely more than a whisper. Her eyes widened even further. "You know the creation story, I assume."

"But…that's been disproven. You said so yourself," Colette blurted, her cheeks flushed.

"Colette," Audric began, touching her hand. She gave him a doe-eyed look and he tried not to chuckle at her vulnerability. "Part of being a teacher is that you must teach what your employer wants you to teach."

"So…the creation story is real?"

"As real as evolution."

She shook her head. "That doesn't make sense. Do you mean…one led into the other?"

Audric smiled. "That's exactly right."

"So the gods are real?" she asked incredulously.

"Were. They were real."

"Rhumein, the thinker; Nharyav, the evil spirit he created…"

"Who was 'a god like him, but dark in matters of spirit'," Audric quoted from Existence, the book that documented the beginning of time.

"And Aluveina, the Everlasting Melody." Audric nodded. "Then why have they stopped letting you teach that?"

Audric smiled. "Why indeed?"

"What are they trying to hide?"

"And that, my dear Colette, is my new project." He patted her hand. "Remember," he began sharply, and the smile disappeared from her face, "this knowledge is for no one but us."

VII

"Does this hurt?"

Jade winced. Her leg felt like it was on fire. "Yes."

"Sorry." Kahra, whose name she had recently learned, was rubbing a cold, foul-smelling salve on her sore. The thick, white paste oozed down into the black cavity of dead skin.

"Are you sure you're supposed to be doing this?"

"Just because I'm still in training doesn't mean—"

"Wait, what?" Jade snapped. "You're not even a real nurse?"

"Not yet," Kahra admitted. "I'm an actress. I'm training to be a nurse for extra money while I'm between shows."

"Great," Jiada said, grimacing again at the pain. She was holding her leg right above the sore, as if that would keep the pain from traveling up her nerves. It was a way to feel in control.

"So, who are you?"

"My name is Jiada." She was about to say her last name, where she was from, and that she was a well-known astronomer back home, but she bit her tongue. That didn't matter anyway. Not here.

"Nice to meet you." Kahra closed the jar of salve and stood up to leave. "More soup?" she asked. Jade's stomach turned over just thinking about it. She'd eaten a bowl of soup yesterday. It hadn't gone well.

"More vomit, you mean," she grumbled.

"We have to keep trying," Kahra said. "I told you that your body would reject it at first."

A few minutes later, Jade held a bowl of warm broth in her hands. Slowly, she lifted it to her lips and took a sip. Last night, the liquid had felt unfamiliar and disgusting on her tongue. Now she wanted to weep with joy. It tasted better than any feast ever had.

VIII

Sven trudged down the underground tunnel, five guards surrounding him. The makeshift lamps on the wall were spaced too far apart; he could scarcely see in front of himself in between their glows. They finally reached a door. Sven opened it himself and stepped inside. Seated at one side of a table was General Karl. There was an empty chair next to him. On the other side of the table was a man with light skin and black hair. His eyes were slanted, a trait of his people that many Gláspeir children mocked. He was Iosif, the king of Kamareng.

Sven sat in the empty wooden chair and folded his hands in front of him, staring at Iosif. The two kings beheld each other and the room was silent.

"I am here to propose an alliance," Sven declared. One of Iosif's eyebrows lifted. "You will give me your daughter in marriage."

"Over my dead body," Iosif shouted.

"It will be. If you try to stop me. You are going to tell your people that our kingdoms are to be united in marriage. Your daughter will come home with me. And you will act as if it is wonderful. If you make it seem like this is unwanted, my men will make sure that both you and your daughter never see another day. This is to protect both of our kingdoms from future wars. Everything will be more peaceful this way."

"How can I give my daughter to a man who talks so wantonly about her death?"

Sven chuckled. "This is war."

IX

Three days later, Sven lay in his own bed again. He was naked, furs covering him. He lay on his back, gazing at his new wife. She sat combing her long, black hair in front of the mirror. Every now and then she'd glance at him in the mirror and quickly look away.

"Will you come to me?" he asked. Slowly, she put down the comb and came to lie on the bed. She was wearing a heavy robe. She would not look at him, but instead turned onto her side, away from him. "Vira," he began, touching her arm. She turned to look at him. She was young; perhaps ten years younger than him. Her skin was like milk. So soft. "Are you afraid of me?" he asked. She stared at him and swallowed.

"No," she said.

He chuckled. "You're lying." She looked away. He held her chin in his hand. "Don't be afraid. I'm a good man, and this is your home now."

"This will never be my home," she muttered.

"Ah, I know it feels that way now. Just wait until morning. I'll show you everything. The castle, the grounds, the river. We can go hunting. You'll fall in love with Gláspeir in no time at all," Sven said, more to convince himself than her. She didn't answer. She lay there staring up at the ceiling. Sven climbed on top of her so that she was staring straight into his eyes. She looked at him with her slanted blue eyes, as if begging him not to, but he untied her robe.

X

It had been two weeks, and Jade was buttoning a white cotton shirt. She packed her bag with the book, the rest of her clothes, and some food she'd saved. Kahra had gone to bed for the night, so Jade knew she had time to leave now.

She left a note on her pillow, after stripping the sheets and folding them and placing them on the foot of the bed. The note only had two words. Thank you. Jiada glanced at herself in the mirror on her way to the door. She smiled a little at her reflection. She looked like herself. A little thin, but her eyes had that glimmer again. She quietly opened the door and slipped out.

Chapter 4

I

The sun was settling into the horizon and it felt like the earth was baking. The farmers slithered from row to row, touching each ear of corn, their heads barely visible above the green leaves of the stalks. Among them was one whose back had not yet begun to curve from the constant stooping that the corn demanded. He was only twenty and he looked at the ears of corn like they were prizes. His hair was thick and black, and he carried himself with shoulders back and head always slightly upturned, constantly daydreaming. He passed the entire day in a haze. He could tell you exactly how the corn silk felt—like jelly—, how the kernels beneath the green skin reminded him of teeth, and how he had stumbled upon a congregation of grasshoppers in the middle of a row he'd been working in—he had formed a sort of vague appreciation for their dull brown husks and liked to watch them leap away from his feet—, but he couldn't tell you how many rows he'd completed, how many ears sat in his bushel, or even the name of the man who had been working next to him the entire day.

When the whistle blew to signal the end of the day, he felt relieved like all the other men. The bushels of green-wrapped corn he carried felt as light as air. He dropped them off at the shed where all the collected corn went and waited in line for his thirty imein. The coins felt gloriously heavy in his pocket. Jingling, he followed the rest of the farmers into the city of Tsaigal. Through the massive, sandstone brick wall that had been built by the hands of his ancestors. A shadow fell on him from the watchtower above, its rusty bell hanging, frozen in time since the last invasion nearly a century ago. The view from the watchtower was a forest of red-roofed, whitewashed houses, closely packed, and the silver snake of the Kalmire, the Swift River, through the heart of the city. On the east horizon, a tiny blue strip of ocean shimmered. To the west, open plains and, farther off, thick green forestland. Down on the streets, however, the view was different: women on their way to the marketplace, grimy farmers plodding home, and dock hands, hooks thrown over their shoulders, rushing to the docks after hearing the blare of an arriving ship's horn. They would sink their hooks into burlap sacks of wheat, barley, sugar and sometimes coffee, and pull them down from the ship; unload crates of rosy apples from Briga and nets of silver, fleshy fish from Porthmôr and barrels of ale from Abhainn. With sore and bruised hands, the dock men would eventually trudge home and eat supper with their wives or alone, or maybe head to a tavern and drink until their stomachs expanded with beer or Tsaigal whiskey.

The young man walked home on stiff legs, greeting acquaintances with a solemn nod. Here was his one-story home, nestled between all the others. But his was different. On each side of the path leading up to his door, and surrounded by a fence, were plants. They ranged from tiny sprouts to leafy bushes. There were pepper plants displaying bright red bells; carrot plants with orange roots; potatoes sticking up out of the soil; squash nestled in the ground; an infant onion plant. He remembered when this ground had once been barren and dry. It could never be like that again. He had promised himself. He knelt next to his pepper plant and gently twisted the biggest, reddest bell off of the vine.

"Yes, you're ready," he muttered, smiling. The pepper felt waxy in his palm. He picked three potatoes, one squash, and two carrots. As he carried his armful of vegetables inside, he began to whistle a fragment of some forgotten tune. Setting them on the counter, he heard his father's voice.

"How was work?"

"Fine," he replied, a little startled. The old man was standing, slowly limping his way down the hallway to the kitchen. "Is it a good day?"

"Yes, Adatares. My back feels wonderful."

"Then you can start dinner," Adatares said, patting the old man on the back on his way to the bathroom. The water he filled the tub with was cold on his skin. It was always cold. He scrubbed away all the dirt, leaving the bathwater brown, and rejoined his father in the kitchen. "What are we having?"

"Oh, just a stew."

"Let me help you."

"No, that's okay," his father said. He held on tightly to the counter, swaying slightly.

"It's alright, I can help."

"No, I don't want you to. You make dinner every night," he replied. He began to breathe heavily, squeezing his eyes shut for a second. The knife shook in his hand as he tried to cut a carrot.

"I don't want you to hurt yourself," Adatares said, placing a hand on his father's shoulder.

"I don't want your help, damn it!"

He leaned on the counter for support, panting. His nose almost touched the chopped carrots. Adatares stared at his father's back. Outside, the sun had completely set. It was growing dark in the house. A child screamed across the street.

"I just want to do this," his father whispered.

"I know."

"I have to be able to do this." Tar fidgeted with a scab on his forearm.

"I don't mind cooking dinner."

His father sighed. "I know, Tar." He turned around. He swallowed, a vein bulging in his temple. It used to be hidden under thick black hair like Tar's, but his had receded, thinned into small tufts, and grayed especially quickly because of his disease. Tar remembered when he'd first gotten sick. It had only been a month since Tar's mother had died of a fever. He'd been ten. Then his father, once the earner of the family, had fallen ill and been left with a crooked, fragile back. It plagued him nearly every day. So Tar had started working.

"I'll take a few of these potatoes to sell," Tar muttered, picking up the leftover potatoes and leaving before his father had time to respond.

II

Tar sat in the tavern, staring at the door. It was dark, even though the windows let in a bit of noon sunlight. A few men sat down the bar from him. Every now and then, one of them would erupt into laughter. A woman, too. Tar traced the outline of her upper thigh with his eyes; she felt him looking at her and returned his gaze. He looked up at the wall above her head, around the bar and back to his drink, cheeks burning.

The room smelled of fried onions and alcohol. Tar held his glass in his hand, swirling it around on the surface of the table. The whiskey sloshed up to the rim, and the sweating glass left rings of water behind. The door of the tavern opened and a young man sauntered in. He glanced at Tar and smiled the way he usually did. It was a smile, but it looked more like a smirk. He leaned over the bar and a shock of black hair fell from its place and obscured his left eye.

"You're drinking?" he asked Tar, finally taking the seat next to him and gesturing at his glass.

"Well, I...no," Tar admitted, wondering why he'd even asked. His glass was clearly full.

"Then what are you doing here, Tar?"

Tar looked around at the sticky tables and smelled the fermented air. "It's not peak season yet. I got off work early." He stared at the last of the white foam on the top of his beer.

"That's not what I asked."

"I don't know. I don't know why I'm here."

Sophrosynes drank his glass all at once. It made a loud, fragile thud when he replaced it on the bar. "Well," he said. "Come with me. I have a fight soon."

Tar looked at his friend. Since they had met when they were eight, Sophro had always been obsessed with fighting. He always won when they wrestled. He made swords out of palm fronds, dueled with trees, and terrorized family pets. This fighting had helped him achieve what seemed to be his only goal in life: to become a featured fighter in the Arena.

"Fine."

"Hide your excitement, jackass," Sophro joked. Tar followed him out of the bar and into the blinding sunlight. Summer in Tsaigal was always brutal. Women caked on their makeup in the morning to go to the market, but by the afternoon, tracks of sweat cut so many tracks in it that they looked as if they'd been to a funeral. The women who prowled the streets of the pleasure district after dark smelled of earthy perfumes: sweat masked by a floral infusion.

They approached the Arena with its huge stone walls looming like slate mountains before them, the heart of Tsaigal. It already resounded with cheers. The outside walls of the Arena were beautifully sculpted with figures of fearsome warriors. There was a painted poster of Sophro bearing his usual smirk.

"Who is the bastard?" Tar asked Sophro, who laughed.

"Alvaro Pantalides," he replied. "The blacksmith." Tar pictured the heavy-set, red-faced blacksmith wielding a hammer and tried not to let his eyes widen. He punched Sophro in the shoulder.

"Kick his ass."

Sophro smiled and began to bounce on his feet. He disappeared into the guarded fighter's entrance and Tar merged into the crowd on its way to the common entrance. On his way through the massive stone archway, he found himself bumping shoulders with Despina Mali.

"Tar, hello. Do you mind if I sit with you? I'm alone," she explained. Tar nodded.

"Anything for Sophro's girlfriend."

Despina smiled. She was beautiful; her large green eyes were captivating. She was very popular in town, and during the summer festival of Elirra, she had been crowned Most Beautiful for four years in a row. Her long, dark brown hair blew in the breeze as she and Tar sat in the front row of the Arena, six feet above the white sand. Tar gazed sideways at her flushed cheeks and wondered what it would be like to hold her the way Sophro did. He breathed away the lust.

"I have to confess, this is the first fight I've been to," Despina told him.

"Really? Well, I'll have to educate you."

"Please."

"The Arena is a large oval, obviously. The fighters will come from that door there...and the opposite door, there," Tar explained, pointing to the two opposite doors.

"What is the purpose of the white sand?" Despina asked.

"To tell when a fighter has drawn blood. It's easier for the people sitting all the way up there to see the blood if the sand is white."

"I see."

"The Arena is always designed differently. Sometimes there are rocks or boulders, sometimes it's completely empty, sometimes they bring in logs or trees or build structures."

For that fight, the Arena was designed with huge stacked boulders in the center and some around the outside. "I bet Sophro will use those boulders right away. He'll use the high ground to his advantage, because Alvaro is heavier. It will be harder for him to climb."

Despina was nodding. She began to pick at her nails.

"Don't worry," Tar said.

She laughed nervously. "Alvaro is so strong," she stated, staring into Tar's eyes with her big green ones.

"But Sophro is faster." He could see Despina gripping the arms of her seat as the fighting commissioner walked onto the sand. When he reached the middle, he cleared his throat. His voice reverberated around the curved walls of the Arena:

"I present a match today between Alvaro Pantalides and Sophrosynes

54

Ilore." All over the Arena, people were rushing, clamoring, placing bets. "No bets taken after the doors open," he concluded and began to walk back to his door. In the few moments after his door closed and the other two doors opened, the sound of the Arena could be heard from the cornfields. During the heart-pounding clamor, Lothario Panes found his way to his usual seat next to Tar, a stub in his hand.

"I have 500 imein on the bastard," he shouted over the cacophony with a toothy grin. He winked at Despina. Lothario had made a total of 5,000 imein on Sophro over the last few months. A notorious gambler, he'd lost his house by betting on cheap dice games before Sophro was popular. Now that he was, Lothario was slowly accumulating wealth. Tar liked him. He knew what it was like to feel out of control. The way he clutched the small paper proved it. It was the same way Tar used to hold a glass. Like a drowning man.

Tar knew Sophro hated Lothario. He'd say that he was a "gutter-dwelling gambler who was using his successes to pay for cheap beer and cheaper women". But Tar also knew he was proud that someone was making so much money by betting on him.

A horn blared to signal the start of the fight and the Arena fell silent. The two large wooden doors slowly opened. From where the two fighters entered the Arena, they were exactly four hundred feet apart. The seat Tar sat in was directly in the middle, on the widest point of the oval.

Sophro's entrance was on his right, Alvaro's on his left. The two fighters appeared in the open doorways, locking eyes.

"They don't wear armor?" Despina whispered. Sophro wore the same cotton shirt he had been wearing all day.

"No," Tar answered. She shifted in her seat. Lothario leaned over the balcony like he always did, as if getting closer to Sophro would help him win.

Alvaro and Sophro slowly began to step toward each other. Sophro held his short sword at his side. Alvaro carried a longer mace with sharp black spikes and was shifting its weight in his hand. Sophro took a quick glance around the Arena and smirked. He took off, racing toward the center stack of boulders. Alvaro lurched forward after him. The white sand flung up beneath his feet. Sophro stood on top of the boulders, smirking, like he was just waiting for Alvaro to catch up. As Alvaro climbed, Sophro waved to the crowd, which erupted in applause. When Alvaro reached the boulder beneath the one Sophro was standing on,

Sophro pointed his sword at Alvaro's face. Alvaro grabbed the blade with one thickly-gloved, monstrous hand and yanked downwards. Sophro came with the sword, stumbling down to the same level as Alvaro, which made it clear that Alvaro was bigger than him in every way. He stood at least a foot taller. His large muscles gleamed in the sunlight like they had been oiled. Alvaro swung his sharp black mace at Sophro, who dodged it easily and lunged forward with his sword. The two of them returned blow after blow this way: the gigantic Alvaro swinging away and the light-footed Sophro circling him, dodging, ducking, always with that amused smirk. Then Alvaro stuck out his foot and Sophro, seeing it too late, tripped and wobbled. There was a wave of surprised cries from the crowd as he began to fall, but Sophro tucked his legs into his stomach and ended up landing on two feet on the sand. Alvaro hopped down and they resumed their fighting. The clash of metal on metal rang throughout the Arena until the round was over. When the horn blared, the fighters stopped and separated. They were handed buckets of water and towels.

"How many rounds are there?" Despina asked.

"Ten," Lothario answered. He had sat back in his seat and was tapping his foot violently.

Sophro dumped the bucket of water over his head and tossed the empty bucket aside. "Sophro!" Lothario called. Sophro looked up, saw who it was, and looked away. "You lost this round. You better get first blood. I've got five hundred on you."

Sophro showed Lothario his middle finger. Tar chuckled.

A horn blared and they began again. The sign on the far side of the Arena showed that Sophro had twenty points and Alvaro had thirty. The huge, lumbering blacksmith wasn't the usual type of fighter that Sophro fought. Each swing with the mace got closer and closer to Sophro's sweaty head until finally Alvaro, with a grunt like a bull, knocked Sophro to the ground. His short sword fell from his grasp.

Despina clutched Tar's arm. Alvaro lifted his mace above his head, one foot on Sophro's chest. The sword lay just out of reach on the sand. Tar's heart pounded. Lothario's eyes were wide. As the mace fell, heading for Sophro's face, he groaned under the weight of Alvaro's foot, finally lurched toward his sword, grasped the hilt, and swung. Alvaro, too stupefied to react, stood frozen. Sophro's sword bit into his bare calf. A crimson gash opened. As the blood marred the virginal sand, an exultation rang out around the Arena. Tar found himself crying out along

56

with the crowd, even standing up involuntarily with everyone else. Despina and Lothario stood on either side of him, cheering wildly. Lothario slapped Tar on the back.

"That son of a bitch!" he shouted, grinning. He kissed his gambling stub.

Sophro won the fight, two hundred to one hundred forty.

Despina, Tar, and Lothario waited for him outside the Arena. He emerged from the guarded doorway a few minutes later, the blood cleaned from his face. He beamed when he saw Despina. She threw her arms around his neck and kissed both of his cheeks.

"Ah, careful," he said, wincing.

"What's wrong?"

"The doctor says my rib is bruised." He shrugged. "I feel great."

"Me, too," Lothario interjected. He was counting his coins for the fifth time, caressing them.

"You've got your share, then. Go on. Go spend the evening in the alleyways, trying to double it," Sophro said with narrowed eyes. Lothario feigned offense and walked away. "Let's celebrate," Sophro exclaimed. "Tar, come with us."

"I don't know," Tar began.

"Oh, come on," Sophro pleaded. Tar had been refusing to go to bars with Sophro for a year. "It will be fine," Sophro promised.

"Alright," Tar relented.

III

The street was dark. Dusk had fallen while Tar had been in the tavern. It was dinnertime. He passed by windows: families seated around tables. Tar walked quickly. The streets were mostly empty; it was too late for the marketplace and too early for the bars. Except for Sophro, who stumbled along behind Tar.

"I don't need her. There are plenty of girls who want me," Sophro spat.

Tar had sat in the bar on a creaking stool, breathing the stifling air. He had stared into a tall glass, sweat forming on his forehead.

"Have a drink already. It's been too long," Sophro had slurred.

Tar had lifted the glass, but he'd felt sick to his stomach. It had smelled just like he remembered. He'd lifted it all the way to his lips,

57

tasting the cold glass, feeling the smell burn down his raw throat. But then he'd put the glass back on the bar. Thankfully, Sophro had turned his back. Tar had lost track of how many times Sophro's glass had been refilled. It had been strange to see this side of his friend. He hadn't seen Sophro drunk in a year, and watching him change again, his hands moving slowly as if through molasses, grabbing at the air; his tongue lolling lazily in his mouth as his eyebrows furrowed, trying to control it, had made Tar's skin itch. He had looked longingly at the door.

"Hey!" Sophro shouted from behind him. Tar kept walking.

"What?"

"I don't need anyone!" he slurred.

"Go home," Tar said.

"The bitch deserved it."

Tar turned around, startling the dizzy, sluggish drunk man. "Go home, Sophro. Go to bed. You're not yourself."

Sophro snorted. "You don't know me."

"Maybe I don't." Tar walked away, listening to Sophro's ranting fade behind him. He'd find his way home eventually, or wake up in the gutters and stumble home with a pounding headache the next morning.

As Tar walked through the quieting city, all he could picture was Despina's body hitting the wall, her head snapping backwards. Her flushed cheeks and the tears that stung her eyelids. Worst of all, Sophro's hands on her shoulders. His smirk, still plastered on his dumb, drunken face, even as she ran out of the bar.

Tar lowered himself onto a bench in the deserted park. It was cold, like dusk had sucked all the warmth out of the stone. He rested his aching forehead in his palms. Being with Sophro was always tiring. He had always been more outgoing. Being around people invigorated him. It drained Tar. Especially this side of Sophro he hadn't seen in so long. That cruel, mocking, violent side. It made him sick.

A cough erupted from the shadows behind Tar. He jumped and looked behind him, squinting in the thick darkness. A figure lay on the bench behind him, under the sheltering braches of the gnarled juniper tree. It shivered and shook with coughs.

"Hello?" Tar called. The figure slowly sat up. Tar came closer until he could see clearly. It was a woman, thin as a scarecrow.

"Look, I just want to sleep," she said. "Please leave me alone." Her auburn hair was tangled.

"Where did you come from?" Tar asked. She couldn't have been from Kahl or Navehn; her clothes were for colder weather. She sighed. "Please?"

"Do you really want to sleep on a stone bench?" Tar asked. She looked up at him, one eyebrow raised. She had nice eyes, he realized. He never really paid much attention to that sort of thing, but hers were a striking blue. Clear. Like looking out over the ocean. She definitely wasn't from Kahl.

"Well, I don't really have any other options, so if you're done mocking me—"

"Come on," Tar said, turning his back.

"I don't need any favors," she called after him.

"I won't tell anyone if you're worried about your pride." Tar watched her look around, tap her foot, and finally stand up and follow him. She carried a leather bag slung over her shoulder. She smelled like she hadn't washed in a long time. She seemed comfortable with the silence they maintained as they walked. The streets were starting to fill with people who exclaimed when they met friends and sang with flushed cheeks. The streets echoed with raucous laughter.

Tar measured the young woman's reaction to the crowds. She kept her sun burnt face emotionless, her eyes straight ahead, until they reached Tar's house. She glanced around at his garden as they walked to the door. Tar opened it. All the lamps were off. The air was close and motionless. Tar fumbled for the lamps and lit them with a match, illuminating small golden circles.

"Here's this," Tar said, handing her a small lamp. "You can take a bath," he added, gesturing toward the bathroom. She nodded. "Sorry about the cold water," he called after her. As the water began to run, Tar put clean sheets on his bed and took one of his blankets to the small couch in the living room of the tiny house. He also checked on his father, who was snoring loudly in his room. Tar realized that she'd need new clothes while hers were being washed, but he couldn't find anything suitable in his closet. And then he remembered. He tiptoed into his father's room and slowly opened the brown suitcase that rested at the foot of his bed. He pulled out a knee-length yellow dress with blue flowers. Carefully closing the suitcase, Tar hurried out of the dark room. He slowly opened the door of the bathroom and heard a frightened splash.

"Relax, I'm just giving you this," he said and slid the dress through a slight opening in the door. She grabbed it.

"Not really my style," she said drily.

She emerged from the bathroom, combing her wet hair. The dress hung elegantly on her body.

"It fits," Tar remarked.

"Yeah." She smoothed a wrinkle in the dress. "It actually doesn't look half bad. Whose is it?" she asked. Tar looked away.

"It was my mother's."

"Ah. Mine's dead too. Both of my parents," she stated. Her cheeks flushed and she shook her head, like she was disappointed with herself for saying that. Tar tried to speak but felt his throat close up. He wasn't sure why. "Well, I'm pretty tired, so…" she began.

"Right," Tar said, finally finding his voice. "Right in there." He gestured at the door to his bedroom. She paused, one hand on the doorknob. It was tarnished from overuse and a fleeting shame crossed Tar's mind. It was because of the way she carried herself. She was obviously weather-worn and exhausted, but she moved like she was royalty. She looked at Tar with her eyes narrowed.

"Why are you doing this?"

Tar shrugged. "I'm…not really sure."

She stared at him for a moment before disappearing into his bedroom.

IV

Dawn came, and then noon. Jiada was awakened by the shouts of children in the street. She was used to wooden ceiling planks and the stale smell of cheap inns. The tiny room she lay in had white walls and a wooden table with a chair and a rich red blanket draped over it. The bed she lay in was narrow but comfortable, and the sheets were light cotton. A warm breeze flowed through the open window. Smell of oranges. Jiada's stomach sank. She threw off the sheets. Her sweater and breeches were lying on the windowsill. They were still damp, but she packed them anyway. She decided the lightweight cotton dress she was wearing would be better suited to the heat, at least until she got further north. She slowly pushed the bedroom door open and she stepped into the kitchen in her damp socks. It was empty. Light from the front window pooled on the floor, warming it. Jiada jumped as the front door burst open. Tar entered the house and smiled when he saw Jade, who was frozen, her boots in her hands.

"You're finally awake," he said in his Kahl accent. It was like everyone here hung onto vowels longer than they should. He wiped his grimy face with his dirt-encrusted shirt.

Jade's mouth twisted at his filthy appearance.

"Working," he supplied. He looked at the leather boots she was holding. "Leaving already?"

She nodded. "I have business to take care of." She was relieved at how easy it had been.

"Can it wait one more night?" Tar asked. "I'd like to show you around the city." Jade's mind raced to find an excuse. "I just have to wash up and then we can go."

Jade was still struggling for words as he closed the bathroom door behind him. Jiada stood in the kitchen, still holding her boots, feeling the sun's warmth dry her socks. She could leave right now, just step outside and be gone, heading north, alone.

She stayed.

V

The sun baked the streets, which gave off a fermented smell. Tanned citizens bought fruit or fish in the bustling marketplace. A violinist played a haunting melody on the corner by the pomegranate stand. The merchant scowled at him.

Jade was dizzy from the merciless rays. Tar had bought her a glass of lemonade, which had helped her headache, but now all the sugar was sloshing around in her stomach. She would have preferred coffee.

"This is the Arena," Tar told her, gesturing one olive-skinned arm at the huge stone walls they were approaching. "Fights happen here. Too bad there isn't one today." They reached the wall. There was a poster of a man with a shock of curly black hair. He was shown in profile, glaring at something in the distance with a short sword in his hand. Every muscle of his upper body was tensed. Jade gazed at his poster's caption. It read: Sophrosynes Ilore: Friday at Sundown.

"That's Sophro. We've been friends since we were eight," Tar said.

"Wow," Jade replied, surprising herself with sincerity.

"There he is." Tar pointed at a young man who had just come from one of the side doors of the Arena, the very image that she had just seen on the poster. "I should have known he'd be practicing," Tar grumbled. Sophro saw them and he hung his head slightly, as if he deeply regretted leaving the Arena at that precise moment.

"Hey," he said when they came face-to-face. Jade thought it was strange that the two men clearly didn't want to see each other but felt unable to simply ignore one another. She was very uncomfortable, a strange feeling for her. There was some sort of shameful thing between them and she felt her cheeks burn simply because of knowing that.

"Working out," Sophro said, staring at his feet. "Trying to get rid of this hangover."

Tar nodded, his eyes wide in a sarcastic expression.

"This is Jade," Tar finally said. Sophro smiled at her and extended his hand. She briefly clasped his sweaty palm.

"You're not from Tsaigal," he stated. She shook her head.

"Briga."

"Ah."

Tar was refusing to look at Sophro. Sophro glanced at Jade hopefully, and she got the idea and wandered away to sit in the shade. From her bench underneath an olive tree, she could still hear their conversation, even though Sophro's back was to her.

"Do you remember?" Tar asked, seething. His arms were crossed.

"Yeah."

"Have you apologized?"

"Yes. But not to you yet." Tar lifted his head and stared at Sophro.

"I guess there's a first time for everything," he said.

"I'm done, Tar. All the drinking, the stupid things—" Tar scoffed. "I'm serious. I've never felt so awful."

Tar must have seen the truth on Sophro's face, because his smirk disappeared. "Have you told this to Despina?"

"Yeah. She'll hold me accountable."

"I guess someone has to. You never wanted my help."

"I wasn't—I wasn't there yet."

"So you had to wait until you hurt someone to change."

"Okay, so I've been wrong. I want to change, and you've wanted me to forever. I didn't support you when you quit drinking. I get it, okay? But I do want to stop. I will. I thought you'd be glad."

Tar was kicking rocks, his eyebrows knitted together. "Don't go back now," he said, and then walked over to Jade's bench. Sophro walked in the other direction. He didn't look back.

VI

Nightfall in Tsaigal always came slowly at first. The sun only dropped a tiny bit at a time, so slow that the bustling ladies in the marketplace would think the dimming light was only a trick of their aging eyes. But then the sun would fall off the earth, the merchants would close up their stalls, and the women would gather up their screeching children and the dock hands would plod home. Then there came the blurry hour when everything turned gray. A calm would settle over the city and darkness crept into every crevice. Families uttered prayers, their heads bowed over the dinner table. Outside the air cooled. The old men sat on their porches, lazy and full, and smoked a pipeful of tobacco before heading back inside to drop into a deep slumber. The streets were ghostly for a few more moments, and then young men with their thin cotton shirtsleeves rolled up would begin to emerge and call to each other as they strolled towards the southern part of the city, looking like just the right amount of hell. Girls would come too, but not as many, and only the ones whose mothers had given up on them. They came if they could swear like the boys and didn't mind taking the chance of waking up in one of their beds. The good girls stayed home and braided their hair; gazing out their windows, they watched the other girls until they were out of sight, looking now at their hands (clasped with a boy's), now at their legs (tanned, bare).

Night in Tsaigal was a force. It pushed the old and tired to sleep, suffocating them with thick, sweaty heat. It pushed young men into the arms of whores with heavily made-up eyelids and tight dresses. It pushed drunks closer to the bottle, the exhausted workers to the gambling tables instead of home, where their wives had left their supper to grow cold on the table and gone to lie biting their nails in bed.

Night punished the good and concealed the lecherous, cradled the impurity in its black embrace.

VII

Tar lay on the small couch that night. He thought of Jade. It was strange to think that her name conjured images of deep green while her eyes spoke of the ocean. Between the two, the sound of her name and the sight of her eyes, she seemed to possess the entire earth. There was one image of her that seemed to stick in his mind, and he didn't know why. It was the sight of her drinking lemonade. It was her first time trying it, and he remembered how her nose had wrinkled at its sourness. He'd laughed, and she'd laughed for a moment too, and it had been real laughter, the kind that makes your cheeks tingle. He was smiling now as he lay in the dark, just thinking of it. But then her smile had fallen away, and how fast it had happened had made his stomach turn over. He sat up and rubbed his eyes. She was leaving in the morning. He gazed at his bedroom door. She would probably be gone before he woke up, and he didn't even know where she was going. The horrible injustice of it hit him. He had to know. He stood up and, just as quickly, lay back down. It was late; she must have been asleep already.

Tar rolled over. He'd catch her before she left. He'd hear her and wake up.

He thought of Sophro with a pang of guilt. His best friend had come to him with a promise. Tar scratched his head, digging his fingernails into it and squeezing his eyes shut. He'd find Sophro and apologize.

Morning could not come soon enough.

VIII

Tar was awakened by a hacking cough. His eyes snapped open. They slowly registered that it was still night and he was calm until he remembered what had awoken him. His bare feet touched the cold floor, sending chills up his spine as he walked to his father's room. The door creaked as he turned the handle and pushed it open. Moonlight pooled on his father's bed. The bed sheets convulsed. He ran to his father's side. The old man shook violently. Blood leaked from the corners of his mouth. Animal grunts escaped his lips. Tar looked frantically around the room, and then ran to the kitchen. Grasping a wooden spoon, he hurried back to the bedroom, pried his father's jaw open, and placed it inside. His teeth bit into it instead of into his poor shredded tongue. Tar held his father's head and chin tightly until the shaking subsided.

"What happened?" Jade stood in the doorway. Her hair was tangled.

"He just started shaking...I—I don't know.." Tar breathed deeply. "We have to take him to the doctor."

Jade looked at the old man. He was unconscious, his head lolling to one side and dried blood crusting on his chin. She nodded.

An old man is very difficult to carry, especially for four blocks. But they managed, although Tar was afraid that with every step, his fingers were bruising his father. He knocked on the door of the hospital. The lamps were all off. After a few moments, a young, tired nurse opened the curtain.

"Yes?"

"My father is sick. Do you have room for him?" Tar asked.

"You're lucky. Bring him inside," she said and opened the door. The three of them deposited the old man on a bed. "Wait here. I'll go and wake the doctor."

Jade and Tar waited. He stood by his father's head and she stood at the foot of the bed. He watched her start awake every few moments. The hospital was only five rooms, with three beds in each, separated by curtains.

"It smells like piss in here," Jade whispered.

The rug on the floor was faded, and in the dim light the color was indiscernible. It was a place that made you grateful for shoes.

The nurse brought the doctor back. He was a large man, fed on corn and pasta. He had lost weight recently, but he still had the waddle of a fat man. His eyes were big and dark and brooding with heavy lids. They bore wrinkles around the edges from reading and squinting during surgery. His hands were leathery, but the fingers were agile enough. Overall, he was a man of high respect in the city, capable of treating everything from a broken arm to the latest epidemic. Sophro owed him, and because of this debt, whenever he treated him for a broken rib or a swollen wrist, he couldn't meet his eyes. But the doctor never spoke of this debt. This actually made Sophro more uncomfortable, and he had told Tar that he would repay every penny he owed once he had the money, all at once too, and even give the doctor tickets to his next fight; "something big like that."

"What do we have here?" the doctor asked Tar as he examined his father.

"I found him. He was coughing, and then he started to shake."

The doctor squeezed his father's fingers, felt his forehead, opened his mouth and examined his tongue, and listened to his heartbeat.

"He has a crooked back, no?" The doctor had remembered treating his father for the illness that had curved his spine long ago. He'd only been an apprentice at that time, but the doctor had been away delivering a baby.

"Yes."

With the help of the nurse, the doctor rolled him over onto his stomach and gently touched each crevice in his spine. Tar heard fingers hitting skin and held his breath when the doctor's fingers settled on the same spot for a long time. Finally he raised his head and met Tar's eyes.

"The spine has curved too much. A nerve has been pinched, I'm afraid."

"Um, what does that mean? Can you fix it?" Tar felt his throat close up.

"To try to align the spine is too risky. Since it's been this way for so long, there is a good chance that it would sever the nerve completely."

Tar gazed at his father. He looked small. "Is there any way to help it?"

"There is one way. A serum that I make from the haelen plant that grows in Gláspeir has a relaxing effect on joints. An injection might help me work the nerve back into place."

"Okay," Tar said.

"But our shipment of medicine from Gláspeir is at least a month overdue," the doctor replied, shaking his head. Tar's stomach dropped. "I don't know when it's going to come."

"Don't you have other medicine that could work? There aren't any other plants that grow here that have the same effect?" It was Jade.

"No, ma'am. Haelen is quite extraordinary in the soothing effects it produces. Enough of it can make even bones quite flexible."

Tar looked at his father again. Ever since his mother had died, it had been the two of them. "What if I go and bring you the plant?" Tar asked.

The doctor scratched his chin. "Traveling to Gláspeir would take at least two weeks. A month to come back. That's if you find the plant right away."

"If a shipment comes while I'm gone, you can give it to him. But if not, then I'll come back with it," Tar said. The doctor nodded solemnly.

"Let me give you this," he said and reached for a book on the shelf behind him. He tore a page out and gave it to Tar. On it was a picture of a dark blue leaf with jagged edges. "Take a lot. And make sure you store them in a dark place after you pick them. Haelen grows mostly in wet places, so it will be near the river."

"Thank you," Tar said. He folded the paper and put it in his pocket. His hand hovered over his father's forehead for a moment before he nodded to the doctor and followed Jade out the door. The sun had tinged the sky with gray. The stars had disappeared. The two of them walked down the empty street toward Tar's house, their footsteps echoing.

When they got there and Tar started packing, he realized that in all the excitement, he'd forgotten that Jade had to leave.

She was standing in the doorway of his bedroom watching him throw clothes into a bag.

"I think I'll come," she said. He turned around. "I mean, I was going that way anyway."

Tar nodded. "Then put this blanket in your bag, will you? Mine's almost full." He handed her the soft red blanket that had hung on the chair in his room. She tucked it into her bag.

They both packed whatever they could find in the kitchen: carrots, a loaf of black bread, a jar of blackberry jam, cold chicken.

When they emerged from the house, the farmers were heading sleepily for the gates. They fell into line with them, their bags slung over their shoulders. Tar felt strange, like he should be preparing for a long day of work. As they left the city, he stared out at the cornfields. He smelled their morning scent: dew and green growth. The smell always made him nauseated in the morning, and today was no different. But the sun rising over the corn, setting the tips of the tassels on fire, he would miss that. The stunning view of the purple clumps of clouds and the green stalks sighing contentedly in the breeze, that was home. The Kalmire shimmered in the distance. They'd follow it upriver to where it was still thawing.

Chapter 5

I

Sven's eyelids drooped. He sat in a hard wooden chair at the desk of his royal communicator in the aquarium-like office, the highest point of Cairblain. The walls were windows, which made it very cold most of the year, but Pietr didn't seem to mind. Sven heard the servants gossip about him often, about his gray, pallid face and wispy hair and the dark circles under his eyes. He looked like a corpse, they'd say. Admittedly, he was a bland and even coarse man at times, but he did his job well. Except for right now, Sven thought. He'd been waiting for a half hour and during that time, the sun had completely disappeared. Sven could see an outline of the forest below him and a light shimmering of the moon on the Kalmire. Everything else was black. Oil burned inside the belly of the glass lamp on Pietr's table. Sven watched the flame flicker, his eyelids slowly closing. The door burst open and he was startled awake. Normally Sven was a patient and kind man, but upon seeing Pietr's unconcerned face, he felt like punching it.

"You've kept me waiting," he said.

Pietr looked at him, his head tilted. Sven had never voiced his impatience with him before.

"I apologize, your majesty."

"Yes, well, carry on." The impatience felt uncomfortable on Sven's face.

Pietr was unpacking a large black machine from a box.

"It arrived last night," he explained.

Sven watched the man assemble it. It had a mouthpiece and on its base, several buttons. On top was a dish-like structure mounted on a stick.

"And this will allow me to communicate with Alain?" Sven asked.

"And Edmund. They've had them for a while now."

"But not Nikola?"

"No, sir."

"Of course Alain didn't give one to him," Sven scoffed.

"This is what allows you to hear them," Pietr explained, pointing to the dish.

"And I just speak into it?"

"Yes, sir. You would press this button to speak to Alain and this one to speak to Edmund."

Sven approached the desk, uncertain. The machine, known as a stemme, was a hulking black mass. Sven pressed the button labeled "Desrala" and leaned so close that his lips nearly touched the mouthpiece.

"Alain?"

A scratchy noise emitted, startling Sven. Then it cleared and Sven heard a voice boom,

"Is this Sven?"

His eyes widened. He beamed at Pietr, who was grinning smugly.

"We need one of these for General Karl in Kamareng, and we definitely need one for Nikola."

II

Outside, the air was warm and moist. Maple buds fell from trees and onto the streets and were eventually mushed by rain boots. The mixing of crushed flowers and mud and wet grass gave off an earthy, sweet smell. Inside a house on the north side of the midway, the professor sat on the floor behind closed curtains. Around him lay papers, a full ashtray, and empty bottles. He'd been sober for a while, but his pounding headache told him he was out of whiskey. Good thing the curtains were closed. A thin ray of sunlight poked around one of them.

Audric began to pick up the pieces of paper that he had strewn across the floor the night before. They were all out of order. He inhaled sharply and restrained himself from ripping the ones in his hands. He sighed and let them float to the floor. He caught his reflection in the wood-framed mirror on the wall. He hadn't noticed the brown whiskey stain on the front of his shirt. He looked different than he had at the beginning of his absence from the university. He'd taken a few weeks off. The chemistry classroom with all of its shining faces had seemed like a prison. Audric had felt a burning need to concentrate on his true work, his research of the Draougari. He was confident that if he ever came in contact with one, he could use its powers. Specifically, its healing powers. With its help, he could make himself immortal. He had a theory that they had an antigen in their blood that kept their cells from aging, but until he found one, there was no way he could prove or disprove his hypothesis. He had

69

scabbed-over cuts on his palms from where he had drawn his own blood to look at it under a microscope. When he'd first stayed home from his classroom, he'd thought seriously about setting out to find the Draougari. But then, after a long night of fervent debating, he'd talked himself out of it. He had a job to get back to; he couldn't risk the dangers of the world just yet. Not while Jade was doing it for him. It had been two months since she'd left, and he wondered what had become of her. He never really thought she'd be able to find them, but it had been a good way to get rid of her. Still, if she ever did find them, he'd finally be able to use her.

She used to worry him. She'd come through the doors of the chemistry classroom, a smirk on her pale face, her hair shimmering as she charted stars in class instead of paying attention. She had too much confidence, and that was dangerous. The first time they'd had sex, she'd barely been eighteen. He had been unable to stop himself, not that he'd wanted to, anyway. She was so fragile in his arms, and her eyebrows had furrowed like she was concentrating on him. The power had coursed through his veins as he cradled her trembling body. He'd lay there after it was over with his eyes closed and his mouth open, seeing on the insides of his eyelids an ornately sculpted, painted masterpiece that could only be heaven.

But then she had shaken off his arms. She had stood up, naked, and looked at his exposed body with a smirk. That was when he knew she could ruin him.

Audric had been surrounded by his own mess for a week. He slept when he couldn't read another word, and only for an hour or two at a time, the alcohol in his stomach invading his rest. He had eaten everything left in the kitchen a while ago, and his stomach was angry. But he had a plan now. He would be prepared if Jade ever returned, because he knew that if she found the Draougari, she'd be different. And her pride would not let her return home if she didn't find them. He wondered if her pride would even let her die out there. He knew that the two things he'd always be able to exploit were her stubbornness and her burning desire to make something of herself. They had both been clear from the first time he'd met her.

Audric looked at his reflection. He was in need of a shave and some real sleep, but he was still wired too tight. He put on a light jacket and left the house. The sunlight burned an ache behind his eyes. The fresh air made him dizzy. He splashed through spring puddles and trudged through thick mud. A warm wind soothed his cheeks. The air tasted thick and floral. He crossed the midway, passing the bakery, the toy shop, and the apothecary. Turning left onto a side street, he glanced around and approached the third house on the right side of the street. He knocked, his bones pounding on the cold wood. It felt like an eternity as he waited for the door to open. A child cried out in the street and Audric jumped. He left the doorstep and walked back the way he had come.

Audric walked back to the midway, the broad street that divided Desrala in half: the university to the north and the residential district to the south. Along the midway were cafés, restaurants, shops, and, near the river on the north side, the hospital. Audric walked along the loud midway toward the river. His shoes hit the road with wet slaps. He watched his feet as he walked, nearly becoming hypnotized by their marching. He lifted his head when he noticed a fading of conversation and the roaring of the falls. The hospital's wide steps and pillars stood, imposing, to his right. The river gushed by on the other side of a railing in front of him. If he leaned over the railing and looked to the left, he could see the river disappear over a cliff, into a cloud of mist. The falls were loud. Audric glanced at the hospital across the midway and saw a mane of lemon-colored hair blowing in the wind. Daina descended the steps as his mind raced. Audric stalked across the midway. When she saw him, her eyes widened.

"Audric."

"What were you doing at the hospital?" he spat in her face.

"Let's talk in private," she said.

"Tell me now," he muttered.

"Come home with me. You look like hell."

Audric sat at the wooden kitchen table. Outside, the sky had turned overcast. Daina placed a mug in front of him. Steam from the tea wafted up around his face. A slice of lemon had sunk to the bottom. He turned it over and over with his spoon.

"I'm going to change," Daina said and disappeared up the stairs. As soon as he heard a door close, Audric bolted out of his chair. He opened cabinets, rifled through drawers, overturned vases. He didn't even know what he was looking for. Some kind of answer. He ripped the cushions off the couch and there lay a letter. It looked like any other letter, except it was stamped with a doctor's seal. He picked it up and opened the envelope with sweaty fingers. Daina came down the stairs just as he was finishing it. She saw the couch cushions on the floor and the letter in Audric's hand and swallowed. Her arms twitched like she wanted to cross them but she left them at her sides.

"Why are you looking through my things?"

"Why didn't you tell me you were pregnant?" Audric clutched the letter, crinkling it.

"I was waiting for the right time," Daina answered. Her hands seemed to instinctively flutter to her stomach as she spoke. Audric's eyes fell on it and he was seize with an overwhelming desire to rip, to tear. He lunged toward her and she dodged away from him.

"Audric," she cried.

"I am not doing this again," he snarled. "Kill it." Daina's eyes widened. "You are not going to have this baby."

"Audric, you're hurting me," Daina whimpered. His hands were clenched around her wrists. She tried to shake him off, but he only held her tighter. She stared at his bloodshot eyes, his unshaven face, with disgust, and that made his teeth clench. He released her, pushed her backwards into the wall. Her head thudded.

"You bastard," she shouted at him. "Do you really think I'll be quiet now?" She was starting to cry, and her tears slipped down her flushed cheeks.

"If you tell anyone about us, you'll ruin yourself, too," Audric sneered.

"I don't care," Daina seethed. Audric froze. "I'm not Jade. It's not my dream."

Audric saw that something in her had decided when he'd pushed her that she had something greater than a future at the university. And that was very dangerous. They stared at each other, panting.

"What do you want?" Audric finally asked.

Daina cleared her throat and swallowed. "Money."

III

It was dark. The plains of Kahl surrounded them on all sides. The city of Tsaigal was a blur in the distance, behind their backs. The Kalmire river rushed past them to their right. They kept away from the bank because the ground was muddy there. The setting sun reflected in the river, trembling pink and orange in pools of dark gushing water.

"We should stop," Tar suggested when they approached a rare stand of olive trees.

Jade threw down her bag. Her legs ached. All the walking had brought back the ache in her calf. She sat on the dry grass and rolled up the leg of her pants. The wound had scabbed over and scarred. It was a deep, puckered ring on her calf, and it throbbed and made her wince.

"What's that?" Tar asked. He pulled out of his bag firewood that he had brought from the stove back home.

"I was sick," Jade replied. Tar nodded.

"How long ago?"

Jade leaned against a tree trunk as Tar lit the fire.

"About a month ago."

The wood began to flame. Tar sat back. They grew quiet as the stars appeared.

"You never told me where you came from."

Jade swallowed. "I'm from Desrala, but I came to Tsaigal from Porthmôr, on the main route." She remembered the heat. The way the sheets had stuck to her sweating body in the cheap inns. How the horizon shimmered ahead of her as she walked, chasing it. The colorful silks that the women from Pruen covered their dark skin with.

"Why were you in Porthmôr?"

Jade shifted. "Traveling." She felt him staring at her. The fire glowed on his face. She looked away.

"Okay."

Jade pulled the red blanket out of her bag and covered her legs with it.

"Tell me about Desrala," Tar said.

Jade raised one eyebrow. "It's cold there," she said.

"Cold? Is that all?

She smiled. His accent, although it had annoyed her before, suddenly felt endearing. "Winters last forever. But then spring comes and it's like everything wakes up again. We have gardens; they're like huge mazes, and all the flowers and trees and hedges are perfectly kept. And we have cafés with real coffee and tea. And the air is so thin there. Down here, it's like soup."

Tar gazed into the darkness, his eyes narrowed in thought. Jade watched the profile of his angular jaw. "Why did you leave?" he asked.

"Why do you care?"

"I don't. I mean, I do. I'm just asking."

Jade picked a blade of yellow grass and twirled it in her fingers. "I had to." She sighed and lay on her back, looking at the stars. She spotted Hiri's sword on the north horizon. They would use those stars as a guide on their journey north. "I was replaced by another woman." Tar lay on his back. The fire separated them.

"And that made you leave?"

"I was forced to. He gave me an assignment," Jade said.

"An assignment?"

"He was my teacher."

"Oh." The fire crackled and spat sparks into the sky. "What's the assignment?"

Jade sighed. "I have to find the Draougari."

Tar propped himself up on an elbow. "That's your assignment?" He laughed. Jade's cheeks burned.

"I know, it's stupid," she muttered.

"It's impossible."

Hearing the words that had been repeated in her head since Audric had dismissed her was dizzying. She fell silent and closed her eyes. She heard Tar rustling around in his bag. The fire crackled.

She felt small, in the middle of an endless plain at night, next to a stranger.

"Do you miss it?" Tar asked.

"Yes," she said instinctively. "Well, I don't know."

"You don't know if you miss it?"

"It's familiar," she said simply. "But I don't think I miss it. I have to get back, though."

"Why?"

"It's where I need to be. I can't make a name for myself anywhere else." Tar brushed a spark from his shirt. "I'm an astronomer," Jade supplied.

"So you know about stars—"

"I've discovered and named most of the constellations known today. I've diagrammed and charted stars and planets and developed a new calendar based on star positions."

"Impressive," Tar said plainly. Jade was caught off guard by his lack of enthusiasm. "Sounds like you've already made a name for yourself."

"I've been working on something for years. If I publish it, it will be so revolutionary...I'll be famous." Jade began. She felt a need to justify her dream to him. "And...I guess it's more than that. I want to show him that he can't control me."

"Your teacher?"

"Audric."

Tar sat up. "What is it with him? You're in love with him?"

Jade laughed. "Not love. Just sex." Tar looked at her pityingly. "Don't look at me like that." She was smiling at first, but as he continued staring at her, she looked away. Tar lay back down. They didn't talk for a long time. The fire burned the wood to ash as Jade dozed off, the blanket keeping away the cool wind.

IV

The theater was dark. The lights on the stage were low. There was an undercurrent of quiet chatter down on the theater floor, but as soon as a single violin played a chilling note, it was silent. Edmund sat beside his pale, skeletal wife. He held her bony hand. He had always loved her fragility. Queen Sema came from a long line of delicate-boned royalty. Everything she ate seemed to vaporize before it reached her stomach. He rubbed her soft hands. They always smelled of vanilla. She smiled at him as the music of the opera began to swell.

A diva waltzed onto the stage, under the eerie glow of a blue light. She sang with a high, clear voice:

"Under clearly glowing stars

Shining sapphire tears remain

Staining my cheeks."

The opera was new; written by the up-and-coming star Deniz Asuman. It was a story of a woman whose lover had been drowned while swimming in the ocean, and she went and sat on the docks every day. One night, she saw his ghost rising out of the water. He asked her to come with him.

The star was a thick-set woman with a beautiful voice and long black hair. Edmund moved slightly with the music, even tearing up when the diva's voice pierced a high note. When she was about to make her decision of whether or not to dive into the ocean to join her lover, a scream erupted from the audience, somewhere in the dark pit below

75

Edmund's seat in the balcony. People began to swarm from their seats and scurry like black ants for the doors of the theater. The diva kept singing, even though she was glancing around. Finally, the orchestra faltered. The diva scrambled offstage. Edmund grasped Sema's hand and pulled her from her seat. Three guards escorted them from the private balcony, down a spiral staircase, and into the muggy evening air. Edmund ushered Sema into their gilt carriage and then ducked into it himself. As the horses clomped along, Edmund stroked Sema's hand. She was biting her lip. Edmund's mind raced. They reached the iron gates of the palace within minutes. The gates clanged shut behind them. They were escorted past the fragrant blue orchids in the courtyard and through the doors of the palace. The guards locked the doors. Edmund pressed Sema's head to his chest. "What happened?" he asked a guard.

"An assassination, your majesty."

Edmund's heart thumped. "Who?" It was all he could say.

"Egemen. The harbor overseer."

"I just spoke with him this morning," Edmund whispered. "Who would do this?"

"Your majesty," a voice interrupted as the front doors opened. It was Edmund's valet, Ahmar. He led the sour-looking chief of police inside.

"Speak," Edmund ordered.

"We have apprehended the criminal. She is being held under close supervision."

"She?"

"Yes, your majesty. We thought you should be there for her interrogation."

"Quite right," Edmund nodded.

"I shall ready the carriage, sir," Ahmar said and left.

Edmund turned to Sema.

"Don't be gone long," she pleaded.

"Don't worry." He smiled and kissed her forehead.

V

The door of the jail cell opened with a creak. Edmund, flanked by guards, stepped inside. The room was dank and cold. A small figure huddled against the far wall. The police chief, Ismet, brought a chair and Edmund sat.

"Who are you?"

The girl lifted her head. She had a pointy nose and small, beady black eyes surrounded by bushy black hair.

"Kahra."

"You are in the presence of the King. Answer him as such," Ismet spat. She smirked and remained silent.

"Why did you kill Egemen?"

"I was given a task."

"By whom?"

"Our leader."

"Leader of what?"

She smiled. "The Silver Blade."

"What is that?"

"I'm surprised you haven't heard of us. We grow in numbers every day."

"Well, you're about to lose a member," Ismet cut in. Edmund held up a hand to silence him. "Forgive me, your majesty."

"What is this organization?" Edmund asked.

"A group of upstanding citizens who are tired of being spat on by the rich. We are tired of overpaying our taxes and working ourselves to the bone so our children will not starve."

"So you think the answer is murder?"

"Assassination of powerful officials, yes."

"See now, I am the most powerful in this province, and I will have you killed," Edmund stated calmly.

"That will only increase our power," Kahra sneered.

"If I may, your majesty, she may be right. Killing her will only make her a martyr."

Kahra grinned. Edmund thought of Sema. Of his daughter Sarila and his son Emre. Murdered in their own beds. "Kill her."

VI

The stable smelled like it always did: manure and sweet, earthy hay. Sven liked to come to the stable when he was tense or sore and just breathe in the air. Today he'd been hunting. It was midmorning and the air was warm. The Kalmire was now flowing freely. Sven led his brown stallion into his stall. He unsaddled, brushed, and fed the horse. Then he stood for a moment more in the stable before plodding back through the mud to the fortress.

The fireplace was blazing in the Great Hall. Sven dried his boots in front of it until the mud caked and he began to sweat. Then he made his way to the bedroom. It was empty. He caught Fyn in the hallway.

"Have you seen Vira?" he asked.

"No, your majesty."

"Well, do you have any idea where she might be?"

Fyn looked uncomfortable. "No," he answered.

Sven stalked past him. He searched the kitchens. Sometimes Vira would stay there with the cook. They seemed to get along. But the cook also had no information. Sven checked the library and the grounds with no avail before finally heading down to the dungeons. He met a maid in the hallway.

"Have you seen the Queen? I haven't seen her in nearly two days."

The maid wouldn't meet his eyes. He grasped her by the shoulders and shook her.

"Where is she?"

The maid began to cry. Sven released her, exasperated.

"She's down the hall."

Sven marched toward the end of the hall and tried the handle on the last door. It was locked. He rapped on the door.

"Is that you, Brione?" Vira called.

"It's your husband. Open the door."

"I have a right to my privacy."

"Not when you disappear for two days."

"I won't open the door."

Sven whistled and the maid turned to him. He motioned her over and held out his hand. After a moment, she placed a key in his palm. Sven opened the door. Vira was lying on a cot in the corner of the room. Water dripped from the ceiling into a bucket. Vira lay on her side, scrunched up. There was another bucket by her feet, filled with a foul-smelling liquid. Sven felt a tinge of guilt at seeing her like that, clearly in pain. He walked to her bedside.

"Why are you hiding yourself? There's no shame in being sick."

She turned away from him. Sven reached for her hand and she pulled it away.

"What's wrong?"

78

The door opened and a short, fat woman came in. Her name was Brione, and she was Vira's maid and had come with her from Kamareng. She carried hot towels, which she set down on the table by the door. When she saw Sven, she froze.

"What's going on?" Sven asked. "Tell me."

"Her majesty needed some privacy," Brione said, crossing her arms.

"Treat me as your king," Sven ordered.

"She has a right to privacy, your majesty."

"There is no privacy anymore. Not when you are hiding something from me." Brione had her hands behind her back. "What's in your hand?"

"Nothing, your majesty," she sneered.

Sven grabbed her arm and wrenched it around.

"Sven," Vira exclaimed. Brione was seething. Sven pried open her clasped fingers and picked a tiny white pill from her sweaty palm.

"What is this?"

Vira rolled onto her back and stared blankly at the ceiling. "My father made it for me. He's always been good with potions. He told me to take three of them, one a day, if I got pregnant."

The blood left Sven's head and he became dizzy. His limbs felt watery.

"You're pregnant?" he whispered.

"I was. It'll be mostly dead by now."

Sven felt hot tears of rage behind his eyes. He crushed the pill between his fingers. All he wanted to do was grab fistfuls of that inky hair and jerk her face toward his and make her feel his anger. But he only said,

"Why? Why would you kill our child?"

Vira sighed. "It's not like it was born." Sven struggled for words. The crushed pill covered his fingers, sticky. "I'm leaving as soon as I'm well. I'm going home."

"You witch," Sven finally spat. He slammed the door behind him as he left.

VII

The next morning, the sun did not rise. It must have risen somewhere, but not in Cairblain. The sky brooded all morning. Sven watched Vira leave. All the while as she packed her floral-patterned hairbrush, her polar bear furs, her books, and her embroidery, Sven knew he should stop her. Hold her prisoner in the dungeon, anything. But when he looked at her, his chest tightened. He wanted her gone. Her high cheekbones and dark, almond-shaped eyes. All he could think about was her voice saying, "It'll be mostly dead by now." His child, dying inside of her. He would never hold it. Sven locked himself in his room for most of the day. It was strange how he felt insulated from the world there, as if it had stopped and was waiting patiently for him to come out. When he finally emerged, it was noon. The sky was still dark and the air out on the balcony was thick and foggy. Sven leaned against the stone wall and surveyed his domain. A green blanket of evergreens covered the land before him. Snaking through, the silver band of the Kalmire River. Past the forest, the fog thickened and sprays of purple heather dotted the hills in the distance. Sven remembered how the servants used to tell tales about the moors on the southern border of Gláspeir. Sometime in everyone's childhood, they all associated the moors with some kind of ethereal, dark feeling. Their beauty was pure during the day, but at night fog obscured them and wolves howled from the hilltops. A man had been killed there once. A messenger. He had disappeared and never reached Tsaigal. A few months later, a group of children had found his decaying corpse in one of the countless honeycombed caves near the river.

Sven thought of Edmund. He had told Sven, nearly three months ago, that he needed a wife. And then there was the prophecy. "Your line will soon end if your eyes are focused elsewhere." He wanted to lie down right there on the balcony and press his face against the cold stone.

VIII

The call came four days later. Sven was awakened by fervent knocking at his bedroom door. He slipped his large feet into his moccasins and stumbled to the door. Pietr was on the other side, a candle flickering in his hand.

"What is it?" Sven grumbled.

"A call, your majesty. From Kamareng. It's urgent."

Sven padded up the steps two at a time. The stemme sat waiting for him on Pietr's desk. Sven leaned close.

"Go ahead, Karl." Adrenaline was sluicing sleep out of his brain.

"This is Lieutenant Feodor. The general has been killed."

80

Sven's head whirled. "What happened?"

Static blared. "No time. Revolt—we need reinforcements—we're at war—"

Silence.

Sven pressed the button. "Lieutenant! Come in, Lieutenant!"

There was nothing. Sven's heart pounded.

"Your majesty?" Pietr ventured. It was the first time Sven had ever seen him look distressed.

"I must call Captain Brahn in Abhainn. And then Nikola."

IX

It was noon. The sun would have been brutal in Tsaigal, but it had been getting cooler every day. The breeze here came from the north, not from the south and across the hot plains like it did in Tsaigal. It was a Gláspeir breeze. Tar and Jade plodded along. The ground wasn't so dry anymore; it had begun to give way a little beneath their steps, like it had a secret. Tar had noticed that Jade looked up as often as she could while she walked. And at night, she always lay on her back, staring at the stars. She had a small telescope that she used sometimes. She said she'd stolen it from her astronomy classroom, but that it didn't matter because she was the only one who used it anyway. Tar liked to watch her gaze at the stars. He started doing it too. He'd never given much thought to it, the same way you don't give a thought to the ceiling above your head until it falls on you. The stars were beautiful. Especially there, in the middle of the plains, away from everything. But although Jade fell asleep every night while looking at them, Tar had to turn over after a while or they burned on the insides of his eyelids and he couldn't sleep.

"The moors," Jade remarked as they walked, pointing ahead to hills with clumps of purple flowers.

That night, a thick fog surrounded them. It was cold. They had set up camp next to the river, in a sort of shallow cave. There were a lot of them around. The fire cast a glow on the gray, puckered rock, and on Jade's face. She was warming her hands. They ate rabbit and then sat staring into the night. The gushing of water on rock echoed on the cave walls.

"What happened with Sophro? Before you met me," Jade asked.

Tar shook his head. "He reminded me why I don't drink anymore."

"Why don't you drink?"

81

Tar sighed and stretched. "I get...mean."

Jiada laughed. "You? Mean?"

Tar nodded. "Worse than mean, actually. And it's not even like I lose my mind and people tell me I'm mean but I don't remember. I remember everything and I'm in control the whole time. I'm just different."

Jade nodded. "I don't drink much either. It makes it hard to concentrate."

"That's the point, I think."

"I guess."

Tar looked at her. She was picking at her nails. She returned his gaze and then quickly looked away.

"You have nice eyes," he said.

She rolled them. "Thanks."

"Really," Tar said. "There's not many people in Tsaigal that have blue eyes."

"So?"

"So, I like them."

"You like them because they're different," Jade concluded.

"No. Well, yes. I don't know. Maybe I like them because people's eyes in Tsaigal are like the earth. Brown, the occasional green. But yours are like the ocean."

Jade laughed. "You should be a poet." Tar shrugged. "I mean it. No one's noticed my eyes before."

"Yes, they have. They just didn't want to compliment you."

Jade raised an eyebrow. "Why?"

He shrugged again. "You're intimidating."

They sat quietly until Jade finally moved to the outside of the cave and lay down on her back. Tar copied her and they stared at the stars for a long time together, separated by the fire.

Tar was awakened by a scream. He jolted up and through his blurry, sleep-filled vision, he saw Jade jump up and run out of the cave. She disappeared into the mist. Tar scrambled to his feet and ran after her. The fog consumed him. He tripped and hit his shoulder on the rocky side of a cave. The uneven ground and all the caves reminded him of a honeycomb. He ran with his hands in front of him. He heard a shout echo and ran as fast as his visibility would let him. Adrenaline clipped his breath. He ran toward the sound and finally a dark figure materialized ahead of him. Jiada was hunched over.

"Jade, are you alright?" Tar asked. She stood up. There was a gash on her right cheek that was dripping blood.

"They were here. One of them. The Draougari. She cut my cheek." Jade pressed a hand to her cheek, smearing the blood. She let out a little gasp of disgust. "I followed her, but I couldn't catch up." Tar heard tears of frustration in her voice. "She must be around still." She began to jog.

Tar caught up and grabbed her arm. "Don't, Jade. It's the middle of the night. There's nothing we can do."

"But she was here!" She was so close, and I could have asked her where she came from. I could have—" She sighed.

Tar stood silently while Jade collected herself.

"Let's go back," he said. She swallowed and nodded. Tar sulked behind her, following her back to the camp. "Let me bandage your cheek," he said.

"It's alright."

"It'll get infected. Trust me."

She sighed. "Fine, whatever." She sat down, crossing her legs. Tar pulled a towel and a long white bandage out of his bag. He soaked the towel in the river and, sitting down in front of Jade, gently pressed it against the cut. Jade winced.

"It's deep," Tar muttered. Her eyelashes fluttered against his hand as he gently wiped the excess blood from her face. Drops of water ran down her chin. He unrolled the bandage and began to wrap it around her head, holding her defiant chin in his palm. He felt her breath on his hand and her eyes staring at him.

"Why would they do this?"

Tar looked at her. The bandage was wrapped around her head, below her right eye and over her nose.

"I don't know. I really don't know much about them," he admitted.

"I do. They all have these scars. Two across their cheeks and one down their chest. It's like part of their initiation."

"So...you think they were trying to..."

"Recruit me? Yeah. But why? And why would they leave when I woke up?"

"I don't know," Tar said, although as he did, he realized it was a rhetorical question. "It's late," he remarked.

Jade felt the bandage. She pressed against her cheek and wrinkled her nose. "I don't think I'll sleep now."

"Then I'll stay up. Just in case."

Jade nodded. They sat, mostly in silence, for a long time.

Toward dawn, Tar awoke. He was lying on his side under the blanket. Next to him, on her back, Jade lay with her eyes closed and her mouth slightly open. The blanket rose and fell with her chest. There was something about the way she looked lying there. Fragile. Tar had never seen it before. Her forehead was wrinkled, like she was scared. The bandage covered her cheek and nose. He gazed at her eyes. They flashed back and forth beneath their lids. Tar slowly sat up and draped the other half of the blanket over her. Still asleep, she curled into a ball.

Tar set to work making a fire for breakfast, and she slowly emerged from her slumber.

"I didn't think I would fall asleep," she mumbled. "I would have helped." She slowly unwrapped the bandage from her head. There was a red blotch on it, but the cut had mostly begun to scab over. It was an angry gash.

"I couldn't wake you. You looked too real," Tar said.

"Real? I'm always real."

"No, not really."

"What are you trying to do?"

"What do you mean?" Tar asked.

"You keep saying these things. Things like, I'm not real, and the way you look at me. Just stop." She was turning pink.

Tar was caught off guard. He kept silent until she looked at him again. "I think you're sad. I think you're depressed."

"I still have my dignity."

"Do you?"

"Shut up," Jade snapped, and Tar almost recoiled at her snarl. "What I do with my body is none of your business. No one owns me."

"Except for your teacher. Audric."

"He is nothing."

"Then what does that make you?"

Jade stood up. "Fuck you." She grabbed her bag and began to walk north.

Tar sat in the grass. He picked a handful and scattered the blades over the fire, where they writhed like little snakes, turned black, and broke up into indiscernible ash. Tar wished for a second that he'd gotten them out of the fire before they were completely destroyed. It was one of those short, simple pangs of guilt in the pit of the stomach, a human instinct. Tar seized his bag, stomped out the fire, and began to run. The ground sloped upward through the mist. He trampled rocks and purple heather. The sound of the river crashing surrounded him, echoing through every cave, a cacophony. There was nothing but those things: the heather, the mist, the roaring water. He felt his skin prickle.

"Jade," he called. There was no answer. He had let her go, and just when she was in the most danger. He saw visions of her mangled body in his head. Tar dug his fingernails into his left hand as he walked, holding his hunting knife in the other. It had a long blade that curved a little, almost as long as the machetes the farmers used to cut down brown corn stalks in the fall. He walked to the river, where he knelt in the mud and splashed cold water on his face. The Kalmire was narrower here than in Tsaigal; faster, too. He watched it for a long time, his head resting on his hands. He thought about her. It seemed like she was all he ever thought about. But it was different now. She had changed in his mind. Tar stood up, his knees aching, and turned around. She appeared out of the fog. He wondered how long she had been standing there.

"I got pretty far," she muttered.

"Why did you come back?" Tar asked, coming closer. As he did, he saw the real look on her face again, the scared look, as she struggled for words. "Jade, tell me something real," he said.

She swallowed. "Like what?"

"Anything. Something about you."

She turned away. "No. Nothing is real."

Tar held her arm. He didn't say anything, he just stared at her. Her eyes were filling with tears.

"I think…I don't want to leave you."

Tar swallowed. "What happened to you?"

She shook her head. "I've only done what I've needed to do."

He didn't know why, but he just pulled her close to him, pressed her head to his chest. There was nothing to say. After a long time, she finally sobbed,

"I'm ruined." Tar held her shoulders away from him and looked at her. "I'm ruined," she whispered. "I wish—"

"What?" Tar held her head up.

"It doesn't matter."

He held her again.

X

There was a knock at the door. Sophro lay in bed, an arm around Despina. She was asleep. Sophro sank back into bed, hoping whoever it was would go away. It was the middle of the night and he just wanted to lie there and smell Despina's hair: ginger and vanilla. The knocking became louder and more rapid. She awoke.

"What is it?"

"I'll go see," Sophro said. He left the warmth of his bed. He was naked from the waist up. A cool breeze blew in from the open window and made the sweat on his neck tingle. He walked down the hallway. The knocks on the door stopped. And he waited. Then there was a crash and the door burst open. Three men darted in. Sophro kicked the bedroom door shut and grabbed a knife from the kitchen counter.

"Get the hell out of my house," he shouted. Then he noticed that the three men wore the red badges of the king's guard. Sophro swallowed.

"The great fighter," one of them said. "You think because you're some kind of celebrity, you don't have to go to Kamareng?" They advanced toward him and Sophro tightened his grasp on the knife.

"I don't believe in this war."

All at once, the men rushed at him. He swung at one and another knocked the knife out of his hand. He elbowed one in the jaw. The third man pinned his arms behind him. He grunted as the guard twisted his arm, and he heard the bedroom door open.

"No, Des. Stay in there. Don't touch her."

"Relax. We wouldn't hurt a woman. Although she is...beautiful." The guard looked her up and down.

"Bastard," Sophro spat.

"Say goodbye. Who knows when you'll see each other next?"

"Sophrosynes," Despina called. She was wrapped in the white bed sheet.

"Des." His voice almost broke. "I'm sorry." They began to drag him.

Sophro didn't sleep. He was in a sort of barracks that had been erected in the Arena for the soldiers. Men snored around him. Some let out muffled sobs, covered by coughs. Sophro lay on his one blanket, waiting for morning. It was the longest night of his life. When the sun began to rise, there was a pounding on the door.

"Everyone up!"

Men grumbled and stretched and swore. Sophro searched for a familiar face.

"Sophro," he heard someone call. He turned to see Lothario. The shadow of a black beard was growing on his face.

"They finally got you, huh? I wondered when they would. I heard the ones they brought in last night were the last of 'em. We're leaving today. As soon as they get us all organized, I imagine. They got me the first day, and I've been here four days. The worst part is being so close to home and I can't leave, I think. Like dogs. We're chained up here. But we'll be leaving soon."

Sophro listened. He was staring at the door, where men had begun to be ushered out.

XI

The sun had completely set when they saw the light in the distance.

"It must be an inn," Jade said. The mist had cleared as they'd left the moors behind them. The entire day had been spent in the mud by the riverbank, looking for haelen. "We should stop there. There's no reason not to. We've been looking all day."

"All right." Tar looked exhausted. His shoulders sagged.

It took twenty minutes to reach the inn, a two-story wooden shack. Inside, the wall lamps cast circles of dim orange light onto the walls and floor. The bar was mostly empty except for a man at the far end, who stared at a blonde woman sitting at a table. It smelled like mold.

"Can I help you?" A short man, maybe fifty years old, hobbled over to them, clearly favoring one leg. He had a few greasy hairs combed over his shining head. He stood a few inches shorter than Jade and nearly a head shorter than Tar. He was wearing a stained white collared shirt with his sleeves rolled up past his elbows.

"We'd like a room," Jade said. He led them up creaking stairs and into a small, cold room. He lit a few lamps and then shut the door on his way out. The room had a bed, a large window, a bucket for a toilet, and a washing basin. "Could be worse," Jade said, throwing down her bag and sitting down on the bed. Tar pulled the blanket out of his bag and spread it over the bed and lay down on his back, rubbing his eyes. Jade unbuttoned her sweater. Tar saw what she was doing and turned away.

She laughed. "You can look if you want." Jade took off her sweater and pants. She saw Tar glance at her lace underwear. He was lying on his side, facing her.

"It's okay," she whispered. Her legs were bent and her feet flat on the bed. She turned to face him and his eyes fell on her bare legs. He reached to touch her. His fingers were warm through the lace. He turned away, looking queasy.

"Nothing is going to happen. Do you understand? I won't do that." He spoke to the ceiling.

"What is wrong with you?"

"Nothing. I'm not Audric. He's obviously the one you want." Tar rolled over and blew out the lamp by the bed.

Jiada didn't sleep for a long time. She wondered if Tar was asleep. Sometimes she'd hear his breathing change or feel his legs move, and she'd know he was awake, but most of the time she couldn't tell. Whenever she saw that queasy look in her mind, her cheeks reddened. No man had ever looked at her that way, except maybe Audric that day in the courtyard. Usually men leered at her, eyes glinting with desire. Like she was something to devour. Tar had looked at her like she was a mangled animal. Disgusted, with some pity. She lay there fuming, three inches away from him. The air in the room was damp, and she was slowly warming underneath the blanket. She turned away from Tar. Just when she thought he might finally be asleep, he said,

"Why did you say you're ruined?"

Jade pretended not to hear him.

"I know you're awake. You're breathing too fast." His muffled voice vibrated in her pillow.

Jade rolled over so they were both on their backs.

"I made a mistake. I got pregnant."

"So you have a kid?"

"No. I…had it taken out of me."

The sheets rustled as Tar sat up. "The baby?" Tar's bare back arched next to her.

Jade nodded. "When I was having it done, the doctor cut me, and now I can't have children."

Tar lay back down. "I'm sorry."

Jade shrugged. "It's okay."

"Fuck. Stop doing that. You don't have to pretend. Don't you get that?" His hands were grasping air above the blanket as he spoke. They

88

made shadows on the far wall in the moonlight, two long black lines.
"Everyone lies," she whispered.
"What?"
"Everyone lies. We have to. It's how we survive."
"It's not how I survive."
"You're not a hero," Jade snapped. Tar fell silent and rolled over. Jade rolled the other way, her back to his back. She rubbed her stomach gently and a solitary tear dripped sideways over her nose. She sniffled. There was an ache in her chest, like a hunger pang, but harder. She breathed deeply, but it was still there. She turned her aching body over and rested her forehead on Tar's back. His muscle tensed and then relaxed.

XII

When morning came, Tar's head pounded. A layer of cold, fine sweat seemed to cover everything in the room, like a frost. He sat up. The sun blared through the window, blinding. Jade's hair was matted with sweat and dried tears. Her jaw was relaxed, her mouth hanging open a little. Tar covered her with the blanket—more of an instinct than anything else. He dressed and left the room, walking down the stairs for breakfast. When he reached into his pocket, his cheeks reddened. Where he should have felt cold coins, he felt empty cotton. He rushed back upstairs to check his bag. As he was throwing clothes out, Jade awoke.
"What's wrong?" she mumbled.
"Someone stole my money," he said.
"What?"
"It's gone." He sat back on the floor, rubbing his face. "Of course the door has no lock."
"Okay, um. Let's just slip out. The place probably has a back door." Jade began to look for her clothes. The door opened. She pulled the blanket up around her chest. The short old man with the limp from the night before stepped in.
"Payment," he stated simply. "Ten imein."
"I'm sorry, but my money was stolen while I slept," Tar said. The short man glared at him.
"What a story."
"It's true, sir. Now, is there any other way I could pay you? I can work," Tar offered.

The short man thought it over. Then he glanced at Jade. His eyes widened. "I know how you can pay me." A film of sweat shone on the man's upper lip.

"No," Tar said. "Anything else. I won't let you touch her." He felt his face burn.

"Tar, it's okay," Jade muttered.

"No. Jade, stop."

Her face was expressionless.

"This isn't happening."

"It's okay."

The old man raised an eyebrow at Tar, who stared at his beady eyes, greasy hair, and the sweat on his lip. "It's the only thing I'll accept," the man said as he eyed Jade's legs.

"It doesn't matter to me," she said plainly.

Tar picked up his bag. He was shaking his head.

"I can't help you," he said and left the room. Tears stung his eyes, painful tears that made him seethe through clenched teeth. He clomped down the stairs and out the door into the raw Gláspeir morning, leaving Jade in her lace underneath the red blanket.

XIII

Shouts outside woke the king. Edmund sat up instantly, alert. He hadn't been sleeping much lately. His sudden movement woke Sema. He held up a finger for silence. Glass shattered. Edmund jumped up. "Get the children."

"I have to dress," she said and rushed to her wardrobe.

"There's no time. Just go."

Sema, her eyes wide, ran in her white nightgown down the hallway. Edmund rushed to the servants' quarters and met Ahmar on his way.

"You must go, your majesty. I have prepared the carriage. Down the east stairs and around the back."

"Ahmar, come with me," Edmund pleaded.

"I must stay with the others, my lord. I do not believe it would be right to abandon the palace. I must stay and fight."

"I release you from your duties. Come with us to Pruen. You are my valet, and I need you."

Ahmar looked distressed. He nodded. "Your will, my lord."

He followed Edmund down the east corridor, down the stairs and out the door. Sema sat in the carriage with Emre on her lap and Sarila next to her. Edmund wrenched the door open and jumped inside, followed by Ahmar. The footman snapped the reins on the horses' backs and the carriage jumped to life. It rumbled through the forest path in the dark, lit only by moonlight. As Edmund watched the palace dwindle behind them, it glowed orange, flames engulfing it. He hugged his daughter close. As they left the city behind them, Edmund thought he heard Ahmar crying.

XIV

It looked exactly like the picture. A small blue plant with jagged leaves. He found it near the river, just where the doctor said it would be. Tar picked as many haelen plants as he could find. It was midmorning and the sun warmed his skin. He put his handful of haelen in his bag. As he began to walk south, he felt increasingly uneasy. He tried to banish the feeling, telling himself that he was going home to save his father, and he needed to get there as soon as he could. He ran until he couldn't run anymore, and then he walked only until he had enough energy to run again. By the time he reached the moors, his chest was aching. He coughed and sat down to rest. There was no time to make a fire. He stood up and tried to squint through the mist. There was a dark mass on the horizon, slowly moving toward him like a seeping black liquid. He didn't know whether to run, hide in one of the caves, or walk toward it out of curiosity. He was paralyzed. As the mass approached, Tar could make out individual shapes of people. They were clearly marching, and there must have been thousands. The only place they could be coming from, right along the Kalmire the same way he had come, was Tsaigal. He decided then to walk toward them. When the leader of the army saw him, he halted the troops. Tar recognized faces, but couldn't put any names with them. He knew he'd seen many of them before. Some of them were farmers, some dock hands. They ranged from old men to almost boys, and they were all dressed in mismatched, makeshift armor.

"Tar," he heard a familiar voice shout.

"Who are you?" the leader asked him.

"I'm from Tsaigal. My name is Adatares."

"You know this man, soldier?"

Sophro pushed his way through the crowd. "Yes, I know him." He slapped Tar on the back. "Listen, Tar, you have to join us," he said.

Tar's head was swimming. "Where are you going?" he asked, scanning the crowd for he didn't know what. No one made eye contact.

"Kamareng. They called every man in the city to fight. There's nothing back home."

"But my father—"

Sophro sighed. He looked at the ground. "He's dead, Tar. He died two days ago. There was nothing to be done."

Tar swallowed. He saw that every soldier was staring at him. All of their faces were so similar that they looked like one whole person. His vision blurred for a moment. There were no options. No father, no Jade, no life the way it once had been. This was it.

"I understand," he said.

XV

The sky opened up. Rain poured in torrents, in sheets. Jade could barely see. She had to stop. She had been walking toward the city of Irien for a week. She had walked past the nearest inn ten miles back, thinking that she'd just walk all night and reach the city. Her teeth chattered. The city lay in the middle of a ravine. She had entered the ravine and was surrounded by cliffs on both sides. The rain made them waterfalls. There was no shelter to be found, so she kept walking, her head down, placing one foot slowly in front of the other. There was no one else on the ravine road. No one else was insane enough to be caught in a rainstorm, she thought. Jade spotted a dent in the rock that formed a sort of cave. The water poured off the top, and the ground underneath was dry. She ducked inside. It was barely large enough to sit in if she put her bag on her lap. She shivered and her stomach growled. She fished inside her bag for some crackers she'd stolen from the last inn. Her fingers grasped something soft—Tar's blanket. She swallowed. The rain formed a sort of curtain in front of her, and the rock was a place to rest her head. But it was cold. All she could think about was the cold.

She drifted in and out of sleep, seeing Tar's face. Her leg felt wet. Then her arms. She opened her eyes. An arm was reaching through the curtain of rain and spilling water over her legs. She started and tried to run out of the cove. Hands on her legs. She fell. She tasted mud and struggled. Her wet hair obscured her vision. Her heart pounded. She managed to turn over and all she saw was a cloaked figure bringing a rock down on her head.

Chapter 6
I

Tar had never seen a fortress as huge as Cairblain before. It looked like a natural part of the mountains, hewn out of solid stone. The army was camped outside its walls in the forest. The sun had begun to die. There were no tents and all they had were thin blankets. Sophro was practicing loading his rifle.

"It's ironic," Lothario remarked as they sat on the ground around their small fire. Dozens of them glowed like fireflies through the murky trees.

"What is?" Sophro asked; face blank, eyes focused.

"You're the best fighter in Tsaigal and you don't even know how to use a gun."

Sophro smirked. Tar stared into the flames.

"This'll be over in no time," Sophro said.

"You don't know that," Lothario said. "It could last decades. We could be old men when we come home."

"Yeah, well."

"I heard the rebels are famous for sneaking up while you're sleeping and slitting your throat."

"Shut up," Sophro said.

"I heard they eat people, too."

Sophro set his gun down and gave him a piercing stare. "Damn it, shut up." Lothario grumbled and lay down, trying to pull his blanket over both his feet and his shoulders. In a few minutes, he was snoring. "I envy him," Sophro said. "He has nothing to keep him awake."

"He does. It's the whiskey," Tar said, pointing at the flask by Lothario's head.

"Let's have a drink, on him." Sophro unscrewed the cap and tossed back a mouthful of whiskey. He handed it to Tar. "Come on. This time tomorrow we could both be dead."

Tar lifted the flask to his lips and took a swallow. The warmth spread into his stomach. He took another swallow. "Easy, leave some for the poor bastard." Sophro laughed. He replaced the flask next to Lothario's hand.

"How's Despina?" Tar asked.

Sophro sighed. "They came and got me in the middle of the night. I don't know why, but that was worse than it would have been in the day. I think it's because night feels like you're hidden. Anyway, they came and Des was there. She'll be okay, I mean. Better than I would be, that's for sure. She has so many friends. Still, it was bad. She was scared." Tar nodded absently, mostly because there was silence to fill. "What happened to that girl from Briga?"

"Jade," Tar supplied.

"I figured she left with you."

"She did. But we went our separate ways a few days ago. About a week, actually."

"Why?"

"I had Dad to take care of, and she…it just didn't work." Tar swallowed when he thought of her plain face that morning as she sat in bed, covered with his blanket.

As they lay down on the hard ground, Tar remembered the way she had lain her warm forehead against his back.

When the sun rose, a trumpet blared. Tar opened his eyes. The trumpet had shattered the calm of the forest. Men stretched and yawned. Some just rolled over. Tar sat up. His back ached; he'd slept on a tree root. Sophro's hair stuck straight up on one side and he had a confused look on his face. Lothario hadn't budged.

When all the men were woken and packed, they were led into the courtyard of Cairblain, where Sven, the king of Gláspeir, stood on a balcony, looking out over them.

"Men of Kahl," his voice boomed, and the chatter died. He was a tall man with blonde hair like a mane. "You are the heroes of this war. You have heeded the call, and because of this, your king and I have been able to join forces and protect these lands from the hands of rebels. Kamareng is a dangerous land, there's no denying it. But this war is important for all of us, to ensure the safety of our children. Heroes of Kahl, go forth to serve this country, and may you all return safely. Give them hell," Sven roared. His energy was infectious.

The men marched along the Kalmire, on their way to the harbor.

II

She was naked. All she knew was that she couldn't see anything, and she was naked. She only knew she was naked because sometimes she felt a cold breeze rush over her bare stomach. She couldn't move. Her mind could barely even hold consciousness for long. But time wasn't anything. She remembered this same feeling from when she was in Porthmôr. But here, wherever she was, it was all black when she opened her eyes. Her neck muscles strained as she tried to sit up, to make out anything. She wasn't tied down as far as she could tell, but the effort exhausted her and she drifted back to sleep. It was never restful. She dreamed she was home, but it wasn't the way she'd left it. The trees lining the streets were all blackened. Ash rained in clumps onto her hair. She pulled some out and smeared black and gray smudges on her fingers. All of the houses she saw were burned skeletons, charred wooden ribs jutting out. She walked down the empty streets to find her house. It was the only one still intact. She opened the door. Shattered glass coated the floor and ash blew in through the gaping, jagged-edged window. Dead roses on the sofa, where they had fallen when she'd smashed the vase. It felt like so long ago. She ran up the stairs. Outside her bedroom door, she paused. Soft moans came from the other side of the door. She slowly opened it. A mass of sheets moved on the bed, rolling like waves. A foot stuck out, toes curling.

"Jade," a familiar voice moaned. "Oh, Jade."

She watched the form that was herself. She saw her fingernails dig into Audric's back. As she watched, a dark spot began to seep into the sheets, covering the bed. Audric gasped in disgust.

"What is that? Is that blood?" He rolled away. The dream Jade stood up and the sheet slipped down to reveal her stomach. Blood gushed from it. Jade gasped and ran back down the stairs. At the bottom, she ran into something and almost fell. She looked up. It was Tar. He smiled at her.

"You have to help me," she heard herself say. His smile disappeared.

"No one can help you." He pushed her backwards and she stumbled into someone's arms. The room seemed to spin and she was wearing nothing but lace. It was still raining ash and there was a bed covered with it. The man from the inn held her in his arms.

"No," she whispered. He lay her down on the bed. "Tar," she called. She heard a door slam. The man grunted as he ripped her underwear.

She woke up. A wave of guilt and relief washed over her and made her shiver.

III

Audric left the money on the table. Daina heard the slap of the coins and the click of the door closing. She slowly dressed. He hadn't looked into her eyes once that time. Just kept them either closed or focused on the wall above the bed and finished as quickly as he could. They did this once a week; he came to pay her and then he would tell her to take off her clothes. All of them. But he left on most of his. And then as soon as he was done, he'd leave without a word.

Daina walked downstairs, sore between her legs. She made a cup of tea with a slice of lemon and counted her money. Fifty imein. She had three hundred saved up. She never spent any of it. But she liked to feel the cold coins in her hands. She liked the smell they left on her fingers.

IV

The soldiers had set up camp in a clearing in the forest. They were supposed to meet up with a Lieutenant Feodor of the Gláspeir army, but it had become too dark to march any further. Bits of snow still clung to the ground. Wind whistled through the pines above them. Ten men were chosen to stand guard, Lothario one of them. He stood up, grumbling.

"A thousand men and I get picked." He trudged to the perimeter of the camp, his rifle and powder in hand. Tar and Sophro lay down. Tar lay on his back and looked up at the sky through the pine branches. Dark clouds covered the stars. He turned over and fell asleep within minutes. He dreamt of Jade. She lay next to him and gazed up at the stars. Then she climbed on top of him and slowly, silently, drew a knife.

Tar's eyes snapped open. A man knelt over him, holding a knife. Tar grabbed the man's throat with one hand and knocked the knife to the ground with the other. He pressed his thumbs into the man's neck. He heard shouts all around him, shots firing, knives cutting flesh. The man's eyes rolled back into his head until only white was visible and his legs stopped kicking. As his body slackened, Tar felt sick. He threw the dead man off of him and looked around wildly. He saw Sophro shoot one in the chest and stop to reload. His fingers fumbled with the powder. A man was sneaking up behind him, knife in hand. Tar picked up the dead man's knife, crept up behind him, and plunged it into his back. He grunted and crumpled into a heap, neck twisting with a sickening crunch. Death was everywhere. Men shouted for fear of their lives and for the thrill of taking others. Gunpowder smoke made Tar's eyes sting. He fired and reloaded and fired and reloaded. It took longer to use his rifle, but it was easier. It felt better. When the last shot was finally fired, the men all let out a breath. Tar felt like he'd been holding it the entire time. It was still dark, like no time had even passed. It felt like it should have been dawn, but maybe that was just a wish. Smoke drifted heavily toward the purple sky. The air tasted thick and foul. Blood stained the patches of snow, stark even at night. Tar's hands shook. He found Sophro once the men began to move again, to breathe.

"How many do you think they got?" Tar asked.

Sophro shook his head. "Maybe fifty. Maybe a hundred."

"They keep doing this and we'll all be dead before we even make it to the camp."

"Our guards didn't even notice them," Sophro exclaimed.

"They're like a part of the land," Tar agreed.

They sat by the fire. After a long time, Lothario came over. He didn't say anything; they just sat.

V

It was only gray half-light, but it felt blinding. Jade squeezed her eyes shut. She slowly opened them again and looked around. She was definitely naked, lying on a stone table. The room was small and mostly empty; there were shelves with glassware, some filled and some empty. The door had been opened and a light fell onto the wall. A shadow stepped into the room, but Jade could not turn. She was paralyzed. She heard male and female voices speaking in a language she couldn't understand.

"Where am I?"

The voices stopped.

"I'll begin. Jareth, you'll do the cutting. Lumine, you'll incant." Three faces came into view, upside down. A man and two women. The first thing Jade noticed were their cheek scars. One woman took a vial of clear liquid from the shelf and emptied it into a syringe. She tapped it, sending droplets through the air, and cleared her throat as she concentrated on Jade's neck. The tip of the needle was cold. Jade swallowed and closed her eyes as it bit into the hollow of her throat. The liquid smelled sharp and fermented, like alcohol. But instead of warmth spreading through her body, she felt cold, like each blood vessel was slowly icing over. She heard everything as if she were underwater. She saw only shapes, like shadows, overlapping. She could make out every detail in the brick wall, but the faces hovering over her were blurry. She choked on panicked tears. Her heart raced as the man drew a sharp knife, just like the one she'd been cut with back in the moors. As the woman named Lumine began to read from a book in her hand, he pressed the knife into her scabbed cut and reopened the gash. Jade bit her lip. She couldn't understand the words, but it seemed like it hurt more at the repetitive, deep part of the incantation when everyone joined in. Her cheek muscles pulsed like she had eaten too much. The knife bit into her left cheek, tearing flesh. She couldn't even writhe in pain. Then the man leaned over her naked body and slowly cut a perfect red line down her sternum. Blood flowed from her wounds, spilling onto the table. She gasped. The blood was warm on her cold stomach and neck. The woman who had injected her with the clear liquid took the knife from the man and quickly sliced her own palm as Lumine continued to chant. The woman pressed her bleeding hand onto all of Jade's cuts, one at a time. Jade shuddered. The chanting slowed until it sounded like a thumping, sensual drumbeat. Jade saw black spots. She had to gasp for breath. Beads of sweat formed on her exposed skin. She heard someone talking and realized she could understand the chanting.

"Oh wondrous Master of Spirits,
Show us the way.
Let us follow your will
And serve you.
We present to you
A new child,
Born of stone,
Baptized in blood.
Show her your ways
And may your name
Be ever revered."

Searing pain in her cuts. It felt like the blood was bubbling up out of them. Her head began to shake. She bit her tongue. Her teeth dug into it.

She couldn't stop. Finally someone stuck something in her mouth. She choked on her own blood. Her jaw ached from clamping. Every vein burned. Sweat dripped down her temples. The beginning of a scream was coming from her throat. It stayed there, like a growl. She slowly opened her eyes; they were covered with a film of water. She blinked away the tears. The room was empty. She felt her limbs loosen. She could move again. She took the wooden stick out of her mouth. There were deep bite marks in it. She sat up. Pools of blood covered the table and dripped to the floor. Jade got off the table and stood up. The room whirled and she collapsed, hitting her forehead on the table.

VI

Shots thundered above them. A group of men huddled in the bunker, awaiting instructions. It had been hastily dug out by Feodor's men. The walls and floor were black, wet earth and the bunker had been shored up with fresh pine planks. It smelled rich. Tar, Sophro, and Lothario were some of the last men who had been told to wait; they were to be given a special assignment by the lieutenant.

"Is this good or bad?" Lothario asked. No one answered. One man sitting in the corner muttered to himself and jumped every time a shot was fired above.

They had reached the camp two days ago at noon. Tar remembered how loud they had been, clomping through the snow so heavily, so visibly. They had made it unscathed, which was, in a way, more unnerving, like they were being watched. The Gláspeir soldiers had been waiting for them with exhausted eyes and bloodstained clothing. There were maybe a hundred left. Although the warriors from Kahl arrived with a general, the lieutenant was clearly more accustomed to the land, so he immediately took charge of the men. They had lined up and waited, all of their rifles loaded. Tar remembered the way the gun had jumped in his hands, bruising his shoulder. Shoot at the heads darting up from the holes in the field before they shoot you. Then step back to reload while the next men shoot. A man next to Tar had fallen. A bullet had whizzed into his neck, tearing open a crimson hole. Tar's arms still ached. He wondered if he'd ever get the smell of gunpowder out of his nose. There was black underneath his fingernails that wouldn't wash away.

"Where is he?" Sophro muttered to himself. Tar was beginning to

Sarah Jilek

worry about Sophro. He didn't sleep, not that any of them slept much. He didn't eat either. His cheekbones were beginning to show.

Footsteps pounded overhead and the lieutenant marched down the makeshift stairs into the bunker. Grimy soot covered his face.

"Alright, men," he began, pulling a map out of his pocket. It was hand-drawn. "It turns out that I only need two of you. Three, to be safe. The rest of you can go back out there right now. So how about you three stay." He pointed at Tar, Sophro, and Lothario. The other men, including the whimpering one, shuffled out. The lieutenant explained their mission to them. They were to travel to an encampment of rebels and take out as many as possible. Only three were going because any more would make too much noise.

The afternoon air was frigid outside the bunker. Tar shivered constantly. Tsaigal never got quite this cold. They walked north. Birds chirped high up in the trees, oblivious. Lothario tripped over tree roots.

"Are you drinking right now?" Sophro asked.

"All the time." He winked and pulled his flask from his pocket. Sophro grabbed it and emptied it onto the ground. Tar felt a pang in his chest as he watched the brown liquid melt into the snow. Sophro dropped the empty flask. "What the hell!" Lothario shouted.

"We're probably going to die today. Do you even realize that? I don't want to take any more chances. I know you don't have anyone to go home to, but I do. So don't get me killed."

Lothario's cheeks were red, but that might have been from the alcohol or the cold. He tucked his empty flask back into his coat pocket like a child with a broken toy. They kept walking, holding their rifles up to their shoulders and trying to move as quickly and silently as they could. It must have been five miles of walking with shouldered rifles and tiny steps, straining calf muscles and holding breath in their chests until it burned. They didn't speak. The sun began to set. It was nearly dark when they finally reached the camp. It was dug out of a hillside and the three of them stood looking out over it through a stand of pines.

"How are we going to do this?" Sophro said, more to himself than the others as he scratched the stubble on his chin. At some time, it had been decided that Sophro was their leader. Nothing had been spoken, but the other two had naturally followed him.

"There are a lot of tents," Lothario remarked. There must have been fifteen tents set up in a circle. But only a few men milled around.

100

"No way to tell how many there are with all those tents," Tar said.

"Let's watch," Sophro said. They knelt and watched the camp for an hour. Men moved into the tents, but none moved back out. As the sky turned black, the camp fell silent. "Don't make a sound," Sophro said, pulling out his knife.

The three of them climbed down the hillside, feet sliding on loose dirt and clumps of grass. Tar's legs ached from kneeling. They reached the bottom of the hill. It felt strange, like they were intruding. Tar's heart thumped. Crickets croaked in the dark. Far off, a wolf pack began to howl. Sophro pointed ahead to the first tent. They crept toward it, knives drawn and glinting. Lamps hung on a rope above the camp. Tar and Lothario followed Sophro. Snoring broke the silence of the night. Their feet sunk into the mud and pulled it up when they lifted them. Tar saw the shadow of his head appear on the tent and ducked so it disappeared. The wolves grew louder, drowning out the crickets and snoring and filling the air with a cacophony of howling. They stood still. Tar prayed that the rebels would sleep through the noise. Sophro finally motioned them forward and they crept after him and around to the front of the tent. The flaps were tied together with canvas strips. Sophro slowly untied them and a sudden wind burst into the tent and revealed the three men sleeping inside. Sophro, Tar and Lothario filed in and quickly knelt over the men and slit their throats, almost soundlessly. Then Tar felt better. There was some sort of routine in place that he could follow. They killed ten more tents full of men this way. All that could be heard was the wind howling through the opened tents and the snick of sharp metal on skin. Tar felt warm. They had been supposed to take out as many men as possible, and they'd already killed eleven out of fifteen tents full of them. They'd be heroes when they got back to the camp. Sophro darted ahead, head constantly turning this way and that. Lothario trudged behind, looking queasy. Sophro untied the flaps of the tent and they slipped inside again. When Tar looked, his stomach turned over. There were at least ten men asleep on the ground. Sophro's eyes were wide. He froze and then, taking a breath, knelt next to a man and motioned for Tar and Lothario to do the same. Tar leaned over and held his knife an inch from the man's throat. He could feel the man's breath on his wrist. Sophro nodded and they all cut. The sound woke a man next to the one Tar had killed. He sat straight up. Tar held his head with two hands, one on his face and one on the back of his head, and twisted as hard as he could.

The neck cracked between his hands. He let out a grunt that woke three other men. One of them shouted. Tar froze. Sophro had jumped on one and was plunging his knife into his throat. Lothario stabbed one in the stomach. More shouting brought Tar back to the tent. A man next to him was fumbling for his gun. Tar gripped his knife and slashed the rebel's throat. The man clutched his neck, blood spilling over his fingers like a waterfall. He slumped over onto his side, blood spurting onto his dead friends. Tar heard grunts and shouts and the gurgling of slit throats. His head hurt. He fell to his knees and vomited. He couldn't get the smell of blood out of his nose. The dead bodies had fallen on top of each other like a stack of firewood. Tar looked around wildly. Lothario groaned and held his stomach. His knees hit the ground and he fell, writhing. Tar stood up on weak legs and hobbled over to him. His skin was cold. His eyes stared blankly ahead. Tar clenched his teeth. He looked for Sophro. He was still fighting the last two men. One of them was holding a gun.

"Sophro!" Tar shouted. A blast exploded in the tent. Smoke stung Tar's eyes. His ears rang. He ran through the smoke to Sophro and, in the gray fog, picked him up and threw him over his shoulder, heart pounding. He stumbled through the open door of the tent, choking on the polluted air that burned his throat. The night air was sharp; fresh. An alarm was sounding, like a hammer pounding a large, deep bell. Men were ripping open the flaps of their tents on the other side of the camp, stepping out into the clearing. Tar ran. He ran and stumbled and fell and ran again, into the thick cover of the pines. Sophro was heavy. Warmth spread through the back of Tar's jacket where Sophro's body lay. He ran until he finally collapsed, all the adrenaline used up. He was surrounded by pines. He lay Sophro down on his back. Blood covered his chest and arm.

"Damn it," Tar whispered. Sophro's eyes were closed. Sweat covered his face. Tar cut off his Sophro's blood-soaked jacket sleeve with his knife. The bullet was lodged in his shoulder. The skin and muscle had torn; stark white bone was visible. Tar sat back on his heels, breathing heavily. He leaned over Sophro, who awoke with a gasp. His eyes widened and then squeezed shut. His back arched and his jaw shuddered.

"Fuck," he swore.

"What do I do?" Tar asked.

Sophro opened his eyes. "Where's Lothario?"

Tar shook his head. "He's gone."

Sophro blinked. A tear ran down his cheek, cutting through dirt. "Damn, this hurts," he finally said.

"What do I do? How do I fix it?"

Sophro sat up slowly, biting his lip. "You have to take the bullet out."

Tar's face must have been enough of an answer for Sophro. "If it had hit my artery, I'd be dead already," he said. "You have to clean it and then take it out. Then you'll have to sew it up."

"No, I—I can't—"

"You have to."

Tar struggled for words. Sophro stared at him, his eyes unfocusing with every shaky exhale. He shivered.

"Um, okay. What do I do?"

Sophro cleared his throat. "You have any water?"

"No." Tar looked around. "There's some snow."

"Yeah, use that."

Tar used a rag in his pack to pick up a handful of snow. He pressed it to Sophro's shoulder. Sophro grunted. The snow melted and ran red down his shirt.

"Okay, now what?"

"Now take it out." Sophro exhaled through his nose. Tar removed the cloth from his shoulder. The wound was a red and brown hole, flaps of torn skin surrounding it. Blood still trickled from it. "Can you see it?"

The bullet was lodged directly beneath his collar bone.

"Yes." Tar wiped his hands on his shirt, like that would clean them, and Sophro leaned back against a tree trunk. Tar slowly stuck one finger inside the hole in his shoulder. Sophro groaned. Tar moved his finger around in the mess of blood. He felt the collar bone and shuddered. Sophro's eyes were squeezed shut.

"Fuck, that hurts," he moaned. He exhaled loudly.

"I can feel it," Tar said. His finger touched metal and he scraped the bullet toward the entry wound. Sophro cried out. The bullet fell into Tar's other hand. Sophro was panting. Tar tossed the bullet away and picked up the cold cloth. He pressed it into Sophro's shoulder.

"Good, good, good," Sophro muttered, nodding. A film of tears glazed his eyes. "I have a needle and thread in my pack."

Tar pulled them out. It took him five minutes just to thread the needle. The thread was black. "I've never sewn anything in my life."

"You can do it."

Tar took a deep breath and pushed the needle into Sophro's skin. The muscle tensed. He pushed the needle up through the other side and pulled the thread through. "Okay," he muttered. "Okay." He sewed up the hole slowly, leaving little drops of red beading on his skin. The stitches looked angry and painful, but the wound was closed. "It's done."

Sophro looked. "Well, it is what it is." He closed his eyes. Tar picked up a handful of snow and pressed the cold, wet cloth to his shoulder again. He pressed down hard to stop the last of the bleeding and numb the wound. Sophro was drifting off to sleep. "Thank you," he mumbled.

VII

A flickering flame slowly came into focus. Jade opened her eyes. A headache made her close them again. She rubbed her forehead with a cold palm. A raised bump made her shudder as her fingers passed over it. She was lying on a narrow, uncomfortable bed in a small room. The walls and floor were the same as she remembered from the room she'd last been in. The bed was in the corner, away from the door. One candle lit the room, a pool of warm orange light. Jade sat up. The room was mostly plain, with only a bed, a table, and an empty bookshelf, all made of the same wood, like they'd been made from the same tree. She was still naked, covered in a thin black blanket. A black robe hung from a hook on the door. Jiada stood up and walked over to it. The fabric was soft, but thick. She pushed her arms through the sleeves and tied the belt around her waist. A small mirror hung on the wall next to the door. The first things she noticed were her scars. Dark red scabs across her cheeks and down her chest. She touched the scar on her right cheek. It ached. Purple bruises were forming around the scars.

The door opened. Jade backed away. The woman who had cut her own cheek during Jade's operation came in. Jade remembered her red hair and dull brown eyes.

"Oh, you're awake. I see you found your robe." Jade only stood, staring at her. "Well, come on." She pushed the door open and turned around, back the way she had come. Jade slowly followed her, pulling the robe tighter around her. They stepped into an underground hallway, Jade barefoot. The earth was cold and damp. "My name is Fox," the woman said. She was taller than Jade, which made Jade uncomfortable.

104

"Fox?" She walked ahead of Jade. The hallway wasn't big enough for them to walk side-by-side.

"I had a real name once. But I've been called Fox for so long I don't remember it," she explained. The hallway was dimly lit with thin white candles. It wound from side to side and at one point Jade even thought they might be walking back the way they had come. All the same wet gray color and the same wet gray smell. Then she heard a crashing sound growing louder. It was so familiar.

"Is that a waterfall?" she whispered. Fox walked through an opening in the cave and Jade followed her onto the brink of a cliff. A waterfall roared down from an unseen source high above. Some light fell with it, illuminating the cave with a silver hue. A river flowed past their feet into darkness to their right. A bridge had been built across the river. "Where are we?" Jade asked. Fox just smirked and began to walk across the bridge. Jade followed, her bare feet numb on the hard, cold stone. They walked across the river into another cave. This one was well-lit and decorated with paintings and rugs. A man sat in a cushioned chair behind a desk at the far end of the room. Jade recognized Lumine and Jareth standing near him. The man beckoned Fox forward. Jade followed her.

"Your new recruit, my lord," Fox said, gesturing at Jade. He stepped toward her. He had a sharp, angular face with dark eyes and a hooked nose. His hair was black and thick. He lifted Jade's chin and stared at her scars. Then he pulled her robe apart. His cold hands brushed against her bare chest. She didn't flinch. She just waited while he inspected her scar and let his eyes linger on her breasts. When he finally turned away, she pulled her robe closed again.

"Where are we?" Jade asked. She barely saw him turn to face her before his palm smacked against her cheek.

"Show me respect."

Jade bowed her head. "I'm sorry, my lord," she muttered, rolling her eyes at the floor. It was the only way. She recognized Audric's type immediately.

"The initiation was done well. Lumine and Jareth, you may go. Fox, you must go and speak with the Master."

Fox bowed and motioned for Jade to follow her. They left the room and Jade followed Fox down a walkway next to the river, over the cold, dusty ground. Fox lit a lantern on a stone step, picked it up, and held it in front of her as they walked. The flame swayed, dizzying. Finally they reached a wooden door. Fox knocked twice and, hearing no response, opened it. She ushered Jade inside and closed the door behind them. It was dark until Fox lit all the lamps in the room. They were in a sort of chapel, with a stone altar at the end of a hall. The ground was covered with straw, which crackled under Jade's feet and made the air smell like a stable.

"Do exactly what I do," Fox said and knelt on the straw. Jade copied her, kneeling on the hard floor. Fox began to crawl, dragging her knees through the straw, her head bowed the entire time. It was like watching an earthworm struggling across a mound of dirt. Jade hesitated. "You have to." Jade sighed and copied her. By the time they reached the base of the altar, her knees were bruised. Fox picked up the small, circular mirror that lay on the straw, and the rusty knife next to it. "Master, may I stand?" Fox called. Jade's skin tingled. Fox stood up. She held the mirror up with her left hand and used the knife to trace a perfect line across the scar on her left cheek. As blood began to flow, she pressed her hand to the cut and smeared her blood onto the stone altar. Jade felt her skin tingle again. It burned, but gently, like a fire was teasing her skin. She closed her eyes and felt warmth spread throughout her body. She could barely breathe from the explosive, sensual feeling. As it slowly ebbed away, she opened her eyes and realized her mouth was open and she was shaking. Fox knelt next to her, eyes closed. Slowly, she sat up. "We can go now," she whispered. Jade followed her out of the temple, or whatever it was, and back into the hallway. Fox closed the door behind them.

"What the hell was that?" Jade whispered. She wasn't sure why she was whispering; maybe there was some remaining sacredness she felt around them.

Fox stared at her. "I was determining my mission. But now I see it's you who has one."

"Me?" Fox began to walk back upriver, the way they had come. "Hey." She turned around. "Why did I feel like that?"

Fox smirked. "I felt it more than you did. It's like nothing else, isn't it? You normally only feel it when your blood is used. But we're...connected."

"Connected? How?"

Fox sighed. "My blood is inside you. From the initiation. That's why I have to train you."

Jade thought about her book. "If I have your blood, then…"
Fox grinned. Her teeth gleamed. "Congratulations. You're immortal."

VIII

Evening had fallen. Jade could tell before she opened her eyes because she felt a cool breeze on her skin and there was no light behind her eyelids. When she did open them, she saw that she and Fox were standing on a small hill. The ground was covered in yellowed, dry grass as far as she could see.

"Where are we?" she asked. Her head was spinning. The last thing she remembered was standing in the cold, waist-deep water of the underground river and feeling the spray from the waterfall prick her skin as Fox chanted. Then her vision had gone black. Fox pointed to a cluster of orange lights in the distance.

"That's Porthmôr," she said.

"Where is Draoul? How did we get here?"

Fox just smiled and began to walk. The night air was warm, except for the occasional breeze. The ocean roared in the distance. They approached Porthmôr from the south, avoiding the main route. Jade glanced east, toward where she knew the city of Tsaigal lay, somewhere far off in the dark. She swallowed a sudden lump in her throat. When the city began to loom close before them, Fox pulled her hood over her head. Jade copied her. There were two men guarding the open gates. Jade noticed that as she and Fox approached, the guards did not seem to notice them. They kept their eyes fixed straight ahead. Fox slowed down and walked on the outsides of her feet, rolling them instead of firmly stepping. She was completely silent. Jade tried to copy her exact movements. Just as she passed in between the two guards, she stepped on a rock. It stuck to the bottom of her boot and she stumbled. The guards jumped to life, looking around wildly. Fox dashed through the gates and veered right into an alley. Jade lurched forward after her. Pressed against a doorway, they watched the guards run past and eventually return, wary. When they had gone, Jade breathed again.

"You have to be more careful," Fox whispered. "Especially with what you're about to do."

What I'm about to do? Jade thought as she followed Fox out of the doorway and into the marketplace. It was mostly deserted, but groups of soldiers chattered or played card games or patrolled, knives resting on their belts. Jade and Fox made it through the marketplace unnoticed. Jade's feet ached from the unnatural way she was walking. Porthmôr was built around a cove, and the harbor was the main district of the city. The air reeked of fish. Jade saw the hospital where she'd barely hung onto her life. The air made her feel sick. It was clear that the regime of the city had been overthrown; graffiti covered the sandstone walls and garbage littered the ground. Plastered on the walls here and there were white posters with bold black lettering that read:

SUBMISSION
TRUST
PEACE

Jade's skin prickled. They turned onto a wide avenue. A palace, or what had once been a palace, loomed in the distance. Now it was a blackened shell of woodwork, although some parts remained intact. Soldiers surrounded the front of the palace, barely five feet away from each other. Jade and Fox slipped between them and crept toward the entrance. Jade tried not to breathe heavily. The doors had mostly burned away; they were able to step over the remains and into the palace. There was a guard stationed toward the staircase, but he was slumped over and snoring. Jade couldn't see any others. They climbed the stairs silently. Blackened bodies lay on them, faces disfigured. The smell of charred flesh hung in the air. Upstairs, there was a long hallway. Fox seemed to know exactly where she was going. She led Jade to a closed door. Three guards stood in front of it. Fox frowned and led Jade back the way they had come. When they were far from the soldiers, Fox handed Jade a knife. Jade stared blankly at it before closing her fingers around the handle. Fox smirked.

"Get inside that room and kill him," she whispered.

"But the guards—"

"I'll worry about them," Fox said. Her eyes glinted—maybe with adrenaline, but it looked like something more unsettling—as Jade left. Jade felt conscious of every breath she took, every heartbeat. She was sure that the soldiers would hear her heart thumping as she approached them, her feet slowly moving along the hallway. She tried to grip the knife tightly, but her palms were sweating. She took a deep breath. It's nothing. Just this knife in his throat. That's it. What could be easier?

She felt more calm then and approached the door. There was a moment as she stood there in front of them that she was sure that Fox had left her. She couldn't breathe. Then a shrill scream pierced the silence. Jade's heart jumped in her chest. The soldiers jumped up and ran toward the scream. When they had disappeared down the hallway, Jade opened the doorknob with shaking fingers. A candle, barely more than a wick in a pool of white wax, dimly illuminated the room. It cast shadows on the wall. Jade crossed the room slowly. The window opposite the door was closed, but it looked easy enough to open; there was a handle that opened the two halves of the window inwards. A snore rumbled from the lump of blankets on the bed. Jade swallowed. It's nothing. She crept further toward him. One fat arm draped over the bedside and a pamphlet lay on the ground where he must have dropped it. Jade was careful not to step on it, but as she glanced at it, the headline caught her attention. She turned her head sideways to read it. It read,

WAR IN KAMARENG: TSAIGAL EMPTIED

Jade picked up the paper. She didn't know exactly why she felt compelled to read it. She read that all able men had been sent to war in Kamareng. Jade swallowed. If Tar had come with her, maybe it would have been different. She told herself that maybe he'd escaped the war, that he'd saved his father and he was home safe, but she knew that he was gone. Alive still, maybe, but gone. For the first time since she'd bled in the tub at the hospital in Desrala, she was filled with regret. And paralyzed. She thought of the uneasy look on his face when he had touched her. And then the tears in his eyes the next morning. She knew there was no way she could get out. They would come after her, find her, before she made it as far north as Desrala. And wasn't she exactly where she needed to be if she wanted to get home? She thought of Desrala. Of Audric. Her stomach churned. She knew she should want to go back. It was the only thing she could do. She tucked the pamphlet, her only tangible connection to Tar, into her robe. The man lying on the bed stirred. Jade froze. As he became still again, she crept closer. He lay on his back. He had a brown face with black hair and a thick black mustache. His eyes moved underneath their closed lids. Jade took a deep breath, leaned close, and, steadying her shaking hand, held the knife over his throat. She heard footsteps approach the door. She cursed herself for not closing it behind her.

"The door is open," a guard whispered. Jade saw their shadows on the wall. She crept away into a corner of the room. The three guards entered silently, apparently as afraid of waking the man as she was. They checked under the bed and in the mahogany wardrobes. Finding nothing but elaborate clothing, they slunk out of the room, shutting the door behind them. Now she would have to use the window. She slowly turned the handle. It made a barely audible click. She crept back to the bed and held her knife to his throat again. He mumbled something in his sleep. Jade pressed the blade to his skin; lightly at first, then harder, deeper, until beads of blood blossomed. His eyes snapped open and he shouted. Jade gasped and leaned into blade and slit his throat with all of her strength. His eyes grew wide and he made a gagging noise as blood covered his white sheets. Then everything happened at once. His arms flailed and he blindly grasped her hood and pulled it down. The door swung open and the soldiers rushed in. They saw her and shouted incoherently. Then a gust of air from outside blew the unlocked window open. Jade leapt onto the bed, stepping on an arm and dark blood. She ran to the window and climbed onto the sill. There was a balcony ten feet below. She jumped. Landed; sharp pain in her ankle. She pulled her hood back over her head and looked up. The soldiers were looking around the balcony. Their eyes never met hers. She sighed with relief and, when the soldiers disappeared, she began her descent using each balcony on the outside wall of the palace. When she finally reached the ground, she hid in a stand of fig trees, her breathing ragged. She waited for Fox and thought about the knife. She'd dropped it on the floor when the guards had come in. It had been a long knife with a curved blade. She hadn't thought much about it earlier; it had just been a knife. But now she remembered how much work it had taken to puncture the skin; bite into the cords of his neck. Her stomach heaved. There was blood on her fingers. She spat on her hands and rubbed them together, but it was a red-brown stain. It was underneath her fingernails, too. She closed her eyes and shuddered.

"Where's my knife?" a voice called. Jade turned to see Fox strolling over to her.

"Um, I—I—"

Fox raised an eyebrow. "You lost it."

"I was running. I—"

"Okay, it doesn't matter."

Jade felt Fox staring at her out of the corner of her eye. She focused on a rotting fig that lay on the ground. It had been bitten and the rich pink flesh was visible, veiny and earth-scented.

"My first one was hard, too," Fox said. Jade looked at her. Her face was blank. "But after a while, you forget."

"I don't want to forget," Jade said. The idea of immortality, of living so long that memories meant nothing, made her uneasy.

Fox scoffed. "Let's go."

Jade stood up. Fox looked around. There were no soldiers nearby. She began to chant, a low, monotonous drone that Jade could not understand. It was maddening; her ears kept trying and failing to make sense of the words. Her eyelids drooped. As her body began to be transported, she felt like her head was being tightened by a vise. Her limbs felt numb. The last thing she saw was the half-eaten fig lying on the sandy ground, its pink guts spilling out.

IX

When Jade and Fox returned, Jade was summoned to the master's rooms. Fox left her there, closing the door behind her.

"Jiada. I'm here," he called from another room. Jade walked toward the doorway. The chamber, like every room in Draoul, was a network of caves. In the master's rooms, paintings covered the stone walls and rugs lined the floors. Jade stepped into the doorway. He lay, covered with a bear skin, on a large bed that took up most of the room. His bare chest shone in the light of the wall lamps. He nodded at the bed next to him. "Sit." Jade sat on the soft furs. "My name is Blaise. You can call me that when we're alone." Jade looked at him. He was an attractive man. His jaw was sharp; his nose was neither short nor too long, and his eyes were dark blue. He smiled at her. "You're beautiful. I've been waiting for a moment to be alone with you," he whispered, brushing her hair over her shoulder and letting his hand rest on her neck. She shivered. "Come here. It's warmer." He pulled her close and untied her robe in one motion. It fell about her shoulders, exposing her bare chest. As he pulled her on top of him and pressed his lips to hers, something crinkled between them. "What is that?" He pulled a paper from the folds of her robe. Jade saw the headline of the pamphlet she'd found in Porthmôr. He tossed it away. She felt her chest tighten. He smiled at her again and she felt nauseated.

111

Sarah Jilek

Her teeth clenched. She saw the inn owner and she saw Audric. There was no difference. It's nothing. She inhaled and leaned over to unbutton his pants.

When they were finished, he immediately fell asleep. Jade pushed his arm off of her and wriggled out of the bed. She put on her robe and smoothed her hair, closing her eyes for a moment. When she walked, she felt sore between her legs. She picked up the pamphlet from the foot of the bed and crept out of the room. When she left the chamber, she began to run. She ran across the bridge and all the way down the hallway to her room. She threw open the door and shut it behind her. Jade slumped onto her bed, breathing deeply. She reached under her bed for her bag. She felt the book and the telescope and pushed them aside. Her fingers grasped the blanket, something soft. She pulled it onto the bed and covered herself with it, curling onto her side. Her breathing became shallower and shallower until she was gasping for air, sobbing, rocking back and forth. She held the pamphlet close to her chest, underneath the blanket.

X

It was dark outside, but the kind of eerie white night that was so common in a Desrala winter, where the sky turned purple and snow fell in clumps. Daina's eyes hurt from squinting at the needle and black thread in her fingertips and the shirt on her lap. The only light in the room came from the last small, yellow candle that slowly melted.

Daina set down the finished shirt and carefully placed her sewing needle in her basket next to the bed. She was about to blow out the candle when a cough came from the foot of the bed. She froze, holding her breath, but the baby let out a shrill wail. Daina sighed. Her eyes burned. It had been two weeks of crying, of waking at all hours of the night to feed the baby, of sewing until her fingers bled just to make sure she'd have enough money for food the next day. Since she'd gotten home from the hospital, all she had done was take care of her son, whom she still hadn't named, and mend clothes for whoever needed it. She'd leave in the morning with the baby bundled close to her chest and an empty basket, going around the city. When the basket was full, she brought it home and went to work. There wasn't much time to sleep.

Daina picked up the baby. He had grown in the last two weeks and

112

gained weight. He quieted as she held him to her chest. He was warm. "You have to go to sleep now," she whispered. She walked around her bedroom, her nose in the baby's hair. It was soft and blonde, like hers, and it smelled like milk. Holding him made Daina drowsy. She held him up so she could see him. He stared at her with his big blue eyes. "You know, things were a lot different before you. I'm not sure if they were better. I think they were." He yawned. Daina gently placed him in his basket on top of his soft blue blanket. She stroked his hair as his eyes closed. "I just don't know about you," Daina whispered. A tear spilled onto her cheek and down her chin. "I don't know what I'm going to do."

She slowly dozed off on the floor, leaning against her bed. She woke up to pounding on the front door. She was lying on the floor. Her back was sore. She looked around. It was still dark outside and the baby was still sleeping. She ran down the stairs, trying to get to the door before the next knock. She swung it open to find Audric. It was snowing and he was shivering in his large black overcoat. When he saw her, his face remained blank.

"Come in," she said. He stepped inside, fishing through his pockets. He set her money down on the table. "I haven't seen you in a long time."

He shrugged. "I thought I'd bring the money inside. The snow," he trailed off, pointing out the window.

Daina nodded. "Would...would you like to see him?" Her heart thumped as she waited for his response. Audric looked at her.

"Him, huh? A son," he said with a smile. Daina nodded. "Probably best not to wake him." Audric headed for the door.

"Oh, please come see him. It'll be alright. I'm getting good at comforting him."

Audric thought about it. "Okay," he said.

Daina grinned. She led him upstairs and lit her candle. Audric crept over to the sleeping baby and peered into the basket. A smile spread across his face. Daina's heart leapt. "He's...uh, he's.." Audric stammered. He shook his head. "A son," he whispered. "What's his name?"

Daina looked at the wood floor. "I—I haven't named him yet."

Audric's eyes widened. He thought for a moment. "Kieran." He looked at Daina. "Do you like it?"

Daina smiled. "Yes," she whispered. It was as if it had been the tiny baby's name all along. She gazed at his small body. "Kieran."

Audric took her arm and led her into the hallway. Daina tried to read his face. His eyes were glistening.

"I...I don't know how to say this," he muttered.

"I've missed you, Audric," Daina said.

He smiled. "Good, I didn't know if you had or not. That makes this easier. Daina, I—I want..."

"Yes?"

"I want us to be a family."

Daina felt tears sting her eyes. "Why now? Why not when I told you I was pregnant?"

Audric shook his head. He grasped Daina's hands. "I wasn't ready. Now that I see him...he's my son, and I want him to have a father. Of course, it will have to be kept quiet."

Daina felt her heart sink. "What, to be reduced to meeting like this? Forever?"

"I'm sorry, but there's no other way. I'll lose my job, and then we won't have any money."

"I understand," she said quickly. She did. She knew that there was nothing to be done about it, and it was a sort of consolation that Audric had called it their money. She had enough for the moment. "Will you...will you stay the night?"

"Yes, I want to."

Audric undressed in Daina's room and slipped into bed. While he lay there, Daina stroked Kieran's hair and kissed his forehead, tears coming to her eyes. He was her beautiful boy, their boy. He had to be the most miraculous baby ever born.

XI

Jade felt her body come into focus. It was such a strange feeling, although she had gotten used to it by now. It felt like being ripped apart and assembled again: first a visceral mass, unfeeling, and then, slowly, tingling sensations and blurred vision. She opened her eyes. She was standing in the river, the water up to her knees. The falls were deafening. She waded to the bank and climbed the stone steps, her wet robe heavy. Nodding to Lumine as she passed her, Jade walked to the master's rooms. When she stepped into them, Blaise was hunched over at his desk. He looked up when she cleared her throat and smiled slightly.

"Was it difficult?"

"No," she replied.

He looked at her, tilting his head. "You're not going to ask why I think you had to kill them?" Jade shook her head. Blaise stood up and walked toward her. "You know, I have a theory," he began.

"I don't care," Jade said.

He shook his head. "Okay." Blaise placed a hand on her neck. "You've changed these past few months…how many has it been?"

"Six."

"Six already? Huh. You were so young back then. You've grown. Look at you, the best assassin we have. Fearless. Merciless. Stoic." Jade nodded. Her face felt numb. Blaise kissed her lips. She barely moved hers, just let them touch his. She knew it was nothing special; she'd known it since the day after he'd first kissed her when she'd found him kissing Fox. She'd been relieved. "Go get some rest," he told her.

Jade obeyed. She went to her room and locked the door. It was only here that she could feel anything. Anywhere else, it seemed like nothing could touch her. But in her room alone, she felt almost normal. She hated it. She sat down on the edge of her bed and buried her face in her hands. Fingers shaking, she reached under her pillow. She pulled out the paper and reread the article for the hundredth time.

"Tar," she whispered without knowing why. It was involuntary. This only happened here; it was as if he could only reach her here. She felt his presence, remembered her forehead on his back during their last night together, the way his muscle had tensed and relaxed, warm on her cool forehead. She remembered the morning after, cringing. She rocked back and forth on the bed. It had been six months of this. Six months of killing and becoming more and more numb. "Are you even alive?" she whispered, exhausted. She sobbed once, a sudden intake of air, tearless. Jade stuffed the paper back under her pillow and left the room, heading straight for the river. She knelt and cupped her hands, slurping the cold water out of them. Immediately, she felt better. There were no more thoughts of bleeding, dismembered bodies or her stained knife. When she went back to her room, she didn't even think of Tar. The water had done its job again; the more she drank, the less she felt. Jade fell asleep. In the middle of the night, she woke shivering and realized that she had never covered herself with the red blanket like she usually did. It lay on the dusty floor. She pulled the other blankets up around her, leaving it there. It was probably too dirty anyway.

XII

The sky was gray. It was night, but the sky was never black at night; it was always gray because the snow meshed with it. The night smothered the forests of Kamareng, hushing everything, but the wind still howled through the branches of the trees. Snow always seemed to be falling. It was the dead of winter; the only color was the eternal green of the pines. Snow weighed down their branches, thick and frigid. The wretched stuff was everywhere and it never seemed to melt. Tar and Sophro trudged through it, their boots heavy and their collars drawn up around their faces. Sophro had grown a beard, a tuft of thick black hair on the bottom of his chin. Tar still shaved religiously every morning that he was able to.

"Let's stop here for a minute," Sophro said. Tar lay down his pack and Sophro looked around for firewood. They broke a few branches off the pines, needles and all, and stacked them. Sophro lit the fire and they warmed their hands. Neither lay down; they both huddled as close to the fire as they could. "I'm so sick of snow," Sophro muttered. He rubbed his hands together and winced.

"How's your shoulder?"

"It's all right." Sophro's shoulder, as the doctor of the camp had told them, would never regain full mobility. Luckily, it wasn't his sword arm, Sophro had said. He would need that one when he got home.

Tar thought about that night, like he often did. He dreamt about it a lot, too. Mostly his dreams were about Lothario. He knew that Sophro thought about it as well, probably even more often. The day they'd gotten back to the camp, Sophro hadn't spoken. He'd just stared at nothing in particular.

Tar saw by the far-off look on his face that he was thinking about him right then.

"It wasn't your fault," he said.

Sophro scoffed. "Yeah, right."

"You weren't our leader."

"And yet you all followed me."

"Only because we thought you—"

"That I would keep you safe. That I knew what the hell I was doing." Sophro sighed. "Well, I didn't."

116

Tar lay down and looked up. He hadn't seen the stars for as long as he could remember. The snow hid them. It was unfair, really. Just when he had come to value them, even need them, they were gone. Now all he had was a gray slate above his head.

"I need...I need to get home, Tar."

Tar cleared his throat. "I know."

"I miss her. She's all I have, and she might not even be waiting for me anymore. She doesn't know if I'm dead or alive."

"She knows. They send updates."

"Yeah, but they're delayed. If I die, it could take weeks for her to find out."

"She'll wait. She'll be there."

Sophro lay down. "Do you think about that girl still?"

"Jade? Yeah. Probably because I get lonely here." Sophro stayed silent, like he was waiting. "She's messed up. I mean, really. But...she knew it. And she almost wanted to change. And I think...I think I could help her." Tar felt his cheeks flush. Now that he'd finally said it out loud, it sounded cheap. He tried to cover up the silence by coughing. He wished he hadn't said anything. To his relief, Sophro didn't answer. "So, what? Two more miles and we'll be there?"

"Yeah," Sophro said. "Slip in, take the letter, replace it with the fake one. Easy."

They had recently been unofficially named the top scouts. Their new mission was to travel to the rebels' military base and swap a stolen troop movement order for a forged one. The base was eight miles from their camp and near the biggest village in Kamareng. In fact, the royal palace was only a mile from it. Sophro carried the sealed envelope inside his coat pocket. They had been given a route to follow, but no one had been inside the actual base before. All that was known was that it was surrounded by four guard towers and probably a good amount of foot soldiers. Inside, it was a mystery. They would have to find a way in without being seen, find the captain's office, find the stolen order, and replace it with the forged one. If they failed, the rebels would be able to predict their troops' movements and surround them. The order had only been stolen three hours ago and maybe wasn't even there yet. They had to reach it before the captain read it in the morning.

"Let's go," Sophro said, standing up and stomping out the fire. Tar followed him from the camp and they trudged through the forest. The

117

sky stayed just light enough to illuminate the outlines of the trees. Sophro and Tar followed as straight of a line as they could. It was hypnotic, walking through the forest; Tar felt his feet hitting the ground over and over, crunching the snow. It was lulling him to sleep. He shook himself awake, fearing that he'd lose Sophro if he fell behind any further; he could barely see his back already. They walked the two miles like this, as quickly and carefully as they could. Tar knew the camp was close when he saw the lights through the trees. At first they were only golden specks, like fireflies, except it was too cold for any insects. They slowly grew. The lights were beautiful. They looked warm. Tar shivered. He was painfully cold. All his fingers and toes had been numb for hours.

"It's like you can't get away from the cold," he whispered.

"It's everywhere," Sophro agreed. "I never thought I'd miss sweating through my clothes. I miss home."

"I miss the stars," Tar said.

Sophro chuckled. "Poet."

Tar remembered Jade telling him he should be a poet. He'd never written poetry in his life. He actually thought it was kind of stupid.

"We're here."

Tar crept up beside Sophro. "How do we do this?"

Sophro looked around, bending branches to see through. The camp was surrounded by four wooden guard towers. They seemed to be directly between two of them. A guard patrolled the distance between the two towers, walking slowly, a gun propped up on his shoulder. The lamps illuminated the rest of the camp. There were barracks on the far side. Closer to Tar and Sophro were three smaller buildings.

"I'm guessing we need to be in one of those. I'll bet one of them is the captain's house, one is the armory, and I'm not sure about the other. Maybe that's where they keep hostages until they take them to a prison camp."

"So which one is the captain's house?"

"My guess is it's the furthest. They'd protect it from this side."

"How do we get past this guard?"

"Well, I'm working on it," Sophro snapped. He stared at the man, following him with his eyes, and at the two towers. He watched the camp for what felt like forever. Tar shifted his weight and sighed. Sophro was completely still except for his eyes. "I don't know," he muttered. Tar sighed. He sat back on the ground and closed his eyes. "Tar, look,"

Sophro hissed. Tar looked through the trees. The guard was heading to the barracks, abandoning his post. "It might be our only chance."

"What about the towers?"

"See how the trees are cover until right under them? If we stay right in the trees, it'll take longer, but they won't see us."

Without another word, Sophro darted ahead. Tar leapt after him. Sophro veered to the right to avoid the open field and Tar followed, branches hitting him in the face. Sophro led them directly in front of the northeast tower. It loomed above them. Made of wood, it looked like it had been hastily erected. Tar couldn't see anyone inside.

"There's no one," he whispered.

"I know," Sophro answered. He was smiling. "I'm going," he said and began to run. Tar, more cautious, crept after him. He stepped into the open space between the forest and the camp. His heart nearly stopped; he felt naked, exposed. Sophro beckoned him forward and he ran, his feet crunching through snow. Their backs pressed against the tower, they looked around. "Stay in the shadows," Sophro whispered. Tar's heart was pounding. He glanced furtively around. The camp was empty and silent. The only sound was the wind and his own ragged breathing. Sophro, holding his knife, crept ahead toward the far building. Tar drew his own knife, clutching the familiar handle. It was like shaking hands with an old friend. He followed Sophro through the shadows, past the first building. All of them were the same; made of pine; temporary shelters. When Tar and Sophro passed the second building and were standing up against the wall, preparing to run for the third, the guard passed them, heading back to his post. He seemingly came out of nowhere; he saw them out of the corner of his eye and jumped. He opened his mouth to scream and Tar's heart stopped, but Sophro was already on him. He held a hand over his mouth and shoved his knife through his stomach. Sophro kept his hand pressed against his lips, catching the man as he fell, until he stopped moving. When he moved his hand away, it was covered in blood. Sophro smeared it on his shirt and dragged the body into the shadows. Tar stared at the dead body and swallowed. He wanted to close the eyes; they looked like they were staring at him. "Come on," Sophro hissed. Tar followed him through the walkway between the two wooden buildings. The light there seemed so bright. He took a deep breath once they were back in the dark on the other side. The doorway was covered with thick canvas. Sophro carefully pushed it aside. He crept inside and Tar followed him. The interior of the cabin was almost completely black. He could only see shapes and outlines until his eyes adjusted. Tar looked around. The room was filled with tables, upon which rested maps and papers and bottles of ink. He and Sophro walked silently around the small room, squinting at papers, looking for a letter identical to the one Sophro carried. Tar heard snores from the next room.

"Hurry," he muttered.

Sophro sifted through piles of papers, his eyebrows furrowed. Tar peeked through the canvas. The wind caught it and blew it open. He couldn't breathe. Two soldiers were patrolling on the opposite side of the camp, wearing the blue overcoats and fur hats of the rebel guard. Their heads jerked over and their eyes seemed to meet Tar's, even though they were too far away for that to be possible. Nevertheless, he felt them stare at him. They began to run toward him.

"Hide." It was all he could say to Sophro, who was holding up the letter. He stuffed it into his pocket and placed the fake one on the table, pressing himself against the wall on the opposite side of the doorway as Tar. Tar breathed shallow breaths, holding his knife close. The guards tore through the canvas and Tar grabbed the first by the shoulder and plunged his knife into his stomach. The man let out a grunt and sank to his knees. Sophro had slit the other's throat. He glanced at Tar and they ran out through the doorway and began to sprint through the snow, sending clumps of powder flying. The air stung Tar's throat. He couldn't breathe. Snowflakes pricked his face. Blood on the blade of his knife, bobbing in the corner of his vision. He couldn't make his legs work fast enough. A familiar alarm rang throughout the camp. Tar had heard it many times before. It sounded like a huge, deep bell being hit with a hammer. The forest loomed closer and closer and Tar could almost relax. He even slowed down a little. Then a guard jumped out of the shadows, swinging the butt of his gun at Sophro's head. Tar saw him crumple and fall, motionless, on the snow. Tar stumbled and slowed. He froze. The guard pointed his gun at Tar's head. Tar looked at Sophro, who had fallen with his arms splayed out to the sides. He felt his stomach drop as he glanced at the trees. He dropped his knife and slowly knelt, hands in the air, in the cold snow.

XIII

Tsaigal in winter was always depressing; the town didn't have the same energy as it did in any other season. That winter was even worse. The watered-down sun hung limply in the blue-gray sky, blanketed sometimes by clouds. It was still warm, but the electricity of the summer heat was missing. The dock hands dragged their feet when they came back from work under stiff clouds. This winter, there were only the old dock hands. The younger ones had left. There were also no young men to keep the women of the pleasure district company. Those girls sat on the steps of their bars, smearing off their golden eye makeup with the folds of their dresses. Their only business came from the old men now, men whose sagging skin revolted them. They all debated amongst themselves which was worse: no customers or the ones they had. The women who scoured the marketplace instead wandered around it absentmindedly, returning home with items they hadn't meant to buy, like a type of bread a husband liked, only to get home and remember that he was gone. Or a new shirt for a child, only to remember that the child was now a man and he was gone, too. The women stayed up at night, maybe after putting their young children to bed, and hung their heads over the table, hands clasped on their lap or clutching the latest newspaper that contained a piece of the man they missed. Even just a piece of paper with his name on it was comforting. The women gathered in the town square each week with heavy hearts to hear the names of the dead. Some days it was only one. Others it was as many as twenty. Once it was fifty. Sobs echoed throughout the empty city.

Despina Mali was not like most of the women; she did not have a husband. But, like them, her life also revolved around those meetings in the square. That day, she woke up in Sophro's bed. She had started sleeping there when she couldn't sleep in her own, but now she slept there every night. The bed barely smelled like him anymore. Despina rubbed her eyes and dressed, wrapping her black scarf around her head. The air outside held the hint of a chill. She walked on stiff legs to the square. The other women were there and more were arriving. She stood in her usual place by the foot of the small stone stage that was carved out of the city walls. The woman beside her bounced a small boy on her hip. He smiled, oblivious to his mother's anxiety. Despina's heart beat furiously as the king stepped onto the stage. A trumpet blared and all the

121

women knelt, bowing their heads.

"You may stand," Nikola called. Despina rose, her legs shaking. She clasped her hands together as Nikola unfolded a piece of paper. It always looked the same. "We have no dead to report this week." A tremor of nervous excitement passed through the women. They sighed with relief. "However, two men have gone missing." Complete silence. Bowing her head, Despina could see her own heart pounding through her shirt. Nikola cleared his throat. "The missing men are Sophrosynes Ilore and Adatares Taiav."

Despina clutched at the arm of the woman next to her, who caught her as she stumbled.

"Are you all right, dear?"

Despina couldn't meet her eyes. She knew they'd be full of pity. "Thank you," she mumbled. The crowd parted for her and she made her way back to Sophro's house. Shutting the door behind her, she pulled off her scarf and dropped it on the floor. A single tear ran down her cheek as she climbed into bed.

XIV

The first night, Tar didn't sleep at all. He knew Sophro didn't either because his bunk was right beneath Sophro's. Tar tossed around in his bunk, staring up at the pine planks. The prison camp was surrounded by a fence and heavily guarded. In fact, guards strolled past his window every few minutes. He shuddered and turned his back to it. As he lay there, he couldn't help thinking of Jade. He swallowed. During the day, he was able to push her from his mind, but at night just the thought of her made his chest ache. He wondered where she was and if she was safe. The wind whistled through the cracks in the barracks and Tar shivered, pulling the thin blanket up around his neck. He dreamt of Jade; she lay beside him.

Chapter 7
I

Spring had once again come. The magnolia trees lining the streets of the Bright City grew green buds, small and fuzzy things holding future flowers. Perfume filled the air, the clean scent of melting ice mixed with every floral scent from the gardens which, when combined, could only be described as green. It was early morning when Edmund arrived in Desrala. As the sun rose, water dripped from roofs. Citizens, going about their daily routines, saw his carriage and paused, shielding their eyes from the sun. Edmund held his wife's hand. Sarila and Emre slept on the opposite seat and Ahmar sat next to him. Edmund hadn't been able to leave them in Pruen; he didn't take any chances with his family's safety anymore. The ride had taken a week and he couldn't imagine being there without them, even though he'd never brought them to a meeting before. It was strange to think that the kings had last met an entire year ago. He remembered meeting in Cairblain like it had happened last week. Edmund gazed out the window. He'd forgotten Desrala's beauty, especially in the spring. The carriage was crossing the bridge over the river. The falls spilled into nothingness to the left. Up ahead was the palace. Its elaborate gardens made Edmund's teeth clench. It was like a painting: green and yellow and rich red everywhere. Edmund remembered his own destroyed palace with a pang in his chest. As the carriage began to rumble over gravel, the children awoke. Sema held the three-year-old Emre in her lap. His eyes were wild. The carriage rolled up to the steps of the enormous white palace. Servants rushed down the steps, shouting orders to each other, surrounding the carriage. As it stopped and Edmund stepped out onto the gravel, Alain emerged from the palace. He waddled over to Edmund.

"Good day, Edmund. And Ahmar…ah, Queen Sema." Alain kissed Sema's hand.

"It's been a long time," she said.

"Yes, yes. Since the wedding," Alain mumbled, distracted. The two children hid behind Edmund. Alain crouched down. "And who are you?"

"Sarila," the six-year-old girl mumbled.

"No, that's not possible. Sarila is just a baby."

A smile crept across her face.

"I'm six." She beamed. Alain opened his mouth in mock surprise.

"Tell you what, since you're so old, I think that you and your brother can go and play in the gardens, if that's all right with your mother."

Sema nodded and the two children galloped off, Emre stumbling after his sister. Sema strolled leisurely after the children, gazing around the gardens, sighing in the morning breeze.

"The others arrived last night," Alain explained as he and Edmund climbed the steps. "And mind you, I haven't been able to get much out of them. They whisper to each other mostly."

"Well, they have a war to fight," Edmund said.

"They act like it's on our doorstep. That's what I'll never understand. When there is a war on everyone feels like they must act reverently. Otherwise, it's disrespectful. To whom? The soldiers? They're too far away to hear us. So let us eat and drink our fill and sing songs of the old days and forget the war while we can, eh?"

Edmund chuckled in spite of himself, but as he did so, he felt shame creep up the back of his neck. No, he would not find joy here, not even fleeting, shallow joy. He had left that in a previous time and he wasn't sure how or when he could get it back.

The palace was how he remembered it on the inside: ornately patterned, gold wallpaper covered every inch of the walls. Huge paintings of sullen men in elaborate uniforms hung wherever there was room. Edmund found one of the royal family. Alain had been thinner back then; it must have been painted over ten years before. He wore a heavy golden crown. Queen Cerise sat in front of him, a fair woman with flowing golden hair and delicate features. There was something about her eyes, though; Edmund couldn't quite place it. They were too blue. It was unnatural, the kind of color that can't be found anywhere on the earth. Almost every eye color can. There is the steel gray of a stormy sky or the green-brown of tree moss. Even colors that seem strange for eyes can be found in nature, like the light green of a spring leaf. But Cerise's eyes were brighter than sky-blue, richer than ocean-blue. They were a painful blue that people looked away from and then glanced back, unsure if they'd really seen it. Next to Queen Cerise stood Prince Aubrey, who at the time had been only ten years old. He was a good-looking boy with a charming round face and a mischievous smile. It was a good healthy smile, and it made Edmund want to smile too.

When Alain and Edmund entered the meeting room, a grand sitting room, Nikola and Sven looked up. They sat on two uncomfortable-looking white couches. In all, there were four in the room. Edmund sat down on an empty couch. It was stiff and had hardly any padding. Sven still stared at him. Edmund nodded, hoping an acknowledgement was all he wanted. Sven looked different. Much older. More wrinkles creased the sides of his eyes and he seemed paler. Nikola looked more somber than usual. His boyish smile had disappeared.

"Pleasure, Edmund," Sven mumbled. Nikola nodded once.

"Now, what were we discussing?" Edmund asked. Sven and Nikola glanced at each other.

"The war," Sven stated.

"Ah, come now, let's not speak of such things. At least not so early."

"There is nothing else to speak of, Alain. Nothing so important." Some color came to Sven's cheeks as his voice rose.

"What about the hunt? That must be arranged."

"I won't be staying for the hunt. I will ride back to Cairblain in the morning," Sven muttered.

"I also must leave early," Nikola added.

Alain's face fell. He looked hurt.

"Nikola I can understand; you've never liked hunting. But Sven, you and I, the forest-dwellers…hunting is in our blood!"

Sven smiled sadly. "Not this time, old friend."

Alain leaned back in his sofa. He took up nearly the whole thing. It groaned under his weight.

"Well."

The four kings sat in silence. Sven stared out the window. Nikola tapped his foot on the soft red carpet.

"Shall we renew the alliance?" Edmund ventured.

"Before we do, I—well, we have a question," Nikola said, glancing at Sven.

Alain leaned forward. "Do you really believe that a year has changed my mind? Here you two are, like beggars in the street. Well, you'll not have any of my men; I guarantee it. Not a single one!"

Nikola's eyes were wide. Sven hung his head.

"I wish I could help you, but I have had worse luck than you this past year," Edmund muttered.

"I believe you have," Sven said. "I understand. Excuse me." He stood up and left the room, his huge hide boots leaving deep imprints in the thick carpet.

II

It was early morning. A thick, gray blanket of clouds covered the sky. The air was crisp and sweet like an early apple. Sven stood, his arms crossed, in a stand of willows, looking south at the falls. The river gushed by to his left and the fragrant willows trailed their crisp leaves in the water. The sun had not yet risen. A film of calm covered the city. Sven inhaled the minty chale leaf smoke of his pipe and closed his eyes. The first noises of the midway echoed in the empty streets across the river. A flock of sparrows chirped, perched on the hedges. As he stood there with his eyes closed, he became aware of a presence beside him.

"I will ready the carriage, your majesty," Fyn said. It was almost a whisper, like he was afraid to break the king's concentration. Sven glanced sideways at him.

"Thank you," he said. Sven chuckled as he watched him sprint back across the green lawn of the palace. Fyn had become immensely more helpful in the past few months. He had stopped drinking as far as Sven knew (because he couldn't smell it on his breath anymore) and he had become a sort of butler. He managed the fortress when Sven was in Kamareng, gave orders to the maids and the cook, and overall, just made life much smoother. Sven couldn't see how he had gotten along before. Sometime between Vira's departure and that moment, Sven had begun to trust him.

The sky was turning golden, like a healing bruise. Sven trudged up the palace greens to the steps. He glanced at the servants preparing his carriage: oiling the wheels, harnessing the stamping horses. Edmund walked down the steps. There were dark circles underneath his eyes.

"I'm sorry you have to leave so early," Edmund said.

"When will you go?"

"Tomorrow. Alain and I have a few things to discuss." Sven raised an eyebrow. "What? Just because he wouldn't give you any men doesn't mean he won't give me any. I need to retake my city." There was a brokenness in his voice, an audible yearning. He gazed south. "Who knows how it's been defiled? And my citizens, my people, falling prey to whoever promises them a crust of bread..." Edmund clenched his fists.

"You're a good man, Edmund. A true king. I worry that our friend Alain may have lost sight of what makes one. Good luck to you." Sven and Edmund grasped wrists.

"And to you, my brother."

Fyn opened Sven's door and he ducked inside.

As the country rolled by, Sven's eyes were fixed on north on the icy land of Kamareng.

III

It was warm enough in the kitchen that the window had to be opened. It hadn't been opened in months. As Daina creaked it open to let in a cool breeze, a gilded carriage rolled by. Daina peered into the window. A man with a mane of blonde hair sat inside. As she watched, he turned and met her eyes. She backed away from the window, an unexpected shame flushing her cheeks. She closed the curtain. It fluttered in the breeze. Daina walked back into the kitchen, where the aroma of the butterscotch cake was overwhelming. Audric sat at the kitchen table with a cup of tea, his dark hair boyishly mussed. He was naked from the waist up. He stared out the window with his eyes narrowed, steam wafting up around his chin. He looked up when he saw her. She smiled.

"I think it's ready to be cut," she said.

"Good."

Daina picked up the serrated cake knife from the counter. The rich smell coated the back of her throat and made her mouth water. She cut the moist cake and put a slice on a plate. She set it in front of Audric.

"Aren't you going to have any?" he asked.

"Later."

Audric took a bite. His eyelids fluttered in a mockery of ecstasy. Daina laughed.

"It's great."

"Good." Audric stood up and put on his sweater. "Don't go so soon. You're not done yet," Daina pleaded. Audric kissed her forehead. His breath smelled sweet.

"Please, don't make me feel guilty. I have to go."

Daina felt her jaw clenching and tried to force the anger back down. "You always do this. Why do you always have to leave?"

A small smirk hinted at Audric's lips.

"It's light out already."

"Then stay all day. You can go home at night." Audric headed for the door and Daina's stomach dropped. She followed him.

127

"I really should go."

"Please," Daina whispered. She reached for his hands and held them. She thought she saw a hint of a grimace cross his face. "I get so lonely. And Kieran...you're so good with him. He loves you." As if on cue, a cough, followed by a wail, sounded from upstairs.

"Of course I'll stay," Audric said. Daina grinned. She kissed him and let him press her body against his until he began to shudder. Then she went upstairs to the baby.

IV

The evening breeze caressed Daina's legs and rustled her dress. Spring was at its peak and the air was humid. The sky was finally black again; during the winter and early spring its gray or violet hue gave off a bleak, ethereal feeling like winter skies usually do. A black night sky was more comforting, like a blanket. Nothing else could be out there when the sky was black. Daina pulled her jacket closer. Her black dress floated around her. It reached almost to her knees and had a ruffled midsection, which disguised the extra fat she had gained while pregnant. She wore a thin white jacket and a string of pearls around her neck. Her shoes were red heels—the new fashion had cost her a month's worth of pay—and they clicked as she walked down the midway. It smelled like popcorn and salted caramel. A band played on the corner of Midway and University Street. As Daina walked by, the handsome violin player serenaded her with a solo. She smiled and turned onto University. The entrance to the gardens shone with yellow lights. In fact, the entire maze seemed to glow and hum. Daina stepped inside and made her way to the center of the maze, from where the sounds of a band and laughter drifted. On the way, she passed a couple tangled together. They were too busy to notice her as she slipped past. She entered the bright, open clearing in the center of the maze of hedges. Closed pearl-pink tulips lined the edges of the clearing. Lamps hung all over, illuminating the night with a soft yellow glow. Daina recognized every student from nearly all of her classes. It was the spring ball, and the band played a lively melody as couples swayed together in the center of the clearing. Colette wore her red hair in curls that framed her face and hung down to the middle of her back. She wore a peach-pink dress with a corset. It barely covered her ass. She was pressed against Jerome, giggling and stumbling over his feet. One of her hands rested on his chest, inside his shirt, and the other held a glass of pink champagne. Lottë stood in the corner by the long table with food on it, picking pieces of cheese and putting them in her mouth with a guilty glance around to see if anyone was watching. She wore a plain taupe dress that actually made her body seem wider. It blended into her skin and made her look like one big bulge. Daina spotted Audric holding court off to the side, sitting at a table while the waiter filled his glass of champagne, surrounded by four young women. She strode over, picking up a glass on the way and taking a sip. Her heels sunk a little into the moist ground. When Audric saw her coming, the smile fell from his face. Daina sat down across the circular table from him in the only open seat left.

"Daina, what a surprise," Juliette said. She was in Daina's biology class. Her dark hair was braided and the long black braid hung down her back. Against the bright yellow of her strapless dress, it reminded Daina of a bee's stinger. "It's been so long since you've been to class." All the girls stared at her, looking her over, sizing her up. Daina felt their glances like pinpricks: on her slightly protruding stomach, on the extra skin under her chin, on the dark circles under her eyes that she'd tried to hide with makeup. They all smiled: the corners of their mouths turned up, their eyebrows raised, their eyes shining like ravenous dogs'. She was their age, but she had a child. They remembered with delight how she used to waddle from class to class, one hand under her enormous belly.

"I've been busy."

"You certainly have," Lienne muttered. She tapped Elise on the shoulder and the two blondes left the table.

"I have to go...do something," Juliette said vaguely and stood up. "Emeline, weren't you going to join me?"

Just Daina and Audric remained at the table. Daina looked around. Juliette watched her from the dance floor, her eyes narrowed. But they were out of earshot from everyone.

"Why have you stopped coming by?" Daina asked.

Audric took a puff of his cigar and set it in the ashtray. He breathed out a cloud of smoke. "I've been busy," he repeated Daina's own excuse.

Daina sat back in her chair. "It's been a month. Kieran misses you."

"I don't want to talk about this. Not here."

"How many of those girls are you fucking?"

"Daina—"

"How many?"

"Keep your voice down." Audric glared at her, his teeth clenched.

Daina traced the rim of her glass with her finger. Pink bubbles floated up to the surface. "Juliette?"

"No. I'm not—"

"Why is she staring at me?"

"Ask her. Daina, I don't know what you want."

"I want you to come over."

"Shh. After this. Go home and I'll be there after midnight."

Daina felt tears of relief come to her eyes. Later that night, when she began her walk home, she walked back through the hedge maze. When she turned a corner, she jumped. Lottë stood there, facing her, like she'd been waiting.

"Excuse me," Daina said. Lottë didn't move.

"Going home?"

"Yes."

"Already?"

"Yes, Lottë." Lottë's face was unreadable. She licked her lips.

"Right, you have a baby. How old is he? Four months?"

"In two days," Daina replied. A tingle crept up the back of her neck. "I should go."

Lottë seemed not to hear her. "Strange…"

"What is?"

"Well, you must have gotten pregnant around the same time Jade left."

Daina's pulse quickened. She tried desperately to keep her face expressionless. When she didn't answer, Lottë went on.

"Remember her? Jiada Ansel? Auburn hair, those pretty blue eyes?"

"I remember. I suppose that's true; I did get pregnant then."

"You know, I could tell you something about Jade." Lottë's mouth curled up in a snarl.

"Oh?" Daina calmed down, relieved that the conversation was heading into familiar territory. She knew everything about Jade.

"She was Audric's whore." Daina widened her eyes in mock surprise. Lottë smiled. "She was pregnant, too. But she killed her baby. Me and Audric were the only ones who knew. And her, I guess. Ha!" Daina didn't know what to say, so she feigned shock. "I blackmailed her, 'cause I knew she was sleeping with him. Just like I know you are, too." Lottë's eyes turned dark.

"Excuse me?"

"I never saw you with any other guy," she said smugly. Daina narrowed her eyes and opened her mouth in incredulous contempt. Lottë's face fell. Daina relaxed. She was a better actress than Jade.

"I can't imagine what would give you that idea." Daina summoned tears.

"I—I...I'm sorry. Look, I don't have anything against you," Lottë cried.

Daina covered her face with her hands so Lottë couldn't see her smiling.

When Daina closed her door behind her and sent her neighbor home, she looked in on Kieran. The little bundle of blankets slowly rose and fell. Kieran's hair had grown and turned a lovely caramel color. Daina kissed his forehead and his eyebrows furrowed.

"Your father is coming back," she whispered. There was a knock at the door. She crept out of the room and down the stairs. Audric stood on the doorstep. He rushed in and Daina shut the door behind him. They didn't say anything; lust glinted in Audric's eyes and Daina, checking that the curtains were closed, pulled him close by his collar. There was something about the way he looked in a collared shirt and vest. Audric's hands pressed against her back. Daina and Audric knelt on the floor, frantically removing each others' clothing. Audric pushed Daina back onto the floor. The whole time, they didn't say anything. Only small grunts or moans escaped their lips. Afterwards, they lay together on the wooden floor. Audric's eyes were closed and Daina was afraid to break the silence.

"Do you ever want...like, something more?" she asked.

Audric inhaled quickly, the startled breath of the half-asleep. "More than what?"

Daina sat up. "This. Being forced to live in secret, lying to everyone."

"I don't lie. Do you? Who's asked you?"

"I'm just saying. I wish we didn't have to be so secret."

"You know we do. It's the only way."

"Well, I'm tired of it. There's nothing wrong with what we've done," Daina said indignantly.

"Just about everyone else in Desrala would disagree."

"I don't care what they think. I love you, and I love our son." Daina

131

saw Audric's eyes widen and she couldn't breathe.

"I love you, too," he said.

Daina exhaled. "Then why can't you acknowledge me? If you really love me then nothing else matters."

Audric sat up. He looked hurt. "You're asking me to give up my career. My life's work."

"We don't know that. You might be able to stay at the university."

Audric scoffed. "Please. I'd be gone in a second."

"What's more important? Your job or your family?" Daina felt a righteous indignation rising in her. "I've been living my life around these visits for four months. They're all that I look forward to. And sometimes you don't show up. I'm going crazy, Audric. I can't live like this forever."

Audric began to put on his clothes. "We have an arrangement." His voice was cold. "You get your money and I keep my job. My life."

"Audric, don't go. I just...I need more."

"Well, I can't give you anything else." He stood up. Daina, still naked, stood up too. She touched his cheek. He turned away, his face expressionless.

"Fine," she said. "Go, then. I'll wait for my money." She shouted the last at a slamming door. Daina crawled onto the couch, breathing heavily. "What...why did I—" she whispered, rocking back and forth. She began to sob. A crushing loneliness seemed to suck the air out of her lungs. She curled herself into a ball. "I—I didn't want this," she cried. She slammed her head into the wall behind her until she saw stars. Upstairs, Kieran began to cry. He screamed his throat raw; he cried himself back to sleep.

V

Jade put a new candle in the holder by her bed. She struck a match and lit the new wick. The flame trembled and then steadied, orange and bright. Jade lit the wall lamps and then hastily shook the flame out of the match. She nearly singed her fingertips every time. She spread out her astronomy book and her notebook on her bed and sat down, crossing her legs. She began to write, and it was the first time in a long time. She began with something simple: a diagram of the spring constellations. Just as she was finishing the last of Hiri's stars, there was a knock at her door. She had an impulse to hide her work, but decided against it and opened

132

the door. Lumine stood on the other side, her blonde hair in a long braid.

"Hey," she said. She held a bottle of whiskey in one hand.

"Hi."

"Can I come in?" Jade stepped aside. "I brought a peace offering." She set the bottle on Jade's desk.

"You didn't have to—"

"I shouldn't have told Blaise about your stargazing."

"It's okay." Jade absentmindedly rubbed the cut on her cheek where Blaise's ring had hit. "It wasn't too bad. He just didn't want me wasting time." Jade sat down on the edge of her bed and Lumine sat in the desk chair.

"What are you doing?"

"Astronomy."

Lumine peered at Jade's notebook. "It looks complicated."

"Not so complicated. Simple, really. This is just a diagram of spring constellations. I wanted to remember them because the summer ones are here now."

Lumine stared at Jade's drawings. "I need a drink," she said.

"There are cups in that drawer."

Lumine poured a glass for herself and one for Jade. "To you," she said and lifted her glass. Jade nodded. They both drank. The whiskey tasted sweet.

"What's in this?"

"Cinnamon." Lumine refilled their glasses and they drank again. Jade felt her head begin to warm. "So you draw stars."

"I diagram and chart them, yes. And I developed a calendar based on them. It's accurate. We use it in Desrala."

"That's where you're from?"

"Yes."

"Wow, so you must be really smart."

"Not everyone from Desrala is. But yes, I am."

"That's why they wanted you, I think."

Jade swallowed and felt the whiskey burn down her throat.

"I've never been drunk in my life," she admitted.

"You're not drunk yet." Lumine grinned, refilling her glass. Jade looked at her book, but she couldn't make sense of the letters. She put it under her bed. As she was fixing her pillow, the pamphlet fell on the ground. Lumine picked it up. "What's this?"

Jade snatched it out of her hand with numb fingertips. "Nothing."
"Why was it under your pillow?" Lumine's eyes shone with the glaze
of alcohol.
"I don't know."
She laughed out loud. "Bullshit."
"It's nothing." Jade's tongue felt clumsy.
"Then burn it." Lumine stared at her.
"I don't want to."
"If it means nothing to you, then burn it."
Jade swallowed. "Fine." With clenched teeth, she held the pamphlet
up to the candle flame. She watched as the end burned to black, her only
reminder of Tar, what she'd slept with for a year. Lumine jumped up. "I
was just kidding. I'm sorry," she said. Jade pulled it out of the fire and
blew out the flame. Half of it remained. Jade set it on her desk. "I don't
know why I said that. I say stupid things all the time. What does it mean
to you?"
Jade looked at the faded, blackened paper. It was smoking. "I know
someone in the war."
"Someone?" Lumine asked with a wink.
"Not like that."
Lumine nodded solemnly, taking another drink. Jade picked up the
bottle and carried it to her bed.
"I'm sorry. Sometimes I say the dumbest—"
"Are you numb?" Jade interrupted.
"What?"
"Do you...do you still feel...like you used to?"
Lumine sighed. "No."
"It's the water," Jade said.
"I think I knew."
"I kind of like it. I don't know if it's like that for a reason or if it's just
one of those things...but I'm not sad anymore. Or happy. I'm just here."
Lumine nodded. She held out her cup for Jade to fill. "I like it, too."
Jade took a huge gulp of whiskey from the bottle. Her chest felt
heavy and her head felt warm.
"I have to get out of here, Lumine. I need to get home."
Lumine looked confused. "But you can't leave."
"I'm going to. Soon."
"No, you can't—"

"I know how to get there. Desrala isn't far. I've been here for too long. Almost a year. I just have to convince Blaise to let me go."

"Even if you did, you'd still be a part of us," Lumine said, her eyes piercing into Jade's. Jade took another drink.

"That's okay. As long as I don't have to stay here." She bit her lip, deep in thought, and they sat in silence, drinking themselves to sleep.

When Jade awoke, her head pounded. The bottle of whiskey had spilled on the floor. Lumine's chair was empty. The candle had gone out. Jade sat up, holding her head like that would keep the headache from reaching her brain. Her eyes burned. She pulled on her robe and stepped into the puddle of whiskey. She shuddered and wiped her foot on a blanket. As she was about to open the door, she glanced at her desk. The charred pamphlet lay on it, half gone. Jade felt the blood drain from her cheeks. She opened the door and rushed down the hallway to Lumine's room. She pounded on the door. After a moment, it opened. Lumine's eyes were red-rimmed.

"Morning."

"What did I tell you last night?" Jade demanded.

"Uh…that you study stars?"

"What else?"

"That's…all I remember. That whiskey…"

Jade sighed. She smiled. "Go back to bed."

VI

A weak light filtered into the room through the high window, illuminating the stone walls and dirt floor with a gray sheen. Tar opened his sleep-crusted eyes, picked a piece of straw off his cheek, and, seeing the light, scratched a mark into the sandy floor. He counted all of the marks he'd made and, smiling, pounded on the wooden door. "Sophro," he called.

"Yeah?" The muffled shout came from across the hallway.

"Day thirty-one," Tar said. A moment of silence.

"Really?"

Footsteps clomped down the hallway. Tar backed away from the door. A key fumbled in the lock, metal scraping metal, and the door creaked open. A blank-faced guard stood on the other side. Across the hallway, Sophro stood in the doorway. The guards led the two of them to the door and pushed them out into the sunlight with the butts of their rifles. Sophro sighed and looked around. Tar closed his eyes and smelled the air.

"I never thought I'd be happy to be back out here," Tar said as they began to walk through the camp. The camp was a collection of sixty huts surrounded by a ten-foot-high wall. High above that, cliffs surrounded it on all sides; the camp had been blasted out of a mountainside. Ten guard towers surrounded it, on top of the cliffs. Days there weren't bad; just long. The men walked the perimeter of the camp, eyes searching for any way out. They stared forlornly up at the top of the cliffs. When Tar and Sophro had first arrived six months ago, one man had recognized Sophro.

"Sophrosynes, the great fighter," he'd exclaimed, and then his face had fallen.

As they walked to their hut, some friends they'd made clapped for them as they passed and they nodded in return. It was summer in Kamareng, which translated to the temperature of early spring in Tsaigal. The air was crisp; the sun never really reached the earth. But the prisoners took advantage of the sun while it was out, especially the men from Tsaigal who needed heat and sweat and light to think properly. They sometimes sat in the sun all day with three jackets on just to feel at home again. Tar and Sophro entered their hut, their small wooden home. It consisted of two bunks with a stove in the middle and a bathroom in back. They shared the tiny hut with two other men, both from Gláspeir. When Sophro opened the door, the men shouted. Startled, Tar glanced around. Izaak stood in front of the door, holding a light brown, sad-looking cake. Riven sat on his bed, the top bunk.

"Welcome home!" Izaak cried. He was a heavy-set man, at least twenty years older than Tar, with a thick red beard and the bulging, filmy eyes of an alcoholic. Riven, whom Tar only knew by his last name, was a dark-haired, dark-eyed introvert, and would often retreat into pensive silence whenever the room was loud.

"What's this?" Sophro asked. All four men grinned in an infectious wave of happiness.

"I saved our flour rations for a week. And stole some sugar," Izaak explained, setting the cake down on the table.

"Cut me a piece, will you?" Tar sat down on his bed.

Izaak beamed and drew his knife from the inside of his jacket. As he'd said, it had been a bitch to keep the knife out of sight, but he'd managed and he wouldn't be parted from it for anything. She was all he had left. "How was it?"

"The same as always. But just longer."

"I should say so. You've never been in for a month before. A few days, sure. A week, alright. But a month..."

"I don't regret it," Tar said.

"Good," Riven muttered.

"I'd do it again in a minute."

"Would you do it again, Sophro?" Izaak asked.

"Yes. Ten escape attempts." Sophro grasped air with his hand, like he could feel freedom between his fingers. "I thought I found a blind spot, but I guess not. And we have to do more research next time." He let his hand fall into his lap.

"Maybe..." Izaak looked uncomfortable. "Maybe you should lay low for a while. Every guard in this place is already watching you. It was a month this time. What if next time they shoot you?"

Sophro shook his head. "I won't be caught next time," he said.

"Next time will be it," Tar agreed, although he felt a sinking in his stomach. What Izaak had said was only too possible. He remembered taking the bullet out of Sophro's shoulder. He swallowed. "It will work."

"Don't you two want to get out of here?" Sophro cried.

"You're young," Izaak said. "I've got no one waiting for me and even if I could get out of here, I would have to go back to the war anyway. I'm a prisoner no matter what. We all are."

"Isn't freedom worth something? Even if you're still in the war?" Sophro asked.

Izaak shook his head. "To tell you the truth, I haven't enough energy. I'd rather sit out the war here. I'm safe here."

Sophro scoffed and stood up. "Safe." He slammed the door on his way out. The men sat quietly. Tar shifted in his chair.

"He's young. He should be home, not here," Izaak muttered.

"Is he planning something, Tar?" Riven asked from his perch.

Tar followed his gaze and looked out the window. Sophro stared up at the cliffs, his back to them. Tar smiled. "I think he is."

VII

137

The sun hovered high in the sky and the air inside the carriage was stale. Edmund felt nauseated. The carriage rumbled down the sandy road, approaching the gates of Porthmôr.

"Home!" Emre shouted, bouncing up and down. Edmund swallowed. Royal guards were stationed at the gates. The royal army, or what was left of it, along with recruits from Pruen and the few men Alain had given, had been sent in a week ago and Edmund had received a report that the city was secure. As the carriage rolled through the gates, Edmund nodded to the guards. The sight of his beloved city made his heart sink. Graffiti covered the walls; papers littered the ground. There was an eerie silence. "Papa, what happened?" Emre asked, climbing onto his lap. Edmund just held him close and kissed the top of his head. The harbor was destroyed: ships blown to pieces, rotting fish scattered everywhere. Edmund felt his son's quick heartbeat against his chest. The carriage turned down the road to the palace.

"Oh," Sema whispered. The crowd of soldiers carrying lumber and shouting orders could not disguise the fact that the palace was only a black shell. Edmund clutched his wife's hand tightly. Sema swallowed and Edmund watched her struggle to keep her face expressionless. They climbed out of the carriage on stiff legs and stood staring at the wreck.

"Mama, how will we live here?" Sarila asked. Edmund felt a pang in his chest as he looked down at his daughter's huge brown eyes. He tried to speak, but his throat closed up. Sema was fumbling for an answer when Sarila looked around at all the soldiers and nodded her head. "We'll just have to rebuild it."

Edmund felt his heart lift with a soaring, gut-wrenching hope. He picked up Sarila, swinging her high up in the air as she screamed with delight.

VIII

Jade pulled the blanket up to her neck to block the chill seeping into her bare skin. Blaise lay next to her, his eyes closed.

"Jade," he whispered. She turned to him, plastering a smile onto her face. "You're beautiful."

"You say that to everyone."

Blaise leaned over her. He kissed her neck. "No, you're gorgeous." He stroked her hair.

Jade took a deep breath and stared up at him with her big blue eyes. "I've been experiencing something lately that...worries me." Blaise's eyes widened.

"Like what?" he whispered.

Jade knew she had him. "I think..." she rolled her eyes. "Never mind."

"Tell me." Jade felt his breath on her face.

"I think I may have a mission. I think I'm being called."

Blaise narrowed his eyes. "I would have gotten the message first. I hear all the messages; they come through me."

Jade nodded, feeling her grasp on him loosen. She ran her hands over his chest. "I know. But if I was..."

"What is it?"

"It feels like a pinprick at first, right in my scars, and then a pounding in my head." Blaise rolled away, staring up at the ceiling. Jade tried not to smile. He hadn't even remembered that, over a year ago, he'd told her the sensation himself. "So I went to the temple and I heard his voice. He said that I needed to go to Desrala. That a man named Audric was attempting to find us."

Blaise rolled onto his side. "Then you'll go there, find him, and kill him."

Jade also turned to face him. She stroked his cheek. "I think I'm supposed to try to recruit him," she whispered.

Blaise shook his head slowly. "I don't know. Perhaps you misunderstood."

Jade sighed. "I know I need to go. I feel the pull. Even now." She summoned tears. "I feel it all the time."

Blaise kissed her cheek. "I don't doubt that the Master wants to use your talents. But Jade, this is a serious mission. You'd have to observe this Audric for a long time to discern the Master's intent. Maybe even go undercover. And...well, I'd miss you."

Jade held her cheeks firmly in place to keep from grinning. He was doing her work for her. "I will pray about it," she said quietly.

Blaise nodded. "So will I."

Later, when he was asleep, Jade crept back to her room, a grin on her face. She closed her door behind her and lit the lamps. As she climbed into bed, she saw the red blanket lying on the floor. Her stomach sank. She picked it up and dusted it off. She looked closely at it. There was an intricate pattern sewn into it: tulips intertwined with stalks of wheat and corn. She'd never noticed it before. She didn't know why, but she had to struggle to breathe normally. She closed her eyes and remembered Tsaigal. A year ago she had found herself in its stifling summer. She remembered the green corn leaves and the bustle of the marketplace and the taste of lemonade. Jade smiled. She opened her eyes and looked around the small room and sighed, the walls seeming to move closer around her, as if they were waiting for her to fall asleep so they could smother her. Even if I leave Draoul, I will always be a part of the Draougari. They will always know where to find me. But it's worth something, going home. Freedom is worth something.

She sighed down at the blanket. Tsaigal was irrevocably changed. Tar was probably dead. Jade pushed the thought of him out of her mind, pressing her hands against her head like she could block him out. She folded the blanket and lay down, drifting into a dreamless sleep.

IX

The lamps seemed to blur, their bright flames making Tar's eyes water. He lay his head down on the table, unfortunately in something sticky. He was too tired to care.

"Tar, pay attention," Sophro snapped. Tar lifted his head. He looked around. Izaak stared sleepily at Sophro with his filmy eyes. Riven lay on his bed, his eyes closed.

"It's late, Sophro. Let's do this tomorrow."

Sophro seemed not to hear him. He stared down at the map he'd drawn, biting his pencil. He had come in twenty minutes before, woken them all up, lit the lamps, and insisted that they stay awake while he drew a map. He'd been exploring, he said, and he had a plan.

"I'm done. Okay. I'm done," Sophro said, leaning back in his chair. Tar looked over his shoulder at the map. It showed the camp, with every hut and tower and jutting wall. Their hut was marked with an X. There was a path drawn that snaked through the huts and to the wall on the north side of the camp, where another X was drawn. "Two months and I've finally done it," Sophro muttered. His eyes glistened with lack of sleep and delight.

"To be fair, you were gone for one of them," Izaak said.

"Yeah," Sophro mumbled. "Look. Here's where we'll go."

140

"We?" Izaak asked.

"You're coming with us. Both of you," Sophro said.

"And when was this decided?"

"A while ago. When I was sitting in that cell for an entire month. Again. I was sitting on that filthy straw scratching this map into the sand and I knew that the whole time I'd been thinking: the four of us. How will I get the four of us out?"

Izaak shook his head sadly. "I'm afraid I'll only slow you down," he said.

"That's why I'm showing you this map. That's why we're going to go through the steps every day until the new moon."

"The new moon?" Tar asked.

"That's when we'll go. It'll be darkest."

"Well...I might as well. I've never been caught. They've no reason to shoot me. I might as well have one attempt," Izaak said. Riven nodded.

"Attempt?" Sophro scoffed. "This is our escape."

That display of confidence, even from a thin, weakened man, made the room feel more intense. Tar felt as if he was a part of something noble and grand. His pulse quickened. It was a simple statement but it stuck inside his head. This was their escape. Riven climbed down and peered at the map on the table. They all leaned close.

"Now, you see how we move through the camp? Like a snake. That's because we'll spend the least amount of time in the searchlight that way. I've studied the patterns. Now I need to memorize the guards' movements. That will take some time, and even then, they're variables. I don't even know if there is a concrete pattern. But if there is, I'll find it. Now, once we get here—" he pointed to the wall, "We have to climb. The drain is right here." He pointed to a spot on the other side of the wall that was near the western end of the camp. "But this is the spot that is the blindest. The towers are the farthest apart. The guards won't see us from above unless we take too long or make too much noise. Which we won't."

"That's alright for you, but what about me?" Izaak asked. "I'm not as young as I used to be."

Sophro grinned. His cheekbones were so prominent and his eyes so hooded that Tar shivered.

"I've worked it out. We stand on each others' backs. You'll go first, Tar, and hoist yourself up. Then Izaak will go and you'll help him up.

Then Riven, and then me. Only one of us will be on top of the wall at a time, because that's the most dangerous part. As soon as the next man is up, the previous one jumps down to the other side. When we're all on the other side, we'll stay close to the cliffs so the guards won't see us from above. We'll walk all the way to the drain and climb in and we'll be as good as home," Sophro explained. His cheeks were red from exertion; he'd been pantomiming every action and was breathing heavily. All the men sat back. No one breathed. As Tar watched, Sophro trapped a shaking hand beneath his thigh.

Tar couldn't sleep that night. He kept going over the plan again and again in his head, feeling the taste of freedom on his tongue. Above him, Sophro tapped his foot against the wall all night.

X

It was early morning. The sun stretched out its fingers through the window and spread its warmth onto the wooden floor. Daina sat there, sewing. Kieran lay next to her, playing with a wooden horse. He was seven months old and his hair was still soft and smelled like milk and soap. Daina winced as she pricked her finger. Her tired hands had slipped. Beads of blood blossomed from the cut and she jumped up to find a napkin. As she pressed it to her finger, her stomach rumbled.

"Are you hungry?" she called to Kieran. He looked up at the sound of her voice, his big blue eyes wide. She felt a pang in her chest. "I'll...I'll find something." She searched the cupboard. Only a few bruised apples sat forlornly on the shelves. Daina opened cabinets and slammed them, yanked open drawers and shoved them back frantically. She breathed heavily. Hunger crouched in her mind. She had been able to ignore it for a long time; giving most of her food to Kieran, she had lost seven pounds in the last few weeks. There was no money. She'd had to start sewing again. She hadn't heard from Audric in months. She couldn't ignore the hunger forever. She clutched at her aching stomach as Kieran began to cry. "No, no, don't cry," she said, lifting him up. His face was red and distorted. He'd broken his horse's leg. The crippled wooden animal lay on its side. Daina bounced Kieran on her hip. "It's okay. We're okay. See, I have you." She poked his chest. "And you have me." She touched her own. Kieran whimpered. Daina wanted to cry, too. She stuck her tongue out. Kieran smiled. "Good." She hugged his little body close to hers and smelled his hair.

A fist pounded on the door. Daina walked over and opened it, Kieran still teary-eyed and in her arms. A short, fat man stood on her front porch. He wore a navy blue suit and was sweating in the morning humidity.

"Good morning," he muttered. Daina opened her mouth to respond, but he interrupted her. "I represent the tax collection office."

Daina swallowed. "How can I help you?" He opened a folder and pulled out a sheet of paper. He handed it to Daina. Her name was printed all over it, always next to the words 'Past Due'. She swallowed again and shifted Kieran on her hip.

"Are you aware that you have not paid any bills in over a month?"

"I…well, yes. It's just that—"

He sighed. "You have one week to pay the five hundred imein that you owe. If you do not—"

"Five hundred? In one week?" Daina exclaimed.

"If you do not, you will be forced to leave your residence," he finished and nodded to her before turning his back and stepping down from her porch. She watched him walk away down the street, his nose upturned, before she slammed the front door. She set Kieran down on the floor and sat down with him. He picked up his broken horse and tried to make it stand. It kept clattering on the wooden floor. Daina watched him, panic rising from her stomach to her cheeks. She felt angry tears burn her eyes. "Come on, Kieran." She picked him up. He still clutched his horse. Daina hoisted him onto her hip and opened the door into the hot morning air.

XI

The chemistry classroom was humid. Audric had opened a window, but a layer of moisture still clung to every surface. The air was stale. He sat at his desk, glancing up occasionally. His students were taking a test, and the atmosphere in the room was the usual: palpable nerves. There was an undercurrent of scratching pencils, sighing, and tapping feet. These sounds combined to form a sort of silence, which was broken by a shout from down the hallway. More shouts erupted, followed by the sound of running footsteps. Every student's head jerked up and eyes looked from Audric to the door and back to Audric. He walked to the door and peered down the hallway. Audric's face paled. Running down the hall toward him, followed by the red-faced dean, was Daina. She carried Kieran in her arms.

"Miss," the dean shouted after her. Audric ducked back into his classroom, facing away from his students. He took a breath and his nerves calmed. This would have to be the best performance of his life. He had been preparing for it. The door opened and Daina and the dean stepped inside. Murmurs were uttered, a quick flow of unintelligible conversation. "I tried to stop her, Audric. I'll have her removed immediately."

"I need to talk to you," Daina cried. Angry tears filled her eyes. He recognized the clothes she was wearing, but they were dirty. Her hair was tangled. Her gray eyes bored into him. He cleared his throat.

"What do you need?"

"You haven't paid me in weeks."

There was a stunned silence.

"Paid you? For what?"

Daina's eyes widened. A tear spilled onto her cheek. "Don't do this, Audric."

"I don't know what you're talking about."

"You know. How could you not take care of your son?" Daina shouted. The class seemed to draw a collective breath. The dean's mouth fell open.

"Audric…is this true? Is this child your son?"

Audric shook his head slowly. "I've never been with Miss Londe," he said. "She must be ill. She's wearing rags. Look at her. The stress of the child must have—"

"The stress of the child? Audric, you did this to me!" Daina screeched. Kieran began to wail. Audric looked at his son's wrinkled, red face.

"I swear to you, sir, I have never been intimate with this woman. Nor any of my students."

"Bullshit! He fucked Jade, and that's why he sent her away. He didn't want her to do this."

The students' faces were plastered with shock. Daina was quite a scene. She sobbed.

"Miss Londe, I will take the child," the dean murmured. Kieran seemed to be slipping from her grasp. The dean caught him and Kieran continued to scream. Snot dripped from his nostrils.

"Tell them the truth," Daina sobbed.

"I have," Audric stated coldly.

"I'll have to make sure that this child gets the attention he needs."

"She's an unfit mother," Audric said. "Look at her. Look at the child. He's starving. He's too thin. She can't take care of him."

Daina shook her head. "Stop it." She tried to reach for her son and the dean turned away.

"I'll have to take him, I'm afraid. You're not well." He looked sick to his stomach. Kieran kept wailing.

"You can't take my son! No! Audric, tell them that I'm not crazy. Don't let him—"

Audric turned his back on Daina, feigning overwhelming shock. He rubbed his face with his hands. Daina ran out the door after Kieran, whose crying drowned out all thought as he disappeared down the hall.

XII

Blaise's cold lips brushed Jade's forehead. He backed away. Jade looked from him to Fox to Lumine, who all stood in front of her.

"I'll be back soon," she said.

"Of course," Blaise replied. Fox nodded.

Jade held her bag with all of her possessions inside it. It felt good to hold it again. They stood near the falls, so they had to shout to be heard.

"Well," she said.

"Goodbye, Jade," Fox said.

"Goodbye."

Lumine smiled weakly. Blaise looked at the ground. The last thing that Jade saw was the falling water fade to black as her body was transported.

When she opened her eyes, it was evening. She stood in a forest. She followed the sound of gushing water and came to the Melien river. The moon touched it, shivered in it. Jade knelt and cupped her hands. She drank from the river and swallowed the cold water. The air in the forest was close and warm, but cooling quickly. She looked around and tried to slow her pounding heart. She seemed to see shapes moving among the trees, black-robed shadows. She made camp for the night and fell asleep staring at the outline of the mountains through the trees.

Chapter 8

I

It was midmorning. The sun hid behind thick gray clouds. The maple trees lining the avenue had begun to yellow, and the beginning of a storm rumbled overhead. Jade's boots clicked on the pavement. She thought she'd hear that sound and smile, but she didn't. It was a little comforting, though, because it was familiar. She strolled down the avenue, her bag slung over her shoulder. No one seemed to notice her, and she was comfortable in her anonymity. She turned onto her street. There was her house, the same small two-story white stone house it had always been, the third one on the north side of the street. Jade walked up her front steps. The last one creaked like always. She tried the door. It wouldn't budge. She stared at it, confused, for a few seconds before realizing, and then fished her key out of her bag. It fit perfectly in the lock like it always had, and the door swung open. Jade closed it behind her. The living room seemed so small. She breathed in the stale air. Shards of glass littered the floor. Unidentifiable brown crusts were all that remained of the roses on the sofa where they'd fallen a year and a half ago. Jade crunched through the broken glass into the kitchen and picked up the broom and dustpan. She swept up the glass and tossed it into the garbage, on top of her old crumpled astronomy notes. Jade looked around the room. It was so familiar and yet so alienating to be home. She picked up a black dress that lay on the floor and clomped up the stairs. She finally smiled when she saw her bed: the covers were still pulled back into a cocoon. Jade felt tears come to her eyes. She set down her bag and took off her jacket, boots, sweater, and pants. She climbed into bed, feeling the cool sheets against her legs and stomach, and pulled the blankets up over her head. Jiada closed her eyes, waiting for sleep to come. But it didn't. She remembered how she had bled in that bed. How she had sweated with Audric there. When she'd been away from home, she'd thought of her bed as immaculate, a place where she couldn't be harmed. Jade sat up because she could feel the filth seeping into her pores. Nauseated, she stood up. She went downstairs and made herself a cup of tea. As she sipped it, she stared out her window. It faced east.

II

Izaak's knife glinted as he picked it up and tucked it inside his jacket pocket. Riven wiped his forehead with the back of his hand. Tar watched Sophro; he was staring out the black window. The only light in the room came from a candle in the middle of the table. It flickered over their faces. They were tensed, eyes wide, breathing through their mouths. Sophro's cheeks were hollow, his eyes dull. He barely ate. Tar would come inside some days and find him asleep, his face lying on the table on top of one of his maps. He'd only sleep for a few hours at a time. Some nights, Tar would find him standing at the window. He talked in his sleep, muttering Despina's name.

"Let's go," Sophro said. Izaak inhaled. He looked nauseated. Sophro reached for the doorknob. As he turned it, a deafening alarm sounded from outside the hut. Sophro yanked his hand off the doorknob. He ran back to the window. Searchlights burned. Guards rushed into huts. Sophro cursed. "Get into bed. It's a search. Go," he shouted. Riven blew out the candle and all four men jumped into their beds. Tar had barely pulled the covers up around his shoulders when the door was kicked open. He jumped.

"Up. Get out," a guard shouted. They walked out of the hut, their arms raised above their heads. All around the camp, guards were searching huts, overturning beds, pushing men around. The four of them stood in a cluster outside. They shivered in the autumn night air. Sophro looked up.

"The new moon," he said, his voice breaking. "We needed that."

"Tomorrow will be just as good, right?" Tar asked.

Sophro scoffed. "I bet they'll be watching us for a few days," he muttered. "By the time they leave us alone, it'll be too late. We'll have to wait a month. Until the next new moon." Sophro sighed and hung his head. He looked up at the ten-foot-high wall.

III

Jade looked in the mirror. Her scars were completely covered with makeup. The only way they were noticeable was if they were touched. She put on clean clothes: a red dress, a black jacket, and boots. Just feeling the cool, clean fabric against her skin was soothing. She breathed deeply as she looked in the mirror. Jade picked up her leather bag. A gust of cool evening air hit her as she stepped outside. She walked down the avenue and could hear loud music from the midway. She checked the date in her mind and realized it was Eventide. She had never enjoyed parties; they were too loud and she didn't like the way people acted. And Eventide was the biggest party of the year. She decided to take the long way and turned onto Maple and approached the orphanage. It was silent; the children must have been eating dinner. As she strolled by, glancing in the windows, she heard a familiar voice.

"Jade?"

She turned. A blonde woman walked toward her. She had been watching the children through the window. Jade looked closely. She wore rags and her face was dirty.

"Daina?" Daina came closer. Her eyes were frantic.

"I'm sorry," she cried. "I'm sorry I made him send you away." Daina began to cry. Jade felt pity, but tinged with bitter disgust.

"Well, I'm back."

"You're lucky it wasn't you. He's…he's an animal," she spat.

"What happened?" Jade was genuinely interested.

"I had a baby. His baby."

"He let you—"

"He paid me to stay quiet. Everything was okay, but I was so lonely. And it was barely enough to survive on." Daina choked on her words and cleared her throat. "Then after Kieran was born, he came and said he wanted us to be a family. He even named him. Then it was great. Until he stopped coming over. And then he stopped paying me. I lost my house. We were starving. So I went to him. I brought the baby. And in front of everyone, I begged him to acknowledge me. And that bastard, he pretended like he didn't know anything about it. The dean believed him. They took my baby, Jade. They—" Daina pointed at the orphanage and broke down into sobs.

Jade felt horribly awkward. She stared at Daina. "I'm sorry that happened to you. Maybe if you had taken care of it…"

"Like you did?" Daina shook her head. "No. I'm glad that I kept my baby. At least I'm more blameless than you." Jade turned away and started walking. "At least I didn't kill my baby," Daina shouted after her. Jade hurried away, her cheeks burning. Her stomach ached like it sometimes did when she thought about her baby. When she remembered that she was ruined.

Jade walked toward the midway, thinking that the familiar smells would calm her, but the scents of popcorn, sugar, and fried dough only made her stomach churn. You're home. But what was home? Jade caught her breath. The midway was packed with costumed citizens, drinking from opened containers of alcohol or laughing loudly or singing. Bands played in front of stores. People drifted in and out of cafes. She squeezed through groups of people holding hands or stumbling with arms draped around each other's shoulders. Scratchy fabric and soft feathers and warm human skin brushed against her. High heels stepped on her feet. The faces all around her seemed to blur as a trumpet blared over the roar of chatter, hundreds of tongues lolling in mouths, working around teeth, vocal chords humming. Painted faces in every color bobbed in a sea: teal, blood-red, violet. Paper lanterns hung on every doorway or lamppost. And then there were the costumes: tigers prowled the midway; blackbirds with hooked beaks flitted through the crowds; fish with brilliant rainbows of scales slithered, holding hands with iridescent peacocks and sleek black panthers. The scents of caramel, coffee, and strawberry ice cream mingled with the unmistakable smells of rich physical longing and chemicals. Jade tried to breathe. She pushed through the crowds, touching feathers and bare skin. As she turned onto University, the sound began to fade. Jade could hear her heels again. Her heart pounded as the chemistry building came into view. She climbed the steps and opened the heavy door. The halls were dark and silent as a tomb. Jade climbed the steps to the second floor. There was light at the end of the hall. She walked toward it, her heart hammering, and stepped through the door. Audric sat at his desk. He looked so much older. Jade couldn't quite place why. Maybe his hair was grayer. He looked up and his mouth fell open. Jade smirked.

"Jade," he blurted out. She came into the room.

"Hello, Audric." He slowly stood up, like she was a wild animal he was trying to capture.

"You're back."

"Here I am." She glanced around the room; at her old desk, the drawn posters on the walls, the chemicals on the back shelves. It all seemed terribly cramped.

"So..." He gazed at her, his eyes narrowed, as he walked toward her. "Did you..."

"Find them? I wouldn't be here if I hadn't." Jade saw his eyes glint.

149

She realized that he actually wanted to know where the Draougari were. There was some knowledge she had that he wanted.

"Where?" He stopped right in front of her.

Jade smiled. "You'd really like to know, wouldn't you?" she said coldly.

"Why wouldn't I? Everyone would."

"I guess so."

"If you found them, that means you're one of them," he said and before Jade could react, he held her by the back of her head and traced the scar on her cheek with his thumb. Jade breathed heavily through her nose. Audric grinned. "You're one of them," he repeated. She felt his breath on her face and her control leaving her grasp. She pulled herself away. "I would have thought that you would have performed the ritual as soon as you could. Why didn't you?" he asked.

Jade felt the color drain from her cheeks. A ritual? What ritual? To reverse the change? To become normal? She thought back to the book in her bag. It had to be in there. The whole time. She had never even looked. She cleared her throat, keeping her face stoic.

"I am one of them," she said. "Do you know what that makes me? Immortal. Powerful." Audric stared at her. She smiled.

"You still have a dream, don't you?" he asked. She swallowed. "Your astronomy. I can make you famous. If you let me use something of yours."

"What?"

"Your blood. You're a woman. I'm the most well-known professor at the university. If you want your own lab, your own tower; if you want to be rich for the rest of your life, I can help you." Jade inhaled. "Just a drop of your blood. And we'll be famous together." Audric brushed her hair back from her face. "I can only ask you to think about it. I look forward to seeing you in class again." Audric's lips brushed against her temple. He turned away, back to his desk.

"Audric."

"Yes?"

"I wondered if you had any news of the war in Kamareng."

Audric sifted through the papers on his desk and pulled out a stack of newspapers. "I guess you've been away from the news for a while. Take these; I don't need them anymore."

Jade felt the glorious weight of all the papers in her arms as she hurried back to the midway. She went to her favorite café, the one by the falls. She sat in the seat in the corner with the squeaky leather. Jade sifted through the papers for the earliest one. Jade flipped through the paper to the list of the dead. She ran her finger down the list, sighing with relief at the end. Jade tossed it aside and picked up the next paper. She flipped through ten more. On the second to last one, she searched the "Missing" section and her heart fell. There it was, printed in front of her. Tar's name. She slowly opened the last paper. Her finger shook as she searched. Down and down, through unfamiliar names. Her finger touched white space at the bottom. Jade sighed.

IV

The moon was barely visible; a tiny sliver. The darkness was as thick as wool as the four men slithered out of their hut: Sophro, then Izaak, then Riven, then Tar. They'd gone over their plan a hundred times; they'd walked these steps in the daylight, but now, actually being there in the dark, was breathtaking. Tar tired to make his footsteps as silent as possible. They crunched the dry dirt of the camp, leaving footprints that might as well have been painted red. They all had dyed their clothes black with boot polish Riven had stolen. The three men in front of Tar looked like a part of the night so much so that he was afraid if he blinked, he'd lose them. They crept through the camp, one after another, each with his eyes fixed ahead. The extra month had given Sophro time to memorize the patterns of the guards' movements. He had timed them perfectly so that Tar never even caught a glimpse of a guard. The searchlight never touched them. They were a ripple in the night, nearly invisible. They walked through the maze of huts until they reached the wall. Izaak searched his pockets frantically and looked up at Tar, a distressed look pulling his eyebrows together like a stitch.

"I left my knife," he muttered. Tar felt a tinge of loss and looked away. Then Sophro knelt on all fours and Tar climbed onto his back. He touched the top of the wall and pulled himself up with a grunt, his muscles straining. He glanced around and up at the guard towers. They were barely visible. Riven stood on Sophro's back. Tar grabbed his arms and lifted him up. When Riven had pulled himself up and was sitting on the wall, Tar jumped down to the other side and pressed himself against the cliff. He allowed himself a breath. His lungs burned. He listened, watching Riven on top of the wall. It seemed like it was taking forever. Then Riven's head jerked to the right. He swore and leaned over. Tar's heart pounded in his ears. He heard arguing on the other side of the wall. Riven pulled Sophro up and immediately Tar's stomach dropped. Izaak was supposed to be next, not Sophro. Riven jumped down next to Tar. His eyes were wide and he breathed in frustrated sobs.

Then a shout echoed and the blood drained from Tar's cheeks. More men shouted unintelligible, harsh Kamar. Sophro was pulling Izaak up, his back straining. Then a blast echoed off the cliffs, deafening. Tar's hands jerked up to cover his ears. He looked at Sophro instinctively. He was looking down at the other side of the wall. Slowly, Sophro raised his hands in the air, his palms outstretched into the moonless autumn sky. Then the searchlight found him and bathed him in blinding yellow light. He looked like a martyr. The light engulfed Tar and Riven, too, and they raised their hands. Tar climbed back up to where Sophro sat and looked down. Izaak's crumpled body lay sprawled there. A bullet had blown off half of his face. Blood matted his thick red beard. Three soldiers pointed guns at them. Sophro's face was iced over. Slowly, Tar and the others jumped down. The bearded guards wrenched their arms behind their backs and searched them. Then they prodded them along toward the jail. Tar's legs felt watery; with each step he thought they'd break. He didn't even have to look up; he knew the way perfectly. They'd been over the plan so many times. Sophro walked in front of him, head down. The guards had to force the great fighter into his cell; he just stood there in the doorway. As the door closed on him, Tar sank to the ground.

"Sophro?" he called after what felt like hours of silence. There was no answer, just the incessant chatter of crickets and the far-off howling of a wolf pack, somewhere free.

V

The night before, she dreamt that Tar lay next to her. They were back in the moors, underneath the stars, gazing up. It was warm. A fire crackled. The two of them huddled beneath the red blanket. In the dream, Tar rolled over. She saw his green eyes. He smelled like honey. Then she felt something warm spread over her stomach. She pulled back the blanket and stared at a gaping, bleeding hole in her stomach. Somewhere off in the mist, a baby cried. Tar held her hand.

Jiada

"You can't help her."

"It's my fault."

"Be pure," he whispered.

Jade lay in bed. For the moment before she'd opened her eyes, she'd been sure that she felt someone lying next to her. She threw off the blankets and sat up, rubbing her eyes. She swung her bare legs over the side of the bed and her feet touched the cold wooden floor. She stumbled sleepily down the stairs and into the kitchen. Picking out a red apple and a paring knife, she settled into a chair. She held the apple in her hand and pressed the knife through its crunchy skin. The knife, missing the core, bit through and Jade felt a searing pain in her palm. She swore and tossed the apple and knife onto the table. The cut wasn't very big, but it was bleeding. Jade pressed a towel to it and watched red seep through. She remembered Audric's request: just a drop of your blood. She'd gone to see him the day before because she had finally finished what she'd been working on for as long as she could remember. Her model of the solar system. Every planet, every constellation, every major star tracked and its movements recorded and predicted. A heliocentric model of the heavens. The idea that the sun was the center of the universe was not a new one, but as of yet, conclusive proof had not been provided. There it was on the kitchen table in a battered leather-bound notebook. She hadn't shown it to Audric, of course. But he'd told her something that she knew was painfully true: her theory would never be accepted because she was a woman. The irony, he'd said, of Desrala and the university was that because of so many scientific and technological advances, society had begun to shift to more primitive expectations of women. That alone made her skin itch. But, Audric said, if she joined with him, if she gave him her blood, together they would be rich. Her work published. And all of her future work, funded. Her own lab. Jade caught her breath. She wrapped the cut on her hand and closed her eyes. Audric held fame and riches within her grasp. But what did he want with her blood? She thought of Daina, tricked and rejected. Then of the ritual. She'd read it the night before. She knew the incantation.

Something thumped against the door. Jade rushed to it and opened it. She picked up the paper and stood there in her robe reading it. She flipped through the Desrala news and to the Riova news. To Tsaigal. The war. The dead. Only five names. She read them all and sighed. She shut the door and walked upstairs. Jade placed the paper on a stack next to her bed.

VI

It was late autumn when they got out. The three men stood in the camp, still in their black escape clothes, smelling like filthy straw and boot polish. Tar breathed clean air. It burned his throat.

"Winter's coming," Riven whispered. Tar barely heard it. They began to walk. The camp was eerily desolate in the autumn afternoon. Tiny snowflakes fell. Tar watched Sophro. He was a shadow. Skin stretched over bones. Eyes a dull brown like dead leaves. His nose was different, or maybe Tar had just never noticed how beaklike it was before. His lips curled in a constant grimace instead of his usual smirk. His eyes were fixed on the ground. Tar shivered. When they entered their hut, a pall of silence descended. There was no sound, not even the wind. Tar sat on his bunk and Riven climbed up to his. Sophro stood staring at the table. Tar followed his gaze. It was Izaak's knife.

The next morning, Tar woke early. The sun wasn't up but he was cold. The fire in the stove was dead and black. He shoved more firewood into the stove and lay back down, covering himself with the thin, scratchy wool blanket. It felt strange being back, although he was almost certain that he'd known they would be. There could be no escape now. Guards stood at their door at night. Searches went on once a week; they'd heard them while they were away. Tar stared out the window. The sun was gray and the whole sky was awash with it. He fell asleep again.

When he woke, Riven was gone. Tar was about to leave when he glanced at Sophro sitting up in his bunk.

"Come eat," Tar pleaded. Sophro just stared at him. His knees were folded in front of him. He looked like a gargoyle on some old castle wall. Tar swallowed. "It wasn't your fault."

Sophro's mouth opened in a snarl. Tar left. A week passed and Sophro hadn't spoken. He went outside a few times and ate some of whatever Tar brought back for him: black bread, cheese, the occasional vegetable soup. It was getting colder every day.

"Let's go for a walk," Tar said. "This might be the last day we'll be able to." Sophro obediently put on his decaying leather shoes and followed Tar out the door. Fine, powdery snow fell in gusts. Older snow crunched beneath their feet and beneath that, frozen dirt. Beneath that, Tar didn't know. Maybe the bones of some buried monster. Maybe the ruins of a lost civilization. Sophro looked up at the sky. "I see you do that

154

a lot. Why do you do it?" Tar wasn't expecting an answer.

"I don't know." Sophro's voice was hoarse. "Do you think they're up there? Izaak and Lothario and everyone."

"I think so."

Sophro scoffed. "I don't think so."

"Then where?"

"Nowhere. Gone. Worm food."

Tar swallowed. "Maybe. But I don't want to think that."

"That's what we'll be. That's all we are. Just food, waiting to be eaten." They crunched along.

"I wondered when you'd break your vow of silence."

"It's not a vow. I didn't have anything to say."

"But now you do?"

"I guess."

"Then tell me."

"Tell you what?"

"I don't know."

Sophro sighed. He didn't speak for a long time. "I don't care," he finally said. "About anything."

Tar exhaled through his nose. "Stop being so goddamn tragic," he snapped. Color rushed to his cheeks; dizzying regret.

"I'm never going to get home," Sophro said quietly. "And maybe that's okay. She won't want me."

"Despina? Yes, she will."

"She wouldn't if she knew what's happened."

"Sophro, nothing is your fault."

Sophro shook his head. His face was blank.

"I'm not even here."

"What?"

"I'm not here. Not home either. I'm nowhere."

"Stop being so…like this."

"I want to go back now." They trudged back to the hut under a torrent of snow.

VII

Sven Falbjorn and Nikola Krön sat side-by-side in identical oaken chairs in the great hall. A fire blazed at the end of the hall. Across the table sat King Iosif, fresh off the ship from Kamareng. He read a paper intently. When he finished, he sat back.

"What are you willing to offer?" Sven asked.

Iosif ran his tongue over his teeth. "You offer me my own country, free of your tyranny at last, as it should be. What shall I give you in return?"

"You'll think of something, I'm sure. For me and for Nikola. This war has been more trouble than it's worth, I'm afraid, and I am a weary man."

Iosif scratched his beard. "Wives," he stated. "You both need wives."

Sven's stomach dropped.

"That's quite kind, but I will soon be married," Nikola said.

"An island for you, then. Off the eastern coast. I will sign it over to you this evening."

"Very well. We can look over the details later," Nikola answered.

"And you, Sven? I've brought your wife with me. She will not leave you again. Vira, come," he called. Sven saw her inky black hair before anything else; there were at least two feet of it. She looked up at him with almond eyes, expressionless.

"No," Sven said.

"You refuse my daughter?"

"She refused me. I don't want her."

"Your majesty, if I may," Vira said quietly.

"Go on."

"I was foolish when I left you. You are a good man. I would be happy to be your wife once again," she muttered at the ground.

"And what about what you did to my heir? The child you killed," Sven cried. "I want nothing to do with either of you."

"Then what shall I give you?" Iosif asked.

"Land. Wealth. Anything. A great king once told me that I needed a wife. I see now that I took his words too literally. I will not settle again. I will find a proper mother for my children."

Later that night, the document was signed by the three kings and the titles to two islands off the eastern coast of Kamareng were handed over. Sven promised to recall his troops within a week.

VIII

It was a dream. He knew it was a dream because colors were so vivid. The green and purple of the moors wasn't possible. He smelled the heather. He wanted to cry because it felt so real. In the dream, Jade just stood before him and they looked at each other. That was it. But it was all he wanted to do. And she was smiling a real smile.

Tar opened his eyes. His breath was ice. His stomach sank as he looked up at the planks above his head, even though he'd known it was a dream. He put more firewood in the stove. It was early morning and the sun was lurking somewhere high up, concealed by snow. Tar hated the snow, but he marveled at how quiet it made everything. He looked out the window at the cliffs and forest, all covered in white. Their window looked south, and he liked to pretend he could see all the way home. After being in that camp for a year and away from home for a year and a half, he thought of the plains of Kahl with a lump in his throat. It would be warm there. Not hot, but warm, with a salty breeze. He closed his eyes and saw the Kalmire gushing. The forests of corn stalks, lush and crisp with morning dew. The rows and rows of whitewashed stone and red roofs, the thin strip of blue sea on the horizon and the forests in the distance. He opened his eyes. There was nothing bright here.

Riven snored in his bunk. Tar stretched and made his way to the bathroom, which was no more than a hole in the ground through a door toward the back of the hut. He walked, feeling the cold floor through his thick woolen socks. The light in the hut was a pale white, silent. Tar opened the door. Blood pooled on the wooden floor, dark and thick. Tar felt a cry escape his throat. His legs felt weak. Sophro's emaciated body, no shirt on, lay on the floor, curled against the wall. His bare feet looked like an animal's: bony, with long nails like claws, his black curls matted against his forehead with sweat. His spine jutted from his back like a ladder; his skin stretched over each rib, pulled tight. Blue bruises on the white canvas of his back and sides. Something clenched in his hand. Tar recognized the black handle and small blade of Izaak's knife. He felt hot tears of rage on the insides of his eyes. Sophro's body swam. Deep gashes all the way down his forearms. Blackened, dried blood crusting his arms. Staining everything. His pants, his stomach, the floor. Tar struggled to breathe as he gazed at his friend's face. His mouth slightly open, his eyebrows furrowed. Dried tear tracks on his cheeks. Blood beneath his fingernails, smeared on his chest, everywhere. This is how it ends, Tar thought, and he sank to his knees and cradled the fighter's head in his arms, holding the fragile stalk of a neck.

IX

That night, a fire lit the violet sky as Sophro's body burned. Tar and Riven stood next to each other as they watched the funeral pyre ignite, watched the flame catch skin and melt it and burn it black. The clouds cleared for a moment and Tar saw the stars. He wept, and he understood silence.

X

A week later, someone pounded on the door of the hut. Riven opened it and a red-faced man rushed inside, breathless. He shoved a paper into Riven's hands.

"Look," he cried. "The war is over. We're leaving." He was gone and Tar and Riven stared at each other.

"Is it real?" Tar asked, hope bubbling like poison in his stomach. Riven showed him the headline. It read,

KINGS SIGN TREATY

WAR ENDED

Tar felt sick. "Is this real?" he whispered again. All he could think of was Sophro's body. If only he'd waited another week. Tar went to the bathroom and violently threw up. His head ached.

Later, all of their things were packed. Their few miserable possessions. Tar slung his leather bag over his shoulder. Riven did the same. They looked out the window at all of the men coming out of their huts. Some of them grinning, some glancing around nervously, as if they were doing something wrong. Tar and Riven stepped out into the frigid afternoon and joined the crowd on its way to the gate, clomping through snow. One man next to them began to softly sing an old folk song from Kahl.

A southern wind blows
far over the golden plains,

and the Swift River flows.

The setting sun glows—
the harvest moon wanes;
a southern wind blows.

Farmers weave from row to row,
gathering golden grain,
and the Swift River flows.

Land lies fallow,
and in winter, it rains,
but still a southern wind blows.

The arena echoes—
fire in fighters' veins—
and the Swift River flows.

Even in despair, I know
that over the golden plains,
a southern wind blows,
and the Swift River flows.

Tar wanted to smile, but couldn't. They walked in a sea of dead men, the ones who had been given up on, who had gone missing. They were alive again, and they felt it. A kind of warmth was creeping up Tar's neck and into his cheeks. He was going somewhere. Finally. But as they walked through the heavily guarded gates and up the steps cut into the side of the cliff, Tar looked around and wanted to be back in his hut. It was all too much. He didn't deserve to be there; Sophro did. Tar swallowed and climbed step after step, out of breath, until they reached the top. Some men immediately departed southwest to where the last camp had been. Others, like Tar and Riven, gazed around and at each other, breathing heavily.

"Where do we go?" Riven asked.

"Back," Tar said. They began to walk.

XI

Despina stared at herself in the mirror and, for the first time in over a year, smiled. Her green eyes lit up. Her black hair was braided down her back and tied with a white ribbon. She wore a dress with blue flowers and a thick blue headband. She looked around. Sophro's house was spotless. She had dusted every surface, washed the floors and walls, and made his bed. There was nothing left to do but wait. She read the paper again just to make sure that it was real, and then sat in the window seat, gazing down the avenue where he'd come walking up the next day.

XII

Jade entered the chemistry classroom. It was cold. Snow fell on the other side of the windows and collected on the ledge. Hunched over at his desk, Audric looked up from his work. He had shadows under his eyes, but maybe that was just the light.

"Hello, Jade," he said. She walked over and placed her notebook on his desk.

"I'm ready," she said. He looked up at her, wide-eyed.

"Okay." He scrambled to the back of the room and motioned for her to follow him. "Come here." He led her through a door into a small laboratory. It was dim and bare, with only a table, a chair, a microscope and shelves with a few jars. "Sit," he said. He had a glint in his eyes that made Jade swallow. Her heart pounded in her throat. In the pit of her stomach, she knew she shouldn't have come. She closed her eyes as he began to prepare the needle, thinking of what she would have when this was over. Fame. Money. Power. Those abstractions that had fueled her studies for her entire life. They felt empty, her old friends. She felt tears coming as he wiped the needle clean, sterilizing it with an alcohol-soaked cloth. It smelled sharp. Jade leaned back in the chair and took a deep breath as Audric steadied the needle over the soft crook of her elbow. "Did you hear about the war?" he muttered. Jade's heart thumped.

"What?"

Audric stopped and looked at her. "It's over. The war in Kamareng. The soldiers are coming home." Jade's cheeks flushed. She sat up straight. "Hold still," Audric said.

"I have to go," she whispered. "I have to go. I can't do this." She stood up. Audric's face contorted.

"No, you can't. You have to give me your blood." His eyes were wide, his eyebrows pushed together, his mouth open to reveal glinting teeth. He held the syringe between his fingers.

"I don't know what you want with it, but I'm not giving you anything. I've given you enough," Jade spat. She reached for the door to the classroom. Audric caught her arm, his fingers like a vise.

"What about your work? I have your notebook."

"I don't care. Use it or not. No one will believe you. You're a chemist, not an astronomer. Burn it if you want. I don't need it." Audric's eyes flashed back and forth between her eyes, as if they were expecting to find something different in each one.

"Jade, what are you saying? You've worked forever on this," Audric cried.

Jade just laughed. She opened the door. Audric's fingers grasped her wrist and she twisted around to free herself and felt a stabbing pain in her elbow. She swore as she saw the syringe begin to fill. She yanked her arm free and the needle came loose. It rolled onto the floor. Audric scrambled to it and picked it up. As he stood up, Jade knocked him off balance, her knee digging into his shoulder, and then pushed him as hard as she could. He stumbled and hit his head on the corner of the table and collapsed like a rag doll. Jade, shaking with adrenaline, picked up the needle and rushed out the door. Down the hallway, empty and breezeless. Down the stairs, feet clattering like falling rocks. Out the door and into a gust of autumn air. Through the streets. Across the midway. She stood on the bridge over the river. Her blood sloshed in the syringe, the same blood that pounded through her ears. She threw it into the river and watched it float away over the falls.

Back in her house, Jade locked the door. Still shaking, she ran up the stairs and into her bedroom. Pulled the book out from underneath her bed. The Draougari. She flipped frantically to the section, the one she needed. It was clearly labeled, The Ritual to Purge the Draougari. It would make her mortal, would cleanse her of her connection to the Draougari. Jade read the entire section again. Her eyes leaped from sentence to sentence so fast that she had to reread it several times before she even knew where to start. She finally began. She needed a sharp knife and the right incantation. That was literally all it took, and she was surprised by the simplicity. Jade memorized the cuts she would have to make. On top of her scars, like making crosses. Two vertical cuts from beneath her eyes to the middle of her cheeks. One horizontal cut across her chest. She flipped to the incantation and found that she could read the words, although she couldn't remember having learned the language. Just like understanding the incantation at her own initiation. Jade picked up the knife. It was a hunting knife with a long, sharp blade and a wooden handle. The one she'd used so many times for assassinations. She set it against her cheek and felt the cold blade. She began the incantation and slowly cut. Three cuts, three different prayers. But these prayers were not to Nharyav, the Master. They were to the Bright One, Aluveina. She could reclaim souls twisted into immortality and darkness. Jade felt each scar burn and she cried. From pain and also because she knew it was working and she felt free. When she uttered the last prayer, she dropped the knife and fell against the bed in exhaustion. Everything ached. She slowly opened her eyes and gazed in the mirror. Smeared blood on her face like a clown's paint. She wiped it off and gasped. Her scars were gone. Smooth skin beneath her fingertips. She wept and touched the mirror and her face and laughed.

Jiada packed her leather bag. Inside it went as many of her clothes as she could fit, some food, her map, and the red blanket. She put on her boots again, the black leather snug and comforting on her calf. She tied the laces tight. Then she closed her door behind her and walked into the cold night. She could hear her heels clicking on the road.

XIII

Tar's legs ached. He had walked more in the last month than he had in the past two years. The journey from Kamareng to Tsaigal had been brutally cold and rainy. The soldiers looked like shipwrecked sailors as they entered the city. Tar was struck by how quiet it was. Until they entered the square and the crowds began to gather. Tar was swept into a sea of people: crying middle-aged women, children tugging on dresses. He waded through, trying to reach the outside, scanning the crowd for the one face he needed to see. He finally caught her gaze. Despina was as beautiful as he remembered. Her black hair was wavy and she wore a dress that reached to her ankles. As he approached her, he swallowed. She smiled and broke eye contact to scan the crowd. But as he took her arm and led her away, her smile disappeared.

"Adatares," she said. He hugged her because he couldn't talk yet. She placed her fingers on his back. "Where is he?" she finally asked. Tar let her go.

"He's dead," he whispered. Despina swallowed. She breathed heavily, clutching Tar's hand. Her eyes filled with tears. She shook her head.

"How?"

"It was a week before it ended. He…in the middle of the night, he—with a knife," Tar stammered. He exhaled. Despina had her face in her hands. He tried to pull her close again, but she pushed him away.

"That coward," she spat. "He didn't have the courage to stay alive for me."

"He did have courage," Tar said. She looked at him. "Do you know how many times he tried to escape? It must have been at least fifteen. Don't think of him as weak. He died with dignity, no matter how it sounds. There's no shame in what he did," Tar said, feeling heat rise to his cheeks. Despina stared at the ground. After a moment, she turned and walked away. Tar looked around as he swallowed tears. The city was the same. But completely different. Smaller.

He walked home. He stood in his front yard, looking over the desolation. Most of his plants, dead. Some completely gone. Rotten fruit littered the lawn. The sprouting apple tree was the only remaining living thing. It had grown a few feet and thickened, its roots spreading out. But there was a crack in its tiny trunk where the wind had battered it. Tar touched it gently. It felt strange to touch a living, growing thing. The crack would probably be its demise; in the next storm, it would topple. Tar sighed. There was nothing to be done. He walked inside. The house had always been small, but now it was stifling, suffocating. He set down his bag with all his possessions on the table. He walked to his room, opened the door, and closed it. He stopped at his father's door and didn't touch the doorknob. He felt nauseated and left the house. The air was cool outside. Not quite warm. The sun set on the whitewashed walls of Tsaigal. The city was quiet.

Two days later there was a ceremony in the Arena for Sophro and all the others who had fought and died in the war. The way Sophro died was never mentioned. Tar left halfway through and went to the bar and got so drunk that he woke up in the hospital the next day. He woke with a pounding headache and the doctor gave him medicine to make him throw up and then he left, his throat raw and his body weak. He went straight to the bar. He chose the one closest to his house so that he'd have a better chance of getting home when he blacked out. The bar was mostly empty; he was surprised it was even open this early. Tar ordered a glass of whiskey and sat staring into it for a few minutes before he took a sip. It burned, warming his throat and stomach. He set down the glass and held his head in his hands, squeezing it. This is it, he thought. There's nothing left. He felt himself slipping and it was like looking out over the edge of a cliff. Black beneath. It was numbing. Tar drank the rest of the glass, feeling his headache melt away.

"Tar," a voice called. He turned. It was Jade. Standing behind him. Like every dream he'd had in Kamareng. He swallowed, the blood leaving his head. She was really there. Her auburn hair was braided. It was longer than the last time he'd seen it, but of course that was true and it reminded him of the time he'd spent without her, like each half inch of growth was a month, and he could see each one since they'd been apart, spelled out in her hair. He stared at her until she looked away. When she looked back, he was still staring. He stood up, still silent. His fingertips felt fuzzy, like their prints had been coated with cotton. She cleared her throat and gestured at the bar behind him. "I thought you didn't drink," she said. Tar looked back at his glass and felt his cheeks burn. "I'm sorry," Jade muttered.

"I just started again," Tar said, finally finding his voice. She looked up at him. Her eyes were so blue it made his chest ache.

"Why?"

"I don't know what else to do," Tar answered, his voice breaking. He looked at the floor and it swam with tears. Jade touched his arm. He led her out of the bar and into the sunlight. They walked, feet on cobblestone. Stiff legs. Tar felt his head clearing. He didn't know where they were going, but they ended up at the Arena. There were no posters on the walls anymore; just smooth, earth-colored stone. He wanted to lay his head on it, become one with its earthy warmth, become part of the city. The narrow streets were empty.

"How is Sophro?" Jade asked.

Tar swallowed. "Dead." Jade looked at the ground, her forehead wrinkling.

"I'm sorry. I assumed, since I didn't see his name—" she trailed off. Tar nodded. They stood by the stone walls. "How did he die?" Jade whispered.

"He killed himself." Jade closed her eyes. "What are you doing here, Jade?" Tar asked.

"Um, I…I left the university."

"Your work?" Tar asked. She looked calm, he realized. Her forehead was smooth, like she had never worried.

"Yes."

"Why?"

Jade shook her head. "I don't need it anymore. Maybe I needed it to get me to this point, but now it's not my dream anymore. I don't know. It feels like I've been walking down the same road for years and getting nowhere."

Tar slowly nodded. "I know." They looked at each other for a long time. Jade's eyes began to fill with tears. Tar reached for her. Found her hand. Solid bones, flesh. He pulled her to him and felt her body against his. Smelled her hair. She was warm. "You're different," he whispered. She nodded.

"I know."

"What happened?" He kept her head pressed against his shoulder.

"They found me. The Draougari. They took me." They separated and Tar looked at her.

"Where?"

"I don't know. I never knew the exact location. It's hidden. Underground. I was there for over a year."

"You were one of them?" Tar felt a sinking in his stomach.

"Yes. But when I got home, I…I changed it. I purged it. I'm not one of them anymore."

"What if they find you?"

"I don't know," Jade admitted. Tar held her face in his hands. He smiled, and she smiled, too. They began to laugh. It felt good. His cheeks tingled. He shook his head.

"You're here," he whispered. She nodded, her eyes filled with tears. "Stay here." Jade looked at the ground. She mumbled something. "What?"

"I'm not clean." Her eyes were tired. Tar kissed her. Her lips were soft and warm as the earth. There was something fervent in their kiss that had waited so long. By the end they both struggled for breath and broke apart.

"You're not ruined," Tar said. "And you can be clean again." Jade inhaled and lay her head against his chest.

After a while, they began to walk. They walked to the river and sat by its edge, silent, watching fish trail their sleek bodies through the clear water. The sun warmed them.

One Year Later

I

The wooden kitchen table felt sticky beneath Jade's fingertips. She wiped her hands on her cotton dress. The window brought only a thin gray light to the room; all day the sun had been covered. Tar sat across the table from her, his head facing his plate. Both of their plates were untouched: the chicken thighs gazed back up at them.

"Do you think it will rain?" Jade ventured. Tar didn't look up. He lay his head on his closed fist, his elbow resting on the table. His chicken looked like it was drying out, like Tar's gaze was a bright, hot light. The chicken lay on the plate, alone. Severed from the rest of its body. Jade picked up her fork. Staring at Tar's forehead, she pushed it into the chicken, between two bones. He didn't look up. She picked up her knife and began to cut it. He kept completely still. Jade sighed and put down her knife and fork. They clattered on the table. Tar met her gaze, his face completely blank, and looked back down again. Jade picked up her fork and touched the prongs to the ceramic plate. It made a sharp, metal sound. She dragged the fork across the plate.

"Stop," Tar said.

The screeching filled Jade's ears. She grasped the fork in her fist and scraped it along the surface of the plate. Back and forth.

"Fucking stop!" Tar slammed his hand on the table. Jade's heart pounded. He was panting, his eyes wide. Staring at her. Her eyes prickled with tears. He picked up the chicken with his fingers and ripped meat from the bone with his teeth, grease dripping down his wrists. He looked at her. "Oh sure, cry about it."

She stared back at him, biting her wavering bottom lip.

"Well, isn't this great?" He said, gesturing around them with the mangled chicken thigh in his hand. "Isn't this just a fucking dream?" Grease glistened on his upper lip.

Jade swallowed, looking at the table. It blurred with tears. "I shouldn't have come," she whispered.

"What? Speak up, my love. I can't hear you over all this joy." Jade raised her gaze. Tar tossed the chicken; it clattered onto his plate. He stared at her, his jaw set firmly. He began to pick at his teeth.

"I'm sorry about Sophro," Jade said. Tar's eyes widened. He looked

167

down. Jade stood up, leaving her untouched plate on the table. She pushed in her chair and began to walk away. Tar's chair scuffed along the wooden floor. She turned around and caught a glimpse of his dark green cotton shirt. He wrapped his arms around her tightly, his hands clutching her hair. He dug his chin into her shoulder, his hair tickling her neck. He was breathing heavily; shuddering. Jade rubbed his back. He opened his mouth; she felt his jaw move. "I know. I know," she whispered before he could say anything. She felt his arms relax.

II

Noon light streamed across the blanket. Birds cawed. Dust motes swam through the window. Jade stared at the ceiling, her fists clenched. She threw off the blanket. She was sweating. She rolled over, her face in her pillow. She could hear Tar stomping around in the kitchen. Each footfall made her skin crawl. She covered her ears. He finally left and she rolled back over. She lay there until he came back at sunset. When she heard the front door open, she rolled over, her back to the door, closed her eyes, and steadied her breathing. The door creaked open.

"Jade?" Tar called. She didn't move. "I know you're awake. I heard you moving around. Please talk to me." Jade felt the bed move as he sat down. He stroked her back. She swallowed.

"Now you want to talk? You've been gone all day."

"I'm sorry." Jade rolled over. Tar sat by her. He smiled.

"I'm still mad at you."

"I know."

"Why did you say that?"

"I don't know."

"Yes, you do. Why did you say that we're not really married?"

Tar sighed. "I'm not proud of that."

"It's because you weren't my first."

Tar wrinkled his eyebrows. "I'm sorry I said that, Jade." She rolled away. "Come on. I didn't...I didn't think. It wasn't right."

"But you said it. And that's what you think. And you're right."

Tar lay down next to her, their bodies fitting together. "No. You're my wife," he whispered into her hair. "And I wasn't right to say that. I know who you are, and who you used to be, and as far as I'm concerned, they're two different people. You're new."

168

Their chests rose and fell together.

"I'm still mad at you."

"I know."

They drifted to sleep. Toward midnight, Jade awoke and rolled over. She kissed Tar's neck. His skin was warm. His eyebrows furrowed in his sleep. She smiled. She kissed his chin and his lips. Waking up, he stroked her back.

"Hi," he whispered.

"Hi."

He rolled on top of her and touched her cheek. They slowly undressed each other. Skin touched skin. They melted into each other like so many times before; husband and wife, natural.

III

A month later, Jade awoke to an empty bed. She stood up and looked out the window.

Tar was hunched over in the front yard, weeding plants. His skin and black hair shone with sweat. His white cotton shirt was stained with dirt, his sleeves rolled up past his elbows. The summer air was stifling in the small bedroom. Jade was hit with a powerful wave of nausea and held the windowsill to steady herself. She took deep breaths, but it would not go away. Finally she rushed to the bathroom and was violently sick. Acid burned the back of her throat. She gasped for air. She sat back against the tub, weak. Her eyes closed, she went over what she had eaten recently. She went to the window in her underwear.

"Tar," she called. He looked up, squinting. She felt that swelling in her chest, that reminder of love. "Could you come in?"

He was sweaty and his hands were dirty. "What is it?"

"Do you feel okay?" she asked.

He looked confused. "Yeah. Why?"

"I just don't feel very well and I wondered if it was something I ate."

"We ate the same things and I feel fine," Tar said. "What's wrong?"

"Just nauseated," Jade said.

"Maybe we should go see the doctor."

"No, I'm sure I'm fine."

"I'll make some tea," Tar said and set to work.

"Thank you." When Jade smelled the tea in front of her, her stomach lurched. She pushed the cup away. Tar's face fell. "I'm sorry, I just can't drink it."

"You love tea," he said.

"I'm exhausted," Jade said. "Thanks anyway." She went back into the bedroom and got back into bed. Tar came and stood in the doorway. Jade felt him looking at her and rolled over. "I'm sure I'll feel better later," she said.

Tar gently closed the door. His footsteps creaked away into the kitchen. Jade lay on her back. She touched her stomach, staring at it in wonder.

IV

A month later, Tar fell asleep in the red armchair in the living room. Jade crept over and sat on his lap. He stirred. She picked up his hand and placed it on her stomach. He opened his eyes.

"Hi," he said. He yawned and looked at his hand.

"Hi." Jade smiled.

"What's going on?" Jade just placed her hand on top of his. He looked from her stomach to her eyes. "I don't understand."

"Neither do I."

"I thought…"

"So did I."

"How do you know?"

"I just do."

Tar stared at her stomach. A smile grew on his face. He grinned. He pulled Jade close and kissed her, his palms to her cheeks. She smiled beneath them. Later that night, while they were in bed, Tar kissed her bare stomach and fell asleep with his hand on it.

V

The sky was bright blue as Tar trudged through the tall grass. He had to keep slowing down for Jade. He carried the basket in his arms. She carried the red blanket.

"Wait," she called.

"You're so slow."

"Shut up." She was getting more tired every day, but as yet, she hadn't begun to show. She wore a white sundress and a straw hat. "This hat is dumb," she called.

"Do you want to burn? It's for your own good." Tar set the basket down and waited for her to catch up. He took the blanket from her and spread it out on the ground. She sat down, her cheeks red. The sun was oppressive. Tar squinted as he opened the basket.

"What's in there?"

Tar tossed her an orange. She stuck her thumbnail into its leathery peel and began to tear it off. Tar pulled another out and peeled it. He watched Jade place the wedge in her mouth, still holding it as she bit it with her front teeth and sucked on it.

"Will you just eat it?"

Jade tossed the limp skin away into the grass. "I don't like the skin."

"You have a real problem." Jade laughed. Tar felt his chest tighten at her laugh as a smile came to his lips. He closed his eyes, praying that he would remember this feeling for a long time. The painfully blue sky and the bright orange fruit and Jade.

Jade gasped. Clutched her stomach with both hands.

"What is it?" Tar cried.

Jade swallowed. She took a deep breath. "I—I don't know." Tar scrambled over to her and grabbed her hand. Jade began to sob. She was shaking. "It hurts so bad." Tar swallowed, his heart thumping. Jade shrieked, squeezing his hand.

"Come on, let's go," Tar said, pulling her up to her feet. She leaned on him. Tar caught a glimpse of bright red. The back of her dress was covered with blood. "Jade," he whispered.

"It hurts. Tar, it hurts," she moaned. Tar, hands shaking, grabbed the blanket and wrapped it around her waist. He held her as they walked back into the city and through the streets. Jade was leaning on him more and more. Tar lifted her into his arms. Her eyes were closed and sweat matted her hair. Townspeople stared, some muttering to each other. The air was so hot. They finally reached the hospital.

A few minutes later, she lay in a bed wearing a paper gown. Tar held her straw hat in his hands. She looked tiny. He remembered that small look; it was the way his father had looked the last time he'd seen him alive. Tar held her hand.

"I'm going to be sick," she whispered, and he reached for the metal

171

bowl and placed it in her hands. Her pale fingers wrapped around the sides. She stared into it for a few minutes, a drop of sweat trickling down her temple. She leaned back and closed her eyes. The white curtain was swept aside and the doctor walked into the room. He adjusted his glasses and sat down next to Jade. She was near tears. Tar stood next to her, twisting her hat.

"Jiada, Adatares," the doctor began. His forehead was wrinkled in distress. Tar couldn't breathe. "I'm afraid...the baby is gone." Jade closed her eyes. "You see, the trauma caused by the...the abortion that Jade had years ago; the scar tissue, it, um...it makes it nearly impossible for the baby to attach to the uterus."

Tar turned away. There was a lump in his throat. There was an awful, strained silence in the room.

"What chance is there? For a child," Jade asked quietly. Her voice broke. Tar turned around. The doctor swallowed.

"A full-term pregnancy would be nearly impossible. A perfectly healthy baby, I'd say...definitely impossible."

Jade stared straight ahead. A tear slid down her cheek. Tar sat on the edge of her bed when the doctor left. His eyes were closed. A hand touched his. He opened his eyes and held her hand tightly. He climbed into the bed and lay beside her, holding her.

VI

A year later, Jade sat in the bathtub. Her stomach was visible above the water, a rounded mound. She placed her hand on it. The water was turning cold. She climbed out and wrapped herself in a towel. When she opened the bathroom door, she saw Tar sitting on the couch in the living room. He was writing. He did that a lot lately. Poetry. His eyes always narrowed when he wrote, his mouth slightly open like he could taste the words. He looked up when he saw her and smiled.

"Come here."

She sat next to him. He placed a hand on her stomach.

"This one is strong," he said softly, rubbing her stretched skin. Their eyes met. When they'd found out Jade was pregnant again, there had been a sort of unspoken agreement not to talk much about it.

"What are you writing about?"

Tar cleared his throat. "Nothing worth talking about." He rubbed her

172

stomach softly. His hands were warm. Jade closed her eyes.

"Do you think about Sophro a lot?" she asked after a minute.

"Probably every day. I try to see him alive when I remember him. But mostly I just see him on that bathroom floor." Jade grasped his hand. She rubbed his fingers, smooth skin pulling over jutting bones.

"I saw Despina today when you were working," she said.

"How is she?"

"She's fine."

Tar and Jade looked at each other. Tar looked like he was concentrating on every detail of her face.

"What?"

Tar shook his head. He closed his eyes. "I want to remember everything," he whispered.

"What do you mean?"

"I forget more things every day. I want to remember everything."

"Maybe we're supposed to forget some things."

"I don't want to."

Tar went back to his poem. Jade looked at her stomach.

That night, they lay in bed. Tar was asleep. Jade lay on her side, facing him. Her back ached. Moonlight touched Tar's face. She kissed his neck. His forehead wrinkled.

She sat up, a wrenching pain in her abdomen. She breathed through it and lay back down. When she was nearly asleep again, another came. She bit her lip and rolled over. Five more came. Then ten more. She breathed heavily, her body shaking. It felt like her entire abdomen was being wrung out like a wet towel. No, she thought. You're early. She cried out and grabbed Tar's arm.

"Wake up," she hissed.

He sat up. "What?"

"It's coming."

"What? No. It's too early. You have...you have over a month left," Tar stammered.

"It's coming now, Tar." Tar swallowed, eyes wide.

"Okay." He jumped up and lit the lamps and ran into the kitchen, pulling on his pants.

"Don't leave," she shouted.

"I have to get the doctor," Tar said from the doorway.

"No, please. Stay with me," Jade pleaded.

Sarah Jilek

Tar looked out the window and back to Jade. "It will only take me a few minutes. I have to go," he said.

"Tar, it's coming now. I can feel it. Help me," she cried. Tar rushed to the side of the bed and held her hand. Her eyes were squeezed shut and she clutched the edge of the bed. "It hurts." Tears escaped her closed eyelids. Tar lifted her legs.

"Push," he said and she screamed in pain and adrenaline. "Push," he repeated. She strained, the cords in her neck visible. She lay back, panting.

"Hurts."

"Okay. Push again. Now," Tar said. She groaned. Sweat poured down her face. Tar glanced between her legs. "I can see it, Jade." He grinned. "Just one more." He knelt down and held her legs. "Now." She screamed and Tar gently grasped the baby's head and pulled. "It's a boy," he cried. He cleared the baby's nose and mouth and wrapped him, all slimy and purple and splotchy, in a towel. Jade lay panting. She looked like the first mother and Tar felt like the first father and this was the first baby ever born. Maybe that was how all parents felt.

Jade sat up. "He's not crying," she said. Tar looked at the baby in his arms. He was tiny. His small lips were blue. Tar's stomach dropped. He looked at Jade, horrified. He saw the moment when she understood. Her face fell. Tar stared at his son. He looked up at Jade, his forehead wrinkled, as an awful silence descended. "What do we do?" Tar whispered.

Jade swallowed. "Clean him off. I want to hold him."

Tar brought the baby into the bathroom. He checked the temperature of the water before washing him. Waited until it was warm. He held the baby in his arms as the water flowed over his tiny body and cleaned the blood from his skin.

When he gave him to Jade, they were both silent. She inhaled deeply and tilted her head, her forehead wrinkled and glistening with sweat. Tar stood by the bed. He watched Jade touch the little fingers and kiss the tiny forehead with trembling lips.

VII

She didn't speak after that. Not until a week later. It was midnight and she couldn't sleep. Rain poured outside and thunder roared. She

174

stood in her robe in front of the window.

"What are you thinking about?" Tar asked. She turned.

"Desrala."

He sighed. "Your astronomy? Do you miss it?"

"Yes."

"Well."

"I wonder sometimes."

"Wonder what?"

"If maybe..." Jade began. She looked back out the window.

"Maybe you shouldn't have left," Tar finished.

"Yeah."

He nodded slowly. "Well," he said again.

"I know you think about it, too. You think maybe I shouldn't have come."

Tar sat down on the couch and held his head in his hands. "I don't think that. Give me a little credit," he snapped.

She turned back to the window. The rain cut tracks in it and slid across. In the garden, the fragile stalk of the tomato plant leaned to the side, about to snap like a neck. Tar's silence behind her was as loud as the thunder. She began to tap her foot. "The storm's ruining the garden."

"Fine."

"Fine?" She turned around. He sat down in the red chair, his arms crossed and his face blank. He shrugged. She felt drained, like she had spent these last few years treading water.

Tar leaned forward, staring into her eyes until she wanted to look away. "What do you want, Jade?" he asked.

Jade's cheeks burned. She stared at the floor. "I...I don't know." She sighed. Tar exhaled and let his head fall into his hands. He scratched it furiously. Jade looked back out the window. Back west was Desrala. Audric. Astronomy. She remembered the way the stars used to look: an orderly chart, just like the hedge mazes and flower beds of her hometown. Now, when she looked at the stars, they were just a jumble, just a mass of pinpricks on a velvet sky. She swallowed tears. "I could pick up life there so easily," she whispered. Tar looked up.

"Do you want..." he trailed off, shaking his head. He was breathing heavily.

"It would be easier," she said. "A lot easier."

Tar stood up. He didn't meet her eyes; he just walked back into the bedroom. Jade looked at the front door. The rectangle of wood lodged inside the open space that she could walk through. She touched the cold doorknob with her fingertips. She turned it and pulled. Raindrops pricked her feet, her arms, her lips. Outside, the dirt road was muddy, little rivers of water flowing and pooling. The tomato plants lay on their sides, roots exposed. Jade breathed the air: rain soaked leaves and spring mud. Tears filled her eyes. She blinked them clear and shut the door. The house was silent, except for the rain pattering on the roof. She looked up at the bedroom door. Tar stood in the doorway. He slowly walked through the living room to her and stopped a foot in front of her, the corner of his mouth raised in a hopeful smile. She reached out with one hand and touched his cheek, the familiar ridge of bone and soft skin. She felt her chest suddenly tighten and she gasped for breath, a strangled sob, and it turned into a laugh. Tar smiled, and she felt his skin stretch beneath her hand.

Sarah Jilek was born and raised in DeKalb, Illinois, a town of cornfields and humidity. She is currently studying English Literature and Creative Writing at Southern Illinois University in Carbondale and working at Grassroots Literary Magazine. She owes her love of reading and writing to J.R.R. Tolkien, John Steinbeck, and Sylvia Plath. Sarah is happiest while drinking anything with caffeine, and has cried at 80 percent of all the movies she has ever seen.